MATIKA

AND THE RIVER LION

LATRICE N. SIMPKINS

Printed in the United States of America

ISBN: 0989561208
ISBN 13: 9780989561204

For my dear sister-in-law, Benaleta, who provided the inspiration for me to create the beautiful Matika. You were always there for me through thick and thin.

To Pete for all the hard work you do and allowing me to take Matika to beyond my imagination. I can never thank you enough.

ACKNOWLEDGEMENTS

I would like to formally acknowledge all the women and girls who face gender-based violence, and the associated risks to their health and well-being experiencing such issues daily. Your bravery is not lost and you are not forgotten.

I also give my heartfelt gratitude to those who fight to help them with these struggles. The lives you save are countless.

PROLOGUE

~~~~~~~~~~

There was a time when the gentle splattering of warm rain against the corrugated aluminum roof would have lulled me to sleep, even in the day. During the season of the rain we never wanted to leave the comfort of our huts unless to tend our gardens during the daylong downpour.

The encroaching jungle vegetation, once surrounding our village, had been burned back so we could see the coming advance of the torturous and brutal Lord's Liberation Army. Central Uganda was once more being ravished by another tribal civil war, and our village was in the center of it. All I ever wanted from life was a loving husband, peace, and the opportunity to raise children. That was no longer a possibility, at least not here.

"Matika! Don't move. Listen," my sister, Suda, ordered.

We heard the distant screams of anguish from women and children echoing through the crisp, cool morning air. The River Lion's legion of terror was delivering death to our village.

"Hurry! We've got to run," Suda commanded, and with only survival in our minds we sprinted with all our might toward the tall elephant grass near the jungle. As soon as we reached it we dropped low, scanning the area while our eyes adjusted to the growing darkness.

"Come on, before they see you," she called as I turned to look at a phosphorous grenade exploding nearby. The burst of intense light outlined the huts and the horrific frenzy of our people running to escape the savagery. Ghosts of armed men, mercenaries, were dragging off screaming women and shooting all who resisted. It was chaos. Through the constant gunfire, we raced toward the trees. My heart was pounding, the blood rushing through my veins with every beat so loudly that I couldn't hear Suda yelling at me. Desperately I ran, trying to catch up to her. The plastic water container strapped to my back banged my spine with each lope I took. Only a few moments had passed, but it was an eternity. I couldn't sustain the pace and fell, losing my shoe. Picking myself up, I continued to run for the safety of the trees, which were still so far away.

Determined to live, I lowered my arms, lengthened my stride and concentrated on a steady rhythm, covering as much ground as I could before they shot at me. It wasn't long before I was noticed. Bullets whizzed over my head, slamming into the banana tree I was approaching and spraying wood chunks everywhere.

"Run for your life, Matika!" Suda called as she looked back. With long strides, she loped off like a Thompson's gazelle.

"Help! I can't keep up!" I shouted, the distance between us widening. The jungle still seemed so distant, and my legs were burning from the strain.

The sound of heavy boots reached me from behind. They were gaining quickly.

"Please, Suda, don't leave me!"

CHAPTER ONE

~~~~~~~~~~~~~~~

"This can't be happening," Mama said, talking loudly over Baba's voice. Suda was kneeling outside with her ear to the front door of the hut. We were supposed to be collecting water from the spring for the evening meal and as usual, she had gotten distracted. My arms ached and my hands went numb carrying the large, clay water pot that we had filled.

"You can't do this! I'm your favorite wife!"

"And that is why I need you safe," Baba's baritone voice, normally brusque, was filled with gentleness.

"Matika, shhh," Suda warned, putting her finger to her lips. I quickly eased the water pots to the ground, silently crouched next to her, and pressed my ear against the dusty door.

Baba's visit was unexpected. Usually he came three times a month for four days, sharing his remaining time with his other wives and traveling back to Kampala for military duties. This day, Suda and I did not have time to change into our colorful *kitenge* that we always wore for Baba. Instead we wore our everyday tattered cotton skirts and stained shirts.

My hair was uncombed, my face and hands dirty from chores. I'd never heard Mama speak angrily to Baba. She was showing him her other side, the side we dealt with on a regular basis.

"If Baba knew what Mama was really like, he'd never have chosen her for a wife," Suda had said. Mama was the second of eight wives and although she was not granted "male status," which would have allowed her to behave equally toward a man and a superior toward his other wives. Like Baba's first spouse, she was allowed to speak freely and only knelt when she served him. Mama always held a special place in Baba's heart because she had given him nine sons and three daughters. Three of her sons had made good matches, bringing a higher status to our family. In her youth, Mama was a great beauty and had eighteen marriage offers by the time she was twelve. My father was envied because he was the only one who could pay the thirteen cows and twelve goats required for her dowry. That was still the standing village record, far exceeding the cap of five cows established in 1950.

My family lived a half-kilometer outside the village of Bamuli on Baba's fertile land, on which we grew potatoes, yams, corn millet, beans, and grass for our cows and goats. Akello, my older brother, said that Father was *ana geringa,* or a snob. He had to have it all. Each *numba,* or hut, had two rooms with corrugated iron roofs that consisted of eucalyptus poles and, most importantly, concrete floors, red clay walls and an additional room for the chickens. This was far larger than any other *numba.*

"Woman, listen. Kembei and his family are dead. The rebels are killing all military, government officials and their families," Baba spoke slowly, as if speaking to a child. "Take the children to your family. Because of my rank they'll be coming for me soon. I can't stay in

Uganda. I am leaving tonight. I'm heading to Kenya. When all is safe, we'll be together again."

"I won't do that! My family can't feed and shelter them. They'll starve. What about the money? The bank? What of your business?" Mama shouted in tears. The very thought of being poor put the fear of God in her. Baba was a general in the military, owned a successful bank, land and a few other small businesses in the nearby town. She never went without since marrying Baba. We were fortunate during this time when so many were lacking food, clean water, and shelter.

"And what about Namazzi's marriage next week? They have already given us seven cows as payment and we've postponed the marriage once," she continued.

Namazzi, my oldest sister at age fifteen, had her marriage postponed ten months due to illness. This pushed Suda's marriage back because it would disgrace Namazzi if Suda married first. Mother cleverly had Baba tell the groom's family that Namazzi had not started her woman's cycle so that she wouldn't lose her chances of becoming a wife to a good family. She was sick more often than not and, according to Suda, wouldn't survive the childbirth. The only reason Father agreed to the match was because the groom was prosperous and Namazzi would be his first wife.

"My brother has seen to everything and his son will come for Namazzi in the morning. I'm leaving you money for the family, but you must leave tomorrow," Baba said softly. "I am counting on you, love. I need you to be strong for me."

All was suddenly quiet. Was this the end of our normal life? Dumbstruck, Suda and I just stared at each other. Neither of us dared to enter the house with the water. We would get beaten for not bringing the water on time, or we would get beaten for coming into the house without permission when Baba was there. No matter what, Mama would beat us.

"I'm going to see Baba," Suda announced, picking up the water pot. At fourteen, she was the only sibling who would protect me from Mama's wrath.

"No, Suda," I whispered desperately. My heart was thumping so loudly I could barely hear my own voice. It was too late. Suda had opened the door, walked in and dropped the pot. There was nothing I could do but follow. When I came inside, I was shocked to see the look of genuine compassion on Baba's face as he looked straight at Suda while hugging Mama. It was as if it would be the last time he would ever see us.

"Baba," Suda said fervently, disregarding protocol and running to him. He embraced her as well. My heart ached as I joined them, unshed tears burning my eyes. This was the first time all of us had ever embraced, because Mama never showed any affection toward us.

The other mamas had an active role in rearing the children. They were very strict but fair, unlike Mama, who would beat us for almost anything. She would often strike the younger wives for being clumsy or lazy. Baba's wives that were in their late teens would be at Mama's beck and call more so than Suda and me. They, along with the other junior wives and my brothers, did the laborious work of tending to the small family fields. The senior sister-wives performed the cooking duties and their daughters did the household chores.

Other than lecturing, Baba had no role in child rearing, typically showing little affection. "Suda," he would say, "you always look like you are up to something. Your husband would not like you to look so sneaky."

Tonight was different. I felt like an equal for the first time. Although it was an honor to eat with Baba, the mood was somber. Quietly, we ate the chicken, *ugali* and *matoke,* knowing this might be the last meal we'd ever share together. After eating, Baba gave us each a hug and told us something special. To me he said, "You're made in the image of your beautiful mother. No man will be good enough to be your husband."

That night Mama slumped silently in her chair in the kitchen, deep in thought. It was one of two wooden chairs by a small pull-down table reserved for only Mama and Baba. The table, a customer's gift, was a piece of wood fastened to the wall. Our front room was a fairly large rectangle shape with a little kitchen in the left corner consisting of a fireplace used for light cooking and a door for ventilation. Two large storage baskets made from elephant grass and palm leaves were used to store food and pottery.

Suda and I were engaged in our nightly chore of making the pallets for sleeping in the inner room. Little Adam was asleep in a cotton sling across my back. Namazzi sat on her pallet, sewing a colorful new dress that she would wear for her future husband.

"Matika, go get the boys. They're playing in the village," Mother absently commanded, obviously absorbed in her thoughts.

Suda looked just as alarmed as I was, but, even distracted, there was no arguing with Mama. Normally, Mama would get the boys every night for evening *chai,* a popular tea, and millet bread before we slept. It was not good for a young girl to be out at this hour without a chaperone. Our mamas told us stories of girls getting ruined and disgraced by simply walking alone at night, and sometimes even during the day. I really couldn't understand how a girl might get ruined, but by the way my mamas spoke of it, a monster would get the girls and bite their flesh and make them bleed. I never asked what getting ruined meant, but those stories were enough to make me travel no further than the village spring without Suda.

"*Wangie*, Mama," I replied out of respect and quickly left the hut. My goal was to run all the way to the village center, where I knew my brothers would be with the other boys, without getting attacked. I headed west on the worn path to the village. At a steady run I would be there in ten minutes. I passed the cattle and goats that were grazing and being rounded up by mamas in the field. It had rained yesterday, but I could still smell the sweet fertile earth. The corn millet grew high and was almost ready to harvest.

I hurried along, not wanting to go too fast and trip, and get bitten by the night monsters. As I approached the village I began to feel a floating sensation inside my stomach, like I was falling from an acacia tree. I knew I would be coming upon the hut of the *sangoma*, or witch doctor, shortly. It was a dark, warm night with a thin moon showing, making it harder to see. The *sangoma*'s hut came into view. I wanted to stop and ask her a question about my fate and that of my family. She was a healer and was able to foresee the future for a small gift in return.

Mama once took me to her hut to get herbal medicines to heal Namazzi of her illness. When we approached the hut there was a stench that made me think of rotten meat or the musty smell of too many unwashed bodies sleeping in a *numba*. Mother called to her and I was momentarily suffocated by intense heat and a pungent smell as she lifted the dirty cloth fabric that served as a door.

The *sangoma* was one of the eldest members of the village, extremely thin with many wrinkles on sagging flesh. Surviving a brutal cattle raid fifty years ago, she bore the scars to prove it. Clad only in a faded flower-print skirt that hung to her knees, her exposed sweaty skin hung loosely on her body, with deflated breasts that reached her waist. Her pale gray eyes were like so many other village elders, who were sightless. Yet she moved around her *numba* like she saw everything. Maybe she did.

Momentarily forgetting the putrid stench, I entered and saw the treasures she had collected as payment. Animal skins cushioned the dirt floor and lined the walls of her hut. Myriad vials, various shapes and sizes, filled with different powders and ointments were stacked in woven baskets and bins hanging from the thatched roof. Grass baskets and an array of broken pottery were scattered about. A disgusting, maggot-infested animal carcass lay in the corner, emitting a powerful order. Several strange trinkets hung from the walls, but my attention was riveted on a boiling pot with a peculiar aroma of legume seeds. The rolling liquid was orange-red with green swirls of a stringy plant floating to the top.

When I visited the *sangoma* with Mama that day, I carried a basket of precious *matoke* bananas that Mother gave her for payment. But now, with nothing to give her, I hoped she'd see me. Overcoming my fear, I approached her hut. Not wanting to be seen by the villagers, I glanced over my shoulder and saw that no one was around. Trembling, I ventured into the *sangoma*'s hut.

CHAPTER TWO

"*S*angoma?" I called, my voice horse. Straining my eyes to see in the dim smoky light, there was only one *tadobba* candle burning in a plastic dish on the floor. The hut was the same as before. I noticed a small pot of tea hanging from a metal rod over the low fire. The *sangoma* sat in the corner on a mat, grinding herbs with a stone awl in a clay pot, not bothering to look up. I wondered what to do next but waited out of respect.

Finally she looked up at me from her toil and in a low voice said, "What business do you have visiting my *numba* at this hour?"

"I thought maybe you could help me? I wanted to…," I could not finish my words; my mouth had gone dry. Her sightless eyes bore through me. Could she see my soul? Unnerved, I glanced at my feet, breaking eye contact.

"Out with it, child! What do you seek?"

"The future. I want to know my future," I said expelling a breath I didn't realize I'd held. "Strange things are happening and I want to know what is to become of my family."

There. I said it. Relief swept over me. She continued grinding quietly, not acknowledging that I had spoken. The frigid silence stretched between us.

"Come here," she ordered, setting her work aside. "Who is your father?"

"I am Matika, the daughter of Batalo Okello Naminiha," I replied, kneeling down before her. She reached out and caressed my face as if seeing me for the first time.

"You are as pretty as they say, more than your mother. She was so beautiful to have such a black heart," she mused. "I knew her as a young girl. She came to my hut often when she was your age, hoping to catch the eye of a certain rich man. She wanted to be his first wife."

"But, Baba had a first wife," I said, confused.

"So he did," she continued. "She was so angry when I would not concoct a spell to kill her. That child got so upset she stormed out of here." She chuckled to herself and reached out, touching my breasts with her thin shaky hands. "Oh, I see you're already a woman, and quite shapely."

My breasts were fuller than any of my sisters'. I could not share their clothes because they fit too tight on my bosom. To my dismay, I was the topic of many of my mama's conversations. I wasn't skinny like Namazzi. Mama would say that I was well-formed.

She hesitated a moment, a look of concern clouding her face, then sighed painfully.

"What is it? What do you see?" I wanted to know. I had to know. Whatever it was, it was not good.

"It's nothing. Take care and be cautious," she said.

The *sangoma's* face suddenly grew serious as she reached for my empty hands. "What did you bring for your *sangoma*?"

"I don't have anything. I could bring you something later," I said, hoping she would help me just the same.

"Bah!" she cried spitting in the fire. A flame crackled and leapt into the air. "Everyone has something. Nothing in this life is free, remember that child."

I frantically searched my body for something, anything. Nothing. I reached up and clutched my beloved beads around my neck. It was all I had from Baba. It was a necklace that he gave each of the girls at Christmas. He had purchased them from a merchant in Kampala, where he was stationed about fifty kilometers south of our village. Sand-colored cylinders alternating with black onyx beads, with a small wedge of rhino ivory in the center formed the necklace. It was my most valuable possession. I did not want to part with this precious gift, but it was for the good of my family. I hesitated a few seconds, not wanting to let go of the gift Baba had lovingly given to me. Reluctantly, I released the clasps that held the stringed beads together.

"I have this," I said putting the necklace into her outstretched hands.

"You are willing to give so much," the sangoma said with a toothless grin, exposing her black gums. She clutched the necklace, letting it slip into a nearby rock-filled basket with a clink. She poured tea in a small bowl. I focused on the basket, desperately wanting to retrieve my necklace and run out of the hut, but something compelled me to stay.

"Drink," she said, thrusting the warm bowl into my hands. I hastily swallowed its contents. "Not so fast." She took the bowl from me and put it down.

"The time of Milton Obote is over. I have lived a long time and I have seen the great work he has done in Uganda. He has been our prime minister and president twice. He was a great leader who led our people to independence from the British. The last election ruined his image.

People didn't feel he could be trusted with an election controlled by his friend, Paulo Muwanga. Now, his reputation is soiled by repression and the deaths of many people. This country has been all but destroyed between Milton Obote and Idi Amin. There will be a new era," she said taking my hand. "There is no place in this country for a former commanding general of the Uganda People's Congress. You and your family will be torn apart. Where is your father now?

"Gone," I answered.

"Then you must leave at once. It will be a long journey. You will have no man to protect you. You will be alone, so hide your womanly beauty or it will lead to your destruction."

"I can't leave my family." I was appalled. Run away? Alone!

"Did you hear what I said? There will be nothing here but death!" The eerie shrill of her voice told me she meant what she promised. I quickly stood, feeling nauseous and dizzy. I was terrified.

"Why are you staying?" I shot back. The room was spinning.

"I am old. Why should I run from death?" she replied, picking up my treasure. "Take it. You will need it more than I." She pressed my necklace into my palm and began to laugh.

I couldn't believe she'd given my treasure back. Not wanting to stay a moment longer, I ran out of the hut. I was so disoriented that I was unsure which way was home. My legs felt heavy as I staggered back toward the hut. Sweat began to drip down my face and my hands were clammy. "I must make it home," I said to myself, pressing onward. What was happening? Did the *sangoma* put a curse on me? I was lost, disoriented, but kept running. Finally, I could see our hut, but darkness was closing around me. As I approached the hut I tripped and fell through the door.

"Where were you?" Mama shrieked, her voice abnormally high. Immediately, she kicked my ribs. I curled up, trying to protect my face from the assault. She began pulling my hair as I gritted my teeth from the pain of being dragged back outside. Everything was happening too fast. I got a glimpse of her bamboo stick and I knew what was coming. I was powerless to do anything, let alone protect myself. "You insolent girl, I will teach you to behave!"

"Mama, no," Suda pleaded, trying to stop her. I could hear my brothers mumbling in the background. They must have returned to the hut on their own.

"You, too, want to misbehave to your Mama, Suda?"

"No, Mama, I'm sorry. Something is wrong with Matika."

"Mama, she looks unwell," Akello agreed.

"There is nothing wrong with Matika," Mama said, but she quickly let go of my hair. I knew was I slipping into unconscious as my brother gallantly lifted me off the ground, saving me from her abuse. Briefly, I heard the incoherent voices of my family as I drifted into a rolling sea of darkness.

I was high up in a lush forest. The gentle rain caressed the bamboo leaves before descending to the plants on the ground below. Rain, sweet and fresh, cleansed the earth. It calmed my body as it fell on my skin. Surrounding trees covered the sky with their leafy canopy branches. It was all so beautiful, serene, and picture-perfect. Suddenly, I grew cold and my lips began to tremble. I could hear someone or something approaching, but I could not discern which direction it was coming from. I turned just as a large silverback gorilla pounced on me, knocking the wind from my chest as I hit the ground. I screamed as his large hairy hands grabbed my neck and began ripping me apart...

"Matika, wake up," Suda said shaking me. Suda, Namazzi, and I were in the front room, lying on mats. They must have watched over me while I slept. Although no candle was lit, the moon shone brightly, providing a pinch of light. The memories of the *sangoma* came flooding back with a roar.

"What happened?" I asked.

"You had a nightmare. We're all extremely worried about you. Mama, too," Suda added with emphasis.

"Matika, tell us what happened to you," Namazzi asked with concern in her voice. "Did someone hurt you?" Namazzi and Suda both waited in anticipation for me to tell them what had happened.

"No one hurt me. I started to feel so strange when I was in the *sangoma*'s hut."

"You went to the *sangoma*?" Namazzi asked, startled. She was afraid of the witch doctor, although they had never met, but Namazzi had heard many stories about the old woman. When she was sick, Mama had to force her to drink the *sangoma*'s herb tea. Namazzi was convinced that people would die from her "strange brews," as she called them.

"Shhh, or you'll wake Mama," Suda warned. Each of us sat quietly as we looked at Mama's door and waited. After a few moments, I began my tale. Every so often, Suda and Namazzi let out gasps or "oohs" and "ahhs." When I had finished, they were fascinated.

"That is very bad. She must have put a curse on you," Namazzi said. She touched my forehead, feeling for a fever.

"Don't be silly, Namazzi," Suda chided, always being the pragmatic one. "She must have put something in your drink. Did you see her put anything in your tea, Matika?"

"I don't remember. I suppose she could have put something in it. This is all so strange. What's going to happen to us, Suda?"

Namazzi and I looked up to her, and although Namazzi would never admit it, Suda was our rock, with knowledge and wisdom of things we seemed to miss.

"Baba told Mama to take us to her family in Mumbede. We'll be safe there."

"And I will be married next week," Namazzi added happily while Suda and I exchanged covert glances.

"We're happy for you," I said, but the sadness in my voice betrayed my words.

"You'll be next, Suda," Namazzi added cheerfully, misunderstanding her silence. "Baba may have to find you a new husband if you leave, but I'm sure he will be as great as Ochen."

How could she say that Ochen was a good man when we truly did not know him? Was she optimistic or simply naive? Ochen lived in our village only three years with his two wives, whom had yet to conceive. Baba said Suda was strong and would bear him many children. If this proved to be true, she would be granted "male status." Baba knew Suda was strong and would take over as head wife when she bore him sons.

"It'll be morning soon. We must sleep," Suda said, curtailing Namazzi's happiness. She turned her back to us.

"Sleep well," Namazzi said warmly, letting out a yawn as she lay on her mat. Soon I heard the steady rhythm of her breath signaling sleep.

The hut was quiet and I assumed that I was the only one awake, lying restless on the mat. I felt anxious. Alone. I had much to think about. Although there were more pressing issues to consider, it would be morning soon. Mama would be waking my sisters and me as she did each day to prepare the morning meal. What would I tell Mama? She would demand to know happened to me. There was no option but to tell the truth. I felt a sharp pain splitting through the back of my head at the thought of facing Mama. I closed my eyes trying to meditate, to clear my thoughts. I was afraid to have that nightmare again, but soon I slipped into a fitful slumber.

"Akello, Mama's gone!" Mukassa shouted as he rushed into the hut. I awoke, looking around as my brothers quickly filed into the front room. It was early morning and the sun had yet to breach the sky. As a younger brother, Mukassa's task was to retrieve water daily from the spring for the morning meal.

"Obiajula, check the fields," Akello gave the orders rapidly. "Isoke, Jababri, check the village. Mukassa, Suda, Namazzi, look in our mamas' huts. Matika, look through Mama's things and see if anything is missing. Where is she?"

CHAPTER THREE

As I searched through Mama's belongings, a fear crept into me that she would appear at any moment. Could I have made her so upset that she would leave? Her most valuable possessions were missing, as was the money Baba had given her to take us to her family.

She might have gone to the village to purchase some provisions, but she wouldn't normally go without telling Akello. At eighteen and the eldest male, Akello was the man of the house in Baba's absence. Obiajula, mean and surly, was seventeen and the largest of my brothers. He used his size to bully the younger brothers and had a fierce temper that matched Mama's. Twenty minutes later, my brothers and sisters returned.

"All our mamas are gone, except for Mama Kaikara and Mama Bacia. They, too, will be leaving this morning," Suda said somberly. "The others must have left in the night. They took their children."

I knew she wanted to ask why Mama had not taken us. We all wanted to know but were afraid to ask. To say it aloud would lead to the painful truth that Mama didn't want us.

"Where's mama?" little Adam asked. "I want Mama!" He began crying.

"It'll be okay. Mama will come back," I said, cuddling him in my arms, getting his tantrum under control.

"She's not coming back. She left us," Suda declared.

"Don't say that. She *is* coming back!" Namazzi fired back.

"Enough! Both of you," Akello said, glaring at them. Then his face softened. We stood waiting for his direction. Everything was happening too fast. "We have to leave right away. Here's the plan. I'll take Adam and Mukassa to relatives in Mumbede. I know they can't keep us all, but they can't refuse Adam and Mukassa. Matika, you will come with me also. I will think of something for you when the time comes. Obiajula, take Isoke, Jababri, and Suda to Entebbe to find Baba's uncle, Mablevi. Baba gave me his address in case of an emergency."

"I need money to travel," Obiajula said.

"I have little, but I will give you some. Make good use of it, Obiajula. Pack what you can but you may need to buy provisions along the way," Akello said, handing him a few shillings.

"Is that all? I can't buy anything with this," he complained. Before Akello could reply they were interrupted by a knock on the door. The eldest answered.

"*Aburri*," my older cousin greeted Akello. "I was sent to bring Namazzi to her husband."

"But I thought I was staying with you until the wedding," Namazzi said nervously, her hands shaking. What happened to the girl who relished the idea of marriage the night before?

"It's very bad, Akello. The LLA is closer than we thought," our cousin said, leading him outside to talk. Then over his shoulder he added, "Namazzi, get your things. We leave in five minutes."

"I should hold the money," Isoke argued, his hands on his hips and Jababri at his side. At sixteen the twins were "*mapacha*," inseparable.

"Obiajula, you lose everything-"

"I do not," Obiajula interrupted, puffing out his chest like a rooster ready for a cockfight. "It's mine. Akello gave it to me."

Suda and I followed Namazzi to the back room where she kept her belongings. My brothers' voices faded in the background. Namazzi carefully removed her new dress that was wrapped in cloth. It was a plain-cut, red-and-orange floral-print dress with a scoop neck, but it was new.

"I was hoping to wear it to my wedding," Namazzi said holding the dress up. "We were going to have a big feast."

"You may still have a wedding feast at a later date," I said trying to lift her spirits.

"I wanted everyone to be there," she continued. "I didn't get to say goodbye to Mama."

"None of us did. Here, let me help," Suda said, taking the dress from her.

I helped her take off the old dress she wore. Standing naked before us, Namazzi looked thin and vulnerable. She was taller than me but shorter than Suda. Her childlike breasts were like petite lemons, small but firm. Her narrow hips, not much wider than her waist, were inadequate for childbearing. A protruding mound could be seen through the sparse curls that covered her woman's center. Her butt, flat and undistinguished, was far from full and round, like two thin quarter-moons. I gasped as she lifted her arms, exposing a line of protruding ribs.

Suda quickly pulled the dress over her head. I hadn't noticed her emaciated body before. To her advantage, her coffee-colored skin was flawless and smooth. She had inherited Mama's pouty, sensuous lips and Baba's large, round eyes. Namazzi reminded me of a beautiful but delicate bird whose wings had been clipped, preventing flight.

"Let me fix your hair," I offered, noting that her hair was in desperate need of repair. It blossomed out of the braids like an angry cloud over her head. She knelt before me as I picked apart her lose plaits with a small comb - Mama's comb - carved from a thin, pointed bamboo stick woven with raffia, and decorated with carved patterns. There was no time to re-braid her hair so I combed it out carefully, starting at the ends and working my way up to the root to loosen the knots. Her dull black hair hung in a mass of tight curls that fell between her shoulder blades.

Suda came forward and wrapped Namazzi's hair in one of Mama's many colorful headscarves. "You look beautiful," she said, giving her much-needed encouragement.

"Thank you. Do you think I will please him?" Namazzi asked. Wearing the new dress with combed hair, her confidence was noticeably restored.

"Of course you will," we both agreed.

"Namazzi, let's go," my cousin called from the front room. Without another word, Suda and I hugged Namazzi before she hurried out of the house. Our family was being torn apart just like the *sangoma* had said. We joined our brothers in the front room while Akello and Obiajula stood outside watching Namazzi and my cousin walk down the path.

"Akello, Ochen has not paid Baba for Suda. As the eldest, you can deliver her to him now and take the money for our journey," Obiajula said.

"That's something I will consider," Akello said.

"No! I don't wish to marry Ochen!" Suda exclaimed stepping forward with fire emanating from her eyes, ready to erupt at any moment.

"How dare you interrupt us?" Obiajula said with disgust. "Know your place as a woman! It was Baba's wish that you marry Ochen."

"Let her speak," Akello interjected raising his hand to silence Obiajula. Suda cleared her throat.

"Baba no longer wanted the match," she fired off her response to Obiajula. "The last thing he said to me was that he would find me a new husband when we're together again. He also said that I would have a say in who I married."

"She's not telling the truth. Baba wouldn't say that. Akello, if you don't take her to Ochen, I will take her myself!"

He grabbed Suda's arm to pull her out the door. Suda was smaller than him but she was strong and fought like a panther, kicking and clawing. Mukassa and Jababri backed away just in time to avoid her flailing limbs. Obiajula held her tightly, encircling her arms. Then he let out an unmanly scream as she bit his bicep, dropping her to the ground. He had a murderous look in his eyes as he grabbed her by the hair.

"Stop!" Akello said pulling the two apart. "What have we come to? Brother and sister fighting. There is enough violence in our country for the whole world to see. We don't have time for this. Our cousin told me that the LLA was spotted only two kilometers from here. Who do you think they will come after first? There will be no mercy! They are slaughtering men, raping women, and taking the children as soldiers. We live only miles away from Luwero district. The Uganda People's Congress is facing a humiliating defeat and they are taking it out on the innocent Bagandans and others, with murder, torture, and mass starvation. We no longer have one enemy. Baba's army is also our enemy. We leave now. Suda, you will come with me to Mumbede."

"You said she was to come with me," Obiajula argued, devoid of any concern for Suda.

"I will not leave this hut with you," Suda said standing firm. Obiajula stormed out of the hut, snatching the bag he had packed. Isoke and Jababri quickly followed suit, saying their goodbyes as they departed.

"I will not be your burden any longer, Akello. I am going to find Baba," she announced.

"You can't travel alone. You will get yourself killed. Have you not heard? They're taking young girls for a fate worse than death. Besides, you don't even know where Baba is," he said.

"I'm in no more danger than you, traveling with children to Mumbede. You're marching right into danger. I'm a grown woman and I can take care of myself," she said boldly. "I know where Father is. I have studied his maps and I can find him on my own."

"You will not be alone. I will go with you," I said placing my hand in Suda's. I gave her a reassuring smile.

"This is madness. But, I'm man enough to admit that I cannot control you, Suda. You were never one to be controlled. Both of you may be killed or taken," his voice was filled with emotion.

"We have a better chance heading for Kenya than all of you have staying in this country," she returned. With Akello's blessing and one shilling she and I hugged and kissed him before we readied for our journey. Within ten minutes our bothers had gone, our entire family shattered.

I wore my everyday clothes and my brother's work shoes that were too large for my feet. Suda insisted that I cover my shoulder-length hair with a colored headscarf. She was dressed similarly, skirt and shirt, with an old pair of shoes and knotted laces. We each carried a little food in raffia bags and had a container of water to share.

"Wait," she said as we were heading out of the hut. "We have to do something about those." She pointed at me. She ran to the back room and produced a plain brown scarf. I lifted my shirt and she tightly wrapped the scarf around my breasts, constricting them to my chest and making it difficult to breathe. "We don't want added attention. You must keep your head down when we are in the presence of men and let me do the talking." She took a cursory glance at her work and was pleased. She tenderly tucked in a lock of my hair that escaped the headscarf. "Now we are ready."

Leaving the hut we headed southwest, not taking the well-worn path away from our home. Suda thought it best that we avoid all villages, including ours. We were going to make a wide circle around our lands. If the rebels were near they would likely approach from the north. It was still early morning and a good day for travel. We were fortunate that it had not rained the night before.

"What made you stand up to Obiajula?" I asked after we had walked about a half-kilometer southwest. "You are so brave."

"I had no desire to marry Ochen, or anyone for that matter. I saw it as my only opportunity to be free. If I went with Obiajula, he would probably sell me to the nearest merchant. I would not allow him to bully me without a fight. Besides, you know Akello has a soft heart."

She was right. Akello was a good brother to all of us. I wanted my husband to be just like him, kind and compassionate. And he was handsome. Yes, I wanted to be married to someone just like him. "You were also courageous for coming with me. I'm glad you did because you are not just my sister, but my best friend," Suda said.

"I couldn't let you go alone. And I am far from courageous," I said sticking my hand out. "See, I'm shaking like a leaf." We both laughed, stopping in our tracks.

"Look at me," Suda giggled barely under control, "I'm shaking, too!" We laughed until tears rolled out of our eyes. And then we laughed some more. It was a good feeling, to finally let out some of the anxiety. Two frightened girls traveling through a war-torn Uganda to Kenya. It was indeed comical. What had we gotten ourselves into?

"No matter what, we must always stay together," she said, holding my hand as we continued on. Suddenly she stopped. "Matika, what was that?"

CHAPTER FOUR

"Matika! Don't move. Listen," my sister Suda ordered. We heard the distant screams of anguish from women and children echoing through the crisp, cool night air. The River Lion's legion of terror was delivering death to our village.

"Hurry! We've got to run," Suda commanded, and with only survival in our minds we sprinted with all our might toward the tall elephant grass near the jungle. As soon as we reached it we dropped low, scanning the area as our eyes adjusted to the growing darkness.

"Come on, before they see you," she called as I turned to look at a phosphorous grenade exploding nearby. The intense burst of light outlined the huts and the horrific frenzy of our people running to escape the savagery. Ghosts of armed men, mercenaries, were dragging off screaming women and shooting all who resisted. It was chaos. Through the constant gunfire, we raced toward the trees. My heart was pounding, the blood rushing through my veins with every beat so loudly that I couldn't hear Suda yelling at me. Desperately I ran, trying to catch up to her. The plastic water container strapped to my back banged my spine with each lope I took. Only a few moments had passed, but it was an eternity. I couldn't sustain the pace and fell, losing my shoe. Picking myself up, I continued to run for the safety of the trees, which were still so far away.

Determined to live, I lowered my arms, lengthened my stride and concentrated on a steady rhythm, covering as much ground as I could before they shot at me. It wasn't long at all before I was noticed. Bullets whizzed over my head, slamming into the banana tree I was approaching and spraying wood chunks everywhere. I flinched but kept going, determined to reach my sister who was still ahead of me.

"Run for your life, Matika!" Suda called as she looked back. With long strides she loped off like a Thompson's gazelle.

"Help! I can't keep up," I shouted, the space between us widening. The jungle still seemed so distant, and my legs were burning from the strain.

The sound of heavy boots reached me from behind. They were gaining on me quickly.

"Please, Suda, don't leave me!"

She slowed down enough for me to catch up and then set a steady pace as we ran through the trees. I labored with each breath, ejecting a sigh every so often as I forced my legs to keep on. For twenty minutes a cramp stitched in my right side, refusing to pass. "Can we rest?"

"Only for a little while," she replied walking in a circle, assessing our location. "We have run about five kilometers."

"Are we safe?" I doubled over, my hands on my knees, gasping for air.

"We won't be safe until we reach Baba," she responded, taking the water container from my pack. Then handing it to me, she said, "Drink, but not too much. We have to cover several kilometers before nightfall or they'll be upon us. There may not be any water source available until tomorrow."

Resisting my desire to drink all the water from the container, I allowed myself a few heady gulps, relishing the cool, quenching liquid, careful not to spill a drop. Handing the container back to Suda, I sat upon the ground to rest and began kneading my tightened leg muscles from the hamstrings to the calves. The soreness of my legs would only get worse as we traveled on.

It was April, the start of the monsoon season. The ground cover was thick with picturesque green landscape and fertile red earth. Bamboo trees provided concealment along the path. This was my least favorite time of the year, I thought, looking up at the sky. The sun alternated between the clouds as though in a game of football. It was only a matter of time before rain would fall, making our journey wet and bleak. Where would we rest our heads tonight? The soil would be cold and wet.

"Matika, we must leave now," Suda said disturbing my thoughts. She stood over me, reaching out. Taking my hand, she pulled me to my feet. My legs had little strength as I followed her through the trees. My stomach growled and I realized that we had not broken our fast.

"Suda, do you think we can have something to eat?" I asked, hoping she would oblige. I got excited as she reached into her bag and pulled out a piece of millet bread. It was a small portion that got even smaller when she split it in half. Disappointment etched my face.

"We must save our food," she said handing me a piece barely bigger than a crumb. Without sauces, the bread was bland but within a few moments I swallowed the dry morsel and eyed Suda's piece as she savored it. She took small bites, chewing each piece like it was gum arabic.

It did little to ease my hunger and I began to wonder when we would have our next hot meal. I wished I had eaten more at the evening meal, already a distant memory. I could have filled my belly to near bursting with *matoke*, but I would have been hungry today. I was always hungry and loved to eat whatever my mamas prepared. I was not interested in how to cook it, but how to eat it. Mama said that I could eat like an elephant and never gain weight.

Suda increased the pace after we had eaten. Although she was walking briskly maneuvering through the leaves and bushes, it was a run for me. Ever so vigilant, she looked expectant, as if something or someone would jump out of the bushes at any moment. We walked several hours in silence as the sun shone high, in and out of the clouds. Without warning, the rain came down like angry tears from the gods. The ground quickly became a soaked stew, creating a slippery mud that seeped through my shoes and drenched my feet.

I sought shelter under the leaves of a banana tree. Suda followed suit. She looked at me. "We must travel in the rain. The LLA will find us if we do not."

She was right. She was always right. Reluctantly, I trekked through the rain with Suda at my side. I knew she felt sorry for me and let me set the pace. It would have been easier had I known where we would stop for the night, giving me something to look forward to. Instead we were cold, wet, hungry, and walking endlessly with no destination in sight.

Loneliness crept into me like the cool night air. Suda's presence didn't comfort me as my mind conjured up horrible thoughts about what was happening in our village. Villagers were being captured or killed at this very moment. Would any survive? Terrifying thoughts raced through my mind as I imagined the murdered bodies littering the paths, pools of blood surrounding their lifeless remains. Had Mama

Kaikara and Mama Bacia and their children escaped? Although I saw my brothers and sister leave the hut, I still questioned whether they had encountered the LLA.

No words could describe the heart-gripping emotions I felt knowing that my family could never return to our huts, our village, or our lives. For once, I longed for the comfort of Mama's embrace that had been robbed from my childhood. Why had she left us without a warning or even a goodbye? She took everything of value and left nothing for us. I must not blame her, I chided myself. She, too, was deserted. Baba had left her, although he did not leave her empty-handed like she had us.

After several hours we came upon a small clearing. Cautiously, Suda surveyed the area as she motioned with her hand for me to stay put. It was getting dark and the rain had slowed to a drizzle. I waited patiently for her to signal me.

"It's a small camp," she said returning to my side. "I think it may have been an LLA advance scout group of about ten or so. They must have hunted for their food by the looks of the fire pit. It hasn't been used for several days." I followed her as she walked to the center of the clearing. There were two rusted tin cans that were filled with rain water. Banana leaves had been pulled off to provide bedding. The elephant grass had been flattened by the soldiers from several days of use.

"Do you think we are safe here for the night?" I asked.

"I think we are safe, but we will travel a few more kilometers to make sure. We would not want them to come back tonight."

"Then let us go now," I responded warily. My feet ached and my body was worn out. I needed to sleep, wherever that might be. Again, Suda took the water from my bag and this time drank liberally. By the time I finished drinking, the container was half-empty. We each took a moment to relieve ourselves before we left the clearing.

Our goal was to travel five additional kilometers. An hour later we made it without my complaining, despite my aching muscles and sore feet.

"We're going to stop for the night," Suda announced, putting her hands on her hips and stretching her back.

Lucky for us, the rain had just about stopped. We covered the ground with banana leaves for our bedding, but to my dismay my blanket was drenched. At this point it did not matter, for I was already soaked. Suda brought out the soggy millet bread that we ate for our meager evening meal. Then she and I curled up together under our wet blankets, trying to keep warm. At first I shook uncontrollably, but soon the heat from Suda's body warmed mine and I quickly fell into an exhausted sleep.

A cold sweat transpired from one dream to the next, following me like a blanket about my body. I dreamed of being chased by an evil man but couldn't see his face. I ran as fast as I could, but my legs were like jelly as they moved in slow motion. I couldn't escape. As my captor neared, I could do nothing, my legs were glued in place. I was alone, always alone and it frightened me. I called out, but Suda never came.

Within moments, the outline of a shirtless man appeared, his face was clouded and unrecognizable. Many scars branded his dark, heavily muscled shoulders and arms. I screamed in horror as he loomed over me.

"Run. Run away child," the *sangoma's* voice broke through my dreams.

I awoke to a teeth-chattering chill running down my spine, tensing my body. My skin puckered with little bumps like a plucked chicken. The night was at its blackest, right before the morning. The moon was hidden, nowhere to be found. I sensed a danger. Something was near. We weren't alone. The quiet rhythm of Suda's breath sharply contrasted the rapid beat of my heart. I wanted to wake her, but was afraid to draw unwanted attention. I had to do something, lest we were caught unguarded.

Cautiously I sat up and reached for Suda, who had rolled a meter from me. I grabbed her shoulder, slowly shaking her awake as I eased closer. She got up with a start.

"Matika, what is it?" she was frightened and it rang clear in her voice.

"Someone is here." I whispered. My eyes were adjusting to the darkness. "I'm afraid," I whimpered.

"Shhhh," she whispered. She held my arm and brought me to my feet. We listened in the darkness as the shadows began to take shape. Then we heard it; a low, horrendous animalistic growl that came from deep within that no human could utter. Instantly, Suda put her forearm across my chest and we began to back away as it crept closer. It was just as aware of us as we were of it.

I could only see the shadowy outline some distance away that seemed gigantic and thoughts of the silverback gorilla from my nightmares stormed my mind. We continued to back away, as it was now about thirty meters from us, until I felt the rough bark of a large fig tree against my back and could go no further. I followed my instinct and began to climb the tree. Suda was quicker than I and scaled the trunk to the few branches above me with ease. I had just reached the first of its thick spiral branches when I lost my footing and slid down.

"Suda!" I screamed, clinging to a branch for dear life. My legs swung back and forth like leaves in the wind.

"Don't move!" Suda yelled.

The sudden movements and noise prompted the animal to launch its attack. The guttural sound vibrated as it leapt toward me. I shrieked when I felt my body being pulled toward the ground. My skirt was in the deathlike grip of its bite. Its powerful jaws swung me back and forth as I struggled to hold the branch. I felt one of the buttons of my skirt give way under the strain. My hands were slipping and my fingers were growing numb. It was only a matter of time before I would fall to my death below.

Desperately, I lifted my legs as the animal gnawed viciously at the fabric. Whimpering, I walked my feet up the tree truck and wrapped my ankles around the first branch. Though, I was far from being safe. Simultaneously my skirt ripped and I watched, horrified, as my hands slipped from the branch. Suda caught my wrist just in time, yanking me onto the branch as if I weighed less than a feather. She had saved me and I was beyond grateful, temporarily.

Then I saw it. Slowly but gracefully, the leopard put its claws against the tree trunk, ripping the bark off, and began to climb. His body was long, camouflaged with circular irregular rosettes, and his legs were short. His paw was bleeding, which explained why he attacked us. A healthy leopard prefers wild prey to humans. Staring at his massive skull and powerful jaw muscles, I imagined my neck being ripped open. We were like sheep awaiting slaughter in the leopard's domain – they stow their prey in trees for future consumption.

There was no reason to continue climbing, as he would only follow. Suda had pulled a branch from the tree as protection and I did the same. A new rush of adrenaline swam through me as we made our stand and faced the leopard.

CHAPTER FIVE

~~~~~~~~~~~~~~~

Suda reached down and stabbed at him with her long stick. She stepped back when a deep rumbling noise gurgled from his throat. Gripping my stick firmly in one hand and holding on to the branch above with the other, I too stabbed at him, infuriating him. He was only moments away and our blunt sticks did nothing to hinder him. I could smell the feral musk as he drew closer.

With hungry jaws wide open, he snapped and growled. Then he launched. I closed my eyes, preparing for the worst. The crack of a rifle deafened my ears and I was thrown from the tree. Stunned, I hit the ground, the force knocking the wind out of my lungs. My head was like a drum beating endlessly in a festival. I attempted to get up but my legs were heavy. I couldn't move them.

"Are you all right?" Suda asked, clearly distressed. She swiftly descended the tree and was by my side stroking my face. Another person appeared and suddenly, my legs felt lighter. The leopard had fallen on them.

"Yes, I think so," I replied feeling my limbs for injury. Had I really survived unscathed? My skirt was torn on the side up to my waist, partially exposing my thighs.

"Matika!" was all she said. She saw the shredded garment and let out a sigh of relief, briefly closing her eyes and arching her head to the sky piously, then faced the stranger who was kneeling on my left.

"What took you so long to shoot? She could have been killed."

"What ever happened to 'thank you?'" he said with a laugh, but abruptly stopped when Suda's eyes shot daggers at him. She was behaving boldly to a man she did not know. "I had to wait until I was close because it was my last bullet."

I gazed at him for the first time and saw that he was not yet a man but a boy in his mid-teens. Even in darkness, I could see he was attractive, with large white teeth, full lips and a strong nose. His large, slightly almond-shaped eyes were the color of coffee beans. Although they were laced with humor, there was an underlying sadness hidden in its pools.

With his hair cut short, a small scar was visible on the right side of his head. His long-sleeved cotton shirt was dark brown with a tear just below the buttoned collar. Too-short cargo pants hugged his backside, exposing his ankles and shins halfway to the knees. His corded calves were sleek and hairless. He wore black boots with a hole near the little toe. His AK-47 assault rifle was an extension of his hand, never touching the ground.

"What's your name? Are you alone?" Suda asked, craning her neck, looking for others.

"Yes, I'm alone," he said. Then with a scripted response, all humor gone, "I am called Fear None."

"You do not expect me to call you that. What is your given name?"

"A name I will never speak again because he's dead."

"Thank you for saving my life," I interjected on a different note as Suda helped me to my feet. "I would've been killed for sure."

"What are you doing out here alone?" she asked, standing in front of him. He was tall, a few inches over six feet.

"I have run away like you," he responded, stepping a scant few centimeters from Suda, looking down into her eyes. His Adam's apple moved up and down as he swallowed hard.

She was quiet for a minute, contemplating something. Her breasts were rising and falling rapidly as if short of breath. "Fine," she said, gathering her composure. "Where are you going?"

"Anywhere but here. Where are you headed?"

"We're going to Kenya to find my Baba," Suda said glancing in my direction. Then taking command, added, "It's almost morning, so we have to get going. You're welcome to travel with us if you would like, but we move quickly."

"You would have me travel with you? How do you know that I would not kill you or take you as a sex slave?"

"You saved my sister's life. I can see that you are a good boy."

"I'm a man, not a boy."

"Very well, you're a kind man. You may travel with us or by yourself," she said walking toward our belongings a few feet away. She bent over and began repacking.

"Is she always like this?" he asked me, staring at Suda's bottom. His eyes seemed to follow every contour of her shapely body.

"Suda has always been headstrong," I said.

"Suda," he repeated slowly, letting the sound roll from his mouth. He watched her, intently licking his lips like a cat. He was like an animal stalking his prey. He wanted her and not in the way that was appropriate. I needed to warn her as soon as possible. To my relief, he walked over to the leopard and bent over it with a knife in hand, his rifle now slung across his back.

I walked over to Suda and she put my packed bag across my shoulder. "I do not like the way he looks at you," I whispered.

"What do you mean?" she asked, both of her brows raised in surprise.

"That look, that hungry leopard look," I said a little louder than I intended to.

"Don't worry, Matika, I can take care of myself," she said dismissing the subject. "I am happy you are all right. He may prove to be valuable. It will be safer to have someone with a rifle traveling with us. Besides, I bet that he knows the location of the LLA, decreasing our likelihood of encountering them. I will feel safer with him. Tonight was a close call and I don't want anything happening to you."

"You know what is best. I trust you," I said hoping she was right.

"Good. Let's go now," she said heading west. "Are you coming?" she called to him, looking saucily over her shoulder.

Without answering, he walked swiftly to her side. I followed the pair, mindful of his every move. Despite my effort to think the best about him, there was something I didn't trust. He was too secretive. We walked in silence for some time.

"I must think of a nickname for you. Let me think." Suda deliberated only a few moments. "I'll call you Walyam because you are our protector."

He was flattered by this and smiled down at her. "Walyam. I like that name."

They began to talk about family life. Suda spoke about our family, omitting the fact that Baba was a general. Instead, she emphasized the banking business as his primary source of income, which was true. Speaking about our mamas, brothers and sisters brought back joyous memories, but ending the tale with the separation of our family brought me back to our painful reality. When Walyam was prompted to talk about his home he abruptly changed the subject, but Suda would not let it go.

"Sometimes it is better to talk about it than to hold it inside," she persisted. With her coaxing he told a little about his life.

"I lived in a small village in the north near Gula. I had three brothers and two sisters. When I was thirteen, me and my younger sister were taken as child soldiers by the LLA, four years ago. The rest of my family was killed in the raid. I ran away a few weeks ago after learning my sister was beaten to death by her 'husband.'

"I told no one she was my sister," he continued, his gaze fixed straight ahead. "Our relationship was kept a secret from all. The only thing that kept me from going crazy or taking the drugs was her. She was my constant reminder that once, I had a normal life. We often spoke of our childhood and the things we used to do. When we got the chance, we planned to run away. We had to get away from that horrible place. Now, I have no family and nowhere to go..." he trailed off, lost in the devastating realities of what had become his life.

"Come with us," Suda interrupted his silent musings. "Our Baba is a kind and generous man. He can find you work."

How could Suda offer such a promise to a man she had just met? Yes, he saved my life, but to bring him to our Baba, that was too much. What was she doing? Walking closer together, they spoke in hushed tones. Walyam was basking in the sympathy she provided while gently stroking his back.

The rain, a constant drizzle throughout the day, emphasized my discomfort with my torn and soiled skirt. We walked for several hours and not once did they look back at me. I could have fallen off a cliff or jumped into Lake Victoria and they would not have noticed. Green with envy, I sulked until we stopped to rest and break our fast.

We shared our food with Walyam, who had a healthy appetite, not caring if there was enough food for tomorrow. Normally, he ate off the land and would steal whatever was needed for survival. I was astonished that Suda let him eat almost all our food when only yesterday she had stressed the need for rationing while my tummy rumbled all last night. Suda's sudden change in behavior made me uneasy.

As the two talked, I began to get afraid. I was forgotten as I walked behind them. Their foolish laughter was exposing us. Suda had forgotten our purpose, our journey. She was traveling as if we were walking to the market or visiting the local village girls. I tried to concentrate on the positive aspects, but it was hard. Worse yet, our pace had slowed since Walyam joined us. At least my legs felt better.

We traveled past a few scattered farms, trying to stay concealed in the vegetation that was now becoming sparse. As the sky darkened, Suda and Walyam agreed on stopping for the night. Walyam went in search for food as we prepared the bedding.

"He's very interesting," she said trying to hide her excitement, but the dreamy look in her eyes betrayed her words. "He's quite handsome, too. I can talk about anything with him. Do you know what? He's going to teach me English." We spoke our tribal dialogue and Swahili. Baba and my oldest brothers were the only ones in our family who studied English.

"Really," I said, uninterested, plopping on the bedding. Bouncing around, making an unsuccessful attempt to search for dry sticks for a small fire, she continued to glorify Walyam, not noticing my noncommittal responses. She didn't care whether I was listening and my mind drifted as she chattered. The setting sun had left a chill in the air and the rain had not abated. It would be another cold night.

"…I think so. What do you think Matika?" she asked, looking at me with a silly grin. I had no idea what she was talking about. She glared at me when I sat mutely. "You haven't heard a word I said. What's wrong with you?"

"I don't want to hear any more about him. That's all you're talking about," I said in my defense.

"I know what it is. You're jealous! You don't like the fact that he's interested in me and not you. For the first time, you're not the center of attention. For once, your sister has gotten the eye of a man before you."

I was momentarily speechless. How could she say such things? The thought had never crossed my mind. She was right, though. All the men and boys gave me attention, but I hated it. I wished just once I could walk by men without their leering eyes, "accidental" patting of my bottom, or their embarrassing comments.

"No, Suda, it's nothing like that," I began.

"Just admit it. You're jealous because you wanted him for yourself," she cried, the muscles in her face twitching, barely controlling her emotions. A bitter mocking smile curved her lips. I would have told her many things had Walyam not appeared with a bunch of unripe *matoke* across his back. His timing was horrid, yet perfect. It burned me to the core to know that she thought I wanted him, that I was jealous. What could I have said to ease her temper and make her understand how I felt?

Suda and I ate in silence as Walyam discussed the location of the rebels and some of their plans that he knew, which really wasn't much. The years he spent in captivity earned him rank, but not enough to be added into the important plans or decision-making among the senior leadership. Despite my best attempt to force myself to eat, I could barely choke down two small plantains, which stuck to my cottonmouth.

Soon after, I mumbled an excuse, rolled in a blanket and pretended to sleep. Suda moved her bedding about a meter away, closer to Walyam. The two continued to talk for another hour before they retired side by side. Every now and then Suda chuckled but I was too emotionally and physically fatigued to care and sleep came upon me like a blessed respite.

My nightmare began again but was greatly intensified. I had been ravished by the unknown captor. It was so realistic that when I awoke right before dawn, I was unable to determine whether I was truly awake. My ears pounded with the thumping of my chest. The headscarf had come off when I slept. I unwrapped the taut scarf around my sore breasts to get a short relief.

Looking over at Suda I took a swift intake of air. There she was, casually sprawled out across Walyam's body and naked as the day she was born, sated from a night of passion. The cover was in a twisted mess as were her legs, entwined around his. They slept without a care in the world when we could be discovered at any moment.

Walyam had one hand behind his head and the other on the small of her back. I watched in appalled fascination. The blood rushed to my face as I saw his manhood hanging limply to the side. I felt an unfamiliar sensation in the pit of my stomach and I felt the peaks of my breasts pucker into little pebbles. My body was behaving in a way that I had never experienced before. I knew I should turn away and silently chided myself as I stared openly at it. Oh my, it was beginning to rise before my eyes.

"You like what you see," he said smugly in a deep sleepy voice with eyes at half-mast. He was looking right at me and made no effort to cover his sword. I turned away. That arrogant man, how I despised him. It was he who put a spell over my Suda and took her from me.

Unable to bear it a moment longer I got up and walked away. For several minutes I walked before I stopped to relieve myself. Then, I sat down against a tree, wishing it would all end and Baba would come for us. Staring at the sky brought a small smile to my face. The sky was a beautiful, untainted blue vista with dry promises. Closing my eyes, I allowed myself to enjoy the warmth of the rising sun. Just as I was beginning to doze off, I was alerted by the sound of hurried footsteps approaching.

CHAPTER SIX

~~~~~~~~~~~~~~~~~

I contemplated drawing up my legs so they would not be visible. Instead, I held my breath, not moving a muscle. Whoever was approaching, I prayed they would overlook me. All noise suddenly stopped. There were no more songs of birds or buzzing insects, but a growing silence. I squeezed my eyes tightly shut and sat trembling, waiting.

"What have we here?" said a low voice. Startled, I gasped as I opened my eyes and stared into the dull black barrel of a rifle only a few centimeters from my face. The man holding the gun motioned with his hand and others came into view. There were at least a dozen uniformed men approaching, laughing, and gaping as they formed a half-circle around me.

The gun was lowered as the largest man, a full head taller than the others, came forward, leering at me. He was missing a few teeth and his nose was large and misaligned, as though it had been broken several times. His arms were massive with muscles that bulged out of his short-sleeve shirt. Large, angry veins ran along his arms like cords of rope.

His legs were small tree trunks and extended beyond his dark cargo pants that came down to mid-shin.

Everything about him was massive as he seemed to fill the entire space around me. When he knelt before me I tried to back away, but he grabbed my shirt and slammed me against the tree. With both hands, he ripped it off, exposing my breasts for all to see. Instinctively I covered them with my arms but he pulled those away. There was a collective sigh before he pushed me against the ground and covered me with his body, using his weight to crush me into the earth. He was so tall and heavy that I could not breathe; my face was buried in his chest. His body odor was foul, reeking of many days of sweat and dirt. I heard the others in the background cheering him on as he ground himself against me.

With every bit of energy I fought him, relentlessly clawing at his body. He ignored my weak attempts and used his knee to push open my legs. When he used his hand to free his member I took advantage of the space created and brought up my knee as hard as I could. For a moment there was a look of utter surprise on his face before he groaned and rolled off me. The others roared in laughter as if they were watching a game. Trying to get away, I stood but to my horror, he clutched my skirt and it was torn from my body. Standing completely naked, I briefly froze in humiliation. I was deafened by their cheers.

"Do you need help, Wandera?" a man called from the group as they circled around me. Smiling down at me, he looked ready to pounce awaiting the response.

"I am…going to… kill her," Wandera moaned, trying to stand while doubled over in pain. He recovered quickly and it was only a matter of time before he would do as he threatened.

"Please, let me pass!" I begged a younger man who blocked my way. He was Walyam's age, maybe younger. For a moment I thought he looked as if he felt sorry for me and for the briefest second I also thought he would let me pass. Then his expression changed and just as quickly he pushed me so hard I fell on my bottom. I pleaded with my eyes but he turned away and I knew I would find no compassion.

"Come here," Wandera snarled like an animal through clenched teeth. He was so angry that I almost obeyed him. Then I thought of Mama. It was better to stay away from her when she was angry, but there was no place to go. Then I saw my only chance of escape. I lunged between the legs of a man, scrambled to my feet and ran, refusing to look back although I knew they were chasing me.

No sooner had I run a dozen strides when I slammed into another man who seemed to appear like a ghost out of nowhere. All the laughter and jokes immediately ceased. It was obvious that everyone knew who he was as they quietly gathered around. My instincts warned me to be exceptionally cautious, so I did not move. He slowly took off his dark glasses. I watched his cold eyes as he scrutinized my naked body from head to foot. Then he grabbed my jaw, forced my mouth open and peered inside.

"Perfect," he said to himself so low it was barely audible. He circled me slowly and I stood shaking in fear. He invoked a terror in me like no other. He was calm and collected and displayed no expression except for the clenching of his jaw muscles. What I feared most was what I saw in his eyes. They were the beady eyes of a snake and as dark as the night. He reminded me of what I imagined a demon would look like in a man's body, the power to brutally kill without remorse. The man was thin, with strong yet sharp facial features, and a square jaw. His clothes resembled more of a uniform than the others and were somewhat clean and neat with a red beret that was tipped to one side. A blade was on his side. "She will come with us back to base camp."

"But Colonel-" Wandera began.

"I said base camp. Is that understood?"

"Yes, Colonel," he replied, clearly disappointed from being cheated of his pleasure.

"I will deliver her to the River Lion untouched. Moses will enjoy her," he said. Then motioning to the youth who would not let me escape before, and who was obviously the most junior ranking man of the group, he said, "It seems that she is a runner?" It was more a statement than a question. "Cover and bind her. We leave now." With a dismissive hand he turned and walked away.

The young man fumbled in his sack and handed me a bundle. It was a dark blue shirt with bloodstains throughout but I was grateful that it was long and loose, hanging midway down my thighs. It was just enough to hide my unbearable shame. I had never been exposed to any male before, not even my brothers, unlike Suda, who didn't have a shy bone in her body. Constantly aware of men staring at my womanly figure, I was always careful not to dress or bathe with others. Beside my sisters, no one could see me, which was a feat in itself considering the lack of privacy we had at our hut.

"Thank you," I said truly thankful for the shirt, but he ignored me. Within moments, my hands were bound with a leather thong so tight I could feel it cutting off the circulation. Why did he punish me? Anyone could see that it was too tight. For some reason, I felt that this young man was my only hope, so I was disappointed in his treatment of me. He picked up the leather leash and pulled roughly, like I was an animal, causing me to lurch forward.

A grueling pace was set and I did everything in my power to keep from stumbling, feeling constantly off balance because my hands were tied. As we traveled north, slipping further away from Suda, my heart cried out. Had she and Walyam gotten away or were they killed in each other's arms? I worried about her more so than my own life. I wanted to ask but feared the answer, and the consequences. I felt a sense of hopelessness deep in my soul. If only I had not harassed her about Walyam traveling with us or stressed over his relationship with Suda. She was a smart girl who could make her own choices in life and she had proved herself time and time again. I could have just turned a blind eye and maybe, just maybe, I would not be in this situation. Walyam was so unimportant to me that I cursed myself for being so selfish.

Mentally replaying the conversations of the previous day, I could not help thinking of different responses I could have said. It could have been my mind that embellished the situation far more than the reality. Thoughts of doubt and hopelessness permeated my mind. What had really happened? Everything had become muddled. No matter what happened during the course of events, I realized that it was too late.

We stopped only once that day for a short break. I asked to relieve myself but was not afforded the luxury of privacy. At this point, I no longer cared whether the young man was watching me, perhaps relishing in my discomfort as I squatted, balancing on unsteady legs. I thought of escaping. Dwelling on Suda and the past was going to get me nowhere. I knew that I would rather die than be a sex slave to this River Lion, or suffer such atrocities that no one should ever suffer. My mind constantly searched for an escape. Although we were a few meters from the group and concealed by light vegetation, with hands tied I would be no match to gain my freedom.

While the others ate I was offered no food, but a drink from the water skin. Wandera sat across from me and his hungry eyes never left my body as he ate his food with a hearty appetite. The others joked and laughed, paying me no attention. The rain started again as I looked up into the sky to take my mind off my rumbling tummy. It had quickly turned gray and I shivered as the raindrops fell upon my naked legs. I ignored Wandera's smile as the shirt shamefully stuck to my body. No one else seemed to notice the rain as they continued their conversations.

I tried to loosen the leather that bound my wrists by wiggling my hands, which currently had no feeling left in them. They were turning a strange grayish color. How much longer were they going to leave me tied like this? It would only be a matter of time before my hands would have to be cut off. I was reminded of the *sangoma*, who had once tightly wrapped a cord around a man's bleeding limb before amputation. That thought was enough for me to ask for it to be loosened.

"Excuse me," I said quietly at first to the young man who was sitting on my left with his back to me. "Might I ask you, please?" I said louder as he pretended not to hear me.

He peered over his shoulder at me but did not respond, so I continued, "Please, I beg you to loosen the ties. I cannot feel my hands any longer."

He looked at me for a few moments with one eyebrow raised.

"Know this. You have no friends here," he said turning his back on me once again.

"I have realized that but I will lose my hands if this isn't taken off."

"Do you think I care?" he said not bothering to face me.

"No, but I do know that you would want to please Moses. The River Lion wouldn't like to see me harmed, as I would be no use to him." That got his attention, for he turned and scooted closer to me.

"There are many girls to take your place," he said looking into my eyes and then carefully untying the leather strap. His words sent chills down my spine. The ties had dug a deep ring around my wrist. I thought I would die from the pain and I cried inside as the blood rushed to fill my hands again. He must have seen the pain in my eyes because he began to rub my wrists and hands to speed up the process. I was extremely grateful, but was smart enough not to say so a second time considering that was how I ended up like this.

"I guess it would be too much to ask for a bite to eat." I knew there was not a chance in this world that I would get food from him, but for some reason it made me laugh inside I'd have the audacity to even ask. It seemed that he, too, had to suppress a smile before he turned around. He may have thought that I was crazy, and for that moment I would have had to agree with him. Like Baba used to say, "Sometimes life cooks you up worms and there is nothing to do but eat them or die of hunger." It was worth a try and I had nothing to lose.

Before we left, the young man tied my wrists once again but this time not nearly as tight. I knew that if I needed to, I would be able to free my hands. Trying to be positive, I focused on my escape. The best plan would be to escape at night. If I could somehow get away and travel west, maybe I could still find Baba and be reunited with Suda. Then it hit me: Suda had not told me where Baba was or how to get there. I depended on her for everything and we did not even have a contingency plan in case something was to happen, such as separation or worse. How foolish we were not to think about that and plan accordingly. I was not a child and should have known better.

I would leave and head west to Kenya. Whatever happened, I would deal with it and think of something, but for now, I had to escape. Time was extremely critical because each hour took me further away from Nairobi and closer to slavery and the agonizing unknown. There was no doubt in my mind that I needed to get out of this situation or die trying.

Late that afternoon, we came upon a little village that seemed to be deserted. There were about twenty huts in a circle situated in a large clearing. The men were on the alert as the colonel dispatched two men to scout the village. We waited in silence. The men were tense and the colonel seemed edgy. This gave me some hope that just maybe armed men from the village or a small military unit had seen us and were hiding, waiting for the right moment for an ambush. I was thrilled with the thought that I may get the chance to run away during the confusion, if I wasn't shot in the process.

CHAPTER SEVEN

~~~~~~~~~~~~~~~~~~~~~~~~~

The village was not deserted, but I was unprepared for what I saw. It was evident that all the livestock had been looted. As we walked through the small village, I was sickened at the sight of maimed bodies of men, women, and children. I don't know if one would call it fortunate or unfortunate, but I had never seen a dead body before that day. I was too young to remember when my brother had died after childbirth. One would say that I was sheltered, and although our country had been at war for years, I had not seen its ugly side.

Some of the villagers had been shot and perhaps died instantly; others had suffered cruelly at the hands of murderers who had not spared a bullet on them. Seeing body parts hacked off and bodies that had been mutilated, I tasted bile and gagged. Although I had nothing in my stomach, I spewed every bit of yellowy acid until there was nothing left. With my stomach empty, I continued to heave to the point of convulsion. My knees weakened and I fell to the ground. How could anyone do something so monstrous and barbaric?

The young man had a little sympathy for me, and with the colonel's permission he carried me into a nearby hut and roughly deposited me on a dirty mat. He began rummaging through the already-ransacked hut. My eyes were clouded and I cried and screamed and cried again to the point of hysteria. Is this what had happened in my village? Maybe my whole family was dead. I felt completely alone in this depraved world. The confines of the hut began to suffocate me and I found myself gasping for breath, unable to fill my lungs.

"Drink," ordered the young man as he handed me a clay bowl filled with water and bits of crushed herbs floating at its surface. I refused it and pushed the bowl back into his hands, a little of its contents spilling onto the floor. I did not want anything from him or anyone. I wanted my family, our hut and our village. I began wailing once again in despair. I thought of the *sangoma* and what she had said to me. She knew this would happen. Why had she not given me more warning? I cursed her.

"They will soon tire of your sniveling," he said. Then he wrapped his arms around me, pulling me in his lap, and forced the bowl to my mouth, hitting my teeth in the process. With my wrist still tied, I had to drink or drown as he poured the liquid down my throat. After I had swallowed the last drops, he told me he had given me something to help calm my nerves and continued to hold me tightly. I soon began to calm down; it was working.

As strange as it sounds, it was comforting to be in his arms and although I knew he was my enemy, I could not ignore his consoling embrace, which had a warmth that radiated throughout my body. My world was unraveling quickly and he happened to be the one holding the strings for now. I wanted to be absorbed into his body and hide until it was over. Without thinking, I nestled my face into his chest, which smelled of Shea butter soap scented with peppermint oil blended with sweat. That Shea butter and peppermint was the scent that we used for washing in our hut. His muscles grew taut as I as savored the aroma that reminded me so much of home.

"You cannot let them see how it affects you," he said bringing me back to reality, adjusting his body and putting a little distance between us.

"How can anyone be so barbaric and heartless?" I cried, looking up at him with eyes on the brink of tears yet again. His eyes grew soft as he held my gaze with a look of what I thought was understanding. For the first time, I really looked at him and saw that he was handsome. Feeling that he somehow read my thoughts, the blood rushed to my face. Blushing, I looked down and lowered my head. What was happening? I was ashamed at how my body responded to him on its own accord.

"There are wicked people here and you are in the center of it. I have watched so many people slaughtered like animals. I've taken part in things that I am disgusted to admit. If you want to live, you must fit in. Do everything they tell you and never question them. You must do it without hesitation because reluctance is a sign of rebellion or weakness, and either will get you killed."

"I will not do anything against my beliefs," I said, perplexed that anyone would do anything against their beliefs. "I will not kill anyone!"

"To save your life or save your family?"

I couldn't answer that. How far would I go to save my life or Suda's? Could I summon the courage to shoot someone in order to save Suda's life? It troubled me to even think that people had to make such decisions. This was different, and there was no reason for the mass carnage.

"Do you want to live?" his frustration rang clear in his deep voice. Then, calming down, he tenderly reached for me and drew me closer to his chest. "I have never spoken to a new recruit because they do not live long enough." He spoke as if he were confessing a great secret that was heavy on his heart. "I will never speak to you when others are around and I will never speak to you again after we reach base camp."

"Why not?" I asked, hurt, as though he had slapped me. Silently, I chided myself for feeling that way, but I was so alone and so desperate for a friend.

"Speaking to you will only bring harm to you and me. I will not take that chance. Never cross the colonel; he is filled with demons. He will give you to Moses, the River Lion, and I have no doubt Moses will be pleased with you." He pulled me back as he swept his eyes briefly over my body, lingering over my breasts.

His next move nearly drove me insane with questions. I didn't see it coming. To my astonishment, he kissed me full on the lips. I closed my eyes to savor the moment, but it was over before I had a chance to register that it even happened. Although the kiss was swift, I remembered every detail because it was my first. Other than family members, I had never been kissed by a man. I could think of a thousand more romantic places and situations it could have occurred. Suda's first kiss was under the moonlight during a village festival last year to a young man she believed herself in love with. Not me. I was kissed by a young man, albeit handsome, whose name I did not even know.

His lips had been warm and soft, so different from how I imagined they would be. I thought they would be firm because they were always pressed tightly together, creating lines in the corners of his mouth. I opened my eyes and looked at him with questioning eyes. His actions went against everything he said. He was a walking contradiction that I simply could not understand.

He sat me aside and only then did I realize I had been sitting so snuggly in his lap. I felt the blood rush to my face for a second time. He then surprised me yet again by sauntering out of the hut without giving me so much as a backward glance. Although I was unattended, I felt it in my soul that it was not the right time to try to escape.

Alone, the fear crept into me at the thought of the bodies outside. Only now did I hear the distant sounds of children crying, some screaming, and the laughter of the men. There must have been a handful of children that remained alive. I imagined they must have been hidden by their mothers in desperation with hopes that they would be overlooked. I tried to tune out what was happening outside but it was impossible to control my imagination.

I don't know how long I sat looking at the hut entrance, afraid to move, but after some time the young man returned. He handed me a plantain and said, "Eat this quickly before someone sees you." He kept watch at the hut entrance, looking uneasy. He must have taken a great risk in giving me food.

Despite the growing sense of dread and the knots in my stomach, I quickly ate the plantain with no complaint. I needed the energy to escape and pride would get me nowhere. When I was done, I drank from the water skin he handed me. We waited in silence, with me sitting on the mat and him standing at the entrance. The children's cries had stopped.

"We will be leaving soon."

"What is happening?" I had to ask. Sometimes I was too curious.

"None of them were worth keeping. They were half-starved and would have died anyway," he explained, sounding a bit defensive.

I left it at that, not wanting to know any details. Soon after, we left the hut, heading out of the village. The men seemed satisfied and carried various provisions. I averted my eyes to avoid the dead but a bright blue-and-white fabric caught my attention ahead. As we neared it, I saw that it was a beautifully patterned girl's dress. It had been ripped in two.

To the left, only a scant few yards away, lay the owner of the dress, eyes wide open, staring at me in utter horror. She could not have been more than eight years old. Blood seeped out of her freshly slit throat, from where small guttural sounds emanated. I turned away quickly, sickened once again, but her eyes were imprinted in my mind and I would never forget them as long as I lived. They were large, innocent, dying eyes, begging for life.

She was moments away from leaving this world and there was nothing I could do. I felt helpless and ashamed; helpless that I could do nothing to save her or the others, and ashamed to be alive. I grew angry at myself, thinking that while she was being brutalized I was safely in a man's arms. When I looked up again, Wandera was smiling and leering at me.

For several kilometers we traveled and I welcome the breakneck pace, feeling that I needed to be punished. Every aching muscle in my body purged the anger within. Wandera would occasionally make grunting sounds to get my attention, making it known that he was walking right behind me. I desperately tried to ignore his intense gaze that burned into my backside.

"We will camp here for the night," the colonel said. "Lutalo, make a fire for tonight." Finally, I knew his name.

Lutalo scurried away, leaving my side for the first time since departing the hut. While the men busied themselves preparing camp I was alone with Wandera, who purposely brushed up behind me, setting my nerves on edge. His touch was acid, nothing like the kindness of Lutalo.

"You think you have escaped me?" he whispered looking out for the colonel. His warm rancid breath, too close to my ear, repulsed me. "Do you think to humiliate me without paying a price? Rest assured, I will have my revenge soon enough."

"Leave me alone, or I'll tell the colonel," I said without facing him before I realized my error. I quickly put my hands to my mouth tightly, squeezing my eyes shut.

"You stupid girl," he said with loathing. "The colonel cares nothing for you. He can always find another to take to Moses." With that he walked away, leaving me alone.

His last words had chilled my bones. How ironic that this River Lion was the only thing keeping me alive, out of harm's way. What if I could not escape before we reached camp? If this Moses did not like me, would I be given to another man, like Wandera?

Lutalo returned, started a fire and saw to the colonel's needs. The colonel told him he had the first watch so I was firmly tied with my hands behind a nearby tree, thrusting my breasts outward, away from the warm fire. The aroma of a delicious soup hovered in a small pot above it, stirring up the sharp hunger lingering in my belly, like a fire that wouldn't be quenched. I was disappointed at being tied again, for I desperately needed rest. I kept my eyes down as the men ate. I hoped Lutalo would be so kind as to spare me a bite, but that was unlikely with the others so close.

I hoped it wouldn't rain and make an uncomfortable situation even worse. I was extremely exhausted, but figured I would not get much sleep with my back against the rough tree bark. I was wrong. Weakened, I fell into a dreamless sleep before the men had even finished eating. Startled, I awoke to an uneasy feeling. It was a cloudy dark night with no moon. The fire Lutalo had started was gone, except for embers that glowed in the ashes. The men lay in scattered snoring mounds, but then I heard movement in the grass.

The quiet of the night returned once again and I closed my eyes, trying to go back to sleep. That familiar smell of rancid breath slipped into my nose. My eyes snapped open. I was face to face with Wandera. Swiftly, I inhaled before he clamped his large hand over my mouth.

"Make a sound and I'll slit your throat." His voice had a heavy unmistakable undertone of what was to come as he waved a shining jagged blade before my eyes.

"Not a sound." He lowered his hand from my mouth slowly.

Before I realized what was happening, my hands were untied, dropping to my sides. He glared at me, warning me to stay quiet. Then he effortlessly lifted me over his shoulder as if I weighed no more than a bag of beans. He was so tall and large that I felt like I was slung over a tree. He quickly walked away from the camp. I was in a dangerous dilemma: cry for help and risk being killed, or be killed in the woods away from the others.

I needed to think fast as the camp disappeared from my sight. I remembered Lutalo saying to do everything I was told if I were to live.

CHAPTER EIGHT

~~~~~~~~~~~

Wandera walked for a few minutes before he threw me to the ground. The back of my head hit the earth with such a force that I saw bright novas in my brain. He came down at me with a wicked grin. There was no way I could get away from him and he seemed prepared for anything I might do. I began to helplessly sob.

"Please do not do this," I pleaded.

"Not a sound!" He struck me across my face with his open hand, forcing my face to one side. I was stunned by his brutal strength and swallowed a scream that threatened to escape. I tasted the metallic rush of blood as it collected in my mouth. My cheek pulsated in complaint.

"If they come, I will say you were trying to run away." His hands were trembling as he ripped open my shirt. I cried out as he painfully squeezed my breasts and pulled my nipples. Crying only made him more aggressive as he quickly pulled his pants down, freeing his oversized sword wrapped in throbbing veins. He tried to force the rounded tip of his erect shaft into my body, which went rigid and would not open for him. His glaringly painful attempts only frustrated him further, softening his member.

"Open for me now or I will cut it open like I did the girl in the village."

I shuddered at the repulsive revelation. I was traumatized as the vision of the girl flashed in my mind. After a few more unsuccessful attempts, he grabbed his knife and I couldn't contain myself anymore. My piercing shriek erupted, cutting through the silent night. He brought his large hand over my open mouth and nose with his knife in tow. With a lethal glare he looked me with crazed eyes before he brought the knife tip to my throat.

There was nothing I could do. I could not get away, for he had covered me with all his body weight. I closed my eyes, terrified of the pain that was to come. I didn't want to die.

Suddenly, there was a sickening thud, followed by an expelling of air, then a deep groan. Before I knew what happened, I was lifted from the ground. I clutched Lutalo tightly, overwhelmed with emotion. I looked over at Wandera, who lay motionless on the ground.

"Are you all right?"

"I…think so," I responded meekly.

"Did he hurt you?" Concern etched his brow. Just then Wandera moaned, jumping to his feet behind Lutalo, his knife in hand gleaming in the moonlight.

"Lutalo!" I cried backing away as Wandera lunged forward, sending Lutalo to the ground face first. I screamed as Wandera's meaty hands solidly pounded the back of Lutalo's head. I could have run away. It would have been the perfect time while all were asleep and Wandera was distracted beating Lutalo. Yes, he had saved my life, but what could I do to save his? I was just a girl and Wandera was a monster of a man.

To this day I can't recall what happened next. Something in me snapped. I wanted to avenge the girl's death. More than anything, I needed to save Lutalo. I would be no better than Wandera if I left him to die. Instead of running away, I jumped on Wandera's rock-hard back, digging my nails deeply into his eyes. I bit the base of his neck. I thought my teeth would crack. It was like biting into the gristle of a crocodile mixed with salty sweat. Yelling, he reared up, dropping his knife. He easily pulled my hands away from his throat; however, separating me from the back of his neck was another matter.

Reaching behind him, he shouted profanities as he attempted to pull me from him by my hair. I held on for all it was worth, doubling my effort and vowing that if I were separated from him, so would be the meat that I clung to between my teeth. When that failed he grew frenzied, sending violent blows to my head at a dizzying rate. One blow sent me into total darkness. I came to with a pounding headache and double vision. The men were standing by and two of them restrained Wandera.

"She was trying to run away and I was merely going after her!" Wandera shouted, sparks of spit flying out of his mouth. "She attacked me. Surely you cannot take Lutalo's word over mine!" Lutalo was standing next to the colonel and relief washed over me knowing that he was okay.

"You have disobeyed a direct order," the colonel said, stepping only a few inches away from me.

"She attacked…" He sputtered as blood flowed freely from his mouth. Enraged, the colonel swiftly tore through him from belly to chest with his double-edged sword. The only emotion he displayed was irritation at getting blood on his hand. He wiped the curved blade with the upper serrated edge on Wandera's chest, making the silver gleam in the moonlight while he looked directly into the eyes of the dying man.

"I will not be disobeyed." Wandera's lifeless body slumped to the ground as the men quickly released him. Then he turned to Lutalo, who stood motionless, waiting for what was to come. I was helpless to do anything but watch. He struck Lutalo across the face, sending him to the ground. The colonel was not a large man but he showed a feral strength that could not be matched by many. "I entrusted you to watch over her."

"Yes, Colonel," Lutalo knelt at his feet with his head before his boots. My heart went out to him.

"If you had done your job, Wandera would still be alive. You tried to protect her, but she should have never left your sight."

"Yes, sir."

"You had better be thankful she was not ruined, but if anything happens to her, I will kill you with my bare hands. Is that clear?"

"Yes, Colonel."

"She will shit, sleep, and eat at your heels. She will be your shadow!"

"Yes, sir."

"Bury him and we move out," he said, and Lutalo rose and took the shovel that was handed to him by another. Then, addressing the men, "We have six days left and I want to make it in five." With that he walked back to the camp. The others followed in his wake, leaving Lutalo and me alone.

There were two valuable things I had learned from the colonel. One was how fragile everyone's position was. Nothing was guaranteed, not even life itself. To live a life on eggshells was no life at all to me. The second thing I learned was that we were only five days away from my living hell. I desperately needed to escape; however, I was faced with a moral dilemma. If I escaped, Lutalo would surely die for my actions. I don't know if he risked his life to save me out of fear or because he cared about me. I would like to think the latter but I knew deep inside it was a combination of both.

There was only one solution. I would have to convince Lutalo to come with me. I watched in silence while he dug and I began to think of the best ways of persuading him to run away with me. For him it was life or death, and why would he risk his life? Did he even want to be away from these people? He seemed to have adjusted a little too well for my comfort. I thought of what Suda would do. I would have to use some of her tactics, I thought, smiling to myself.

"Thank you," Lutalo said when he stopped to rest, wiping the beads of sweat from his brow with the back of his hand.

"No, I thank you for saving my life."

"I should have been there for you. I should have never let you out of my sight. I didn't even hear him take you."

"I could've screamed when he approached so everyone would know."

"When you jumped on him I was able to get up and fight him until the others arrived. If it was not for that bold move I would have been killed. You are a brave woman to have by anyone's side."

That was an incredible compliment. His looked up at me, showing his beautiful teeth in a crooked smile, and I was momentarily lost in the depths of his dark eyes.

"Thank you," I said blushing, down-casting my eyes. The blush quickly faded as I looked over at Wandera's body. For my benefit, Lutalo had covered his face with a square linen cloth. This was one person I felt no remorse for and it sickened me to look at him.

"Lutalo," I said calling him by his name as I edged closer to him. Now was probably a good time as any to bring up running away. "What's going to happen to us?"

"What do you mean us?"

"When we get to your camp."

"*Our* camp. It will be as I have said before." He looked uncomfortable with the idea and began digging the hole once again. I was counting on that, so I pressed a little further.

"I don't want to be with this Moses. I would rather be with you. Why can't you and I be together?"

He stopped his digging and looked at me, melting my heart.

"Don't let anyone hear you say that again. You know that's impossible."

"Nothing is impossible. I thought you liked me?"

"Of course I do, but not at the expense of my life and yours." I was getting somewhere. He liked me and he admitted it.

"We could run away and be together..."

He began to laugh before I had even finished. "You're crazy. If we even got away, where would we go and how would we live?"

"We could go to Kenya and meet my father. He has lots of money and could take care of us. He could give you a job."

"I have a job."

"My father is wealthy. He owns banks and is waiting for me in Kenya. My father is Batalo Okello Naminiha and he-" I clamped my hand over my mouth interrupting myself. Once again I had not thought before I'd spoken.

He grabbed me by the shoulders. "Never mention his name to anyone. Your father is our sworn enemy. Do you know that we slaughtered an entire village looking for him? The village we went through yesterday pales in comparison to what was done to yours."

"My family...oh, please, no!" All my fears came to light. They were all killed!

"Do not worry. All the huts were empty. We found no one. Where are the others?"

With my fears put to rest, I poured my heart out to Lutalo. Since he knew about my father and had done nothing to me, I felt comfortable telling him everything. My blind faith in him allowed me to trust that he would not use that information against me. I had to ask him about Suda and Walyam, and to my relief they were never found. I must have led the men away from them, thus saving their lives. When Lutalo had completed the task, his hands were covered in red earth.

"What's your name?"

"Matika."

"You are full of surprises, Matika." He kissed me again. Unlike the short brief kiss in the hut, this one was longer with passion, full of promise. Our bodies meshed and I tingled from the inside out, wanting more. Suddenly, he broke the kiss all too soon. "We must go now."

As he led me to the others I was thoroughly confused. He hadn't given me an answer. His kiss contradicted his action of returning to the camp, although it was not a good idea to run now. Perhaps he would bring up the subject later. He did have much to think about. There was one question I needed to know.

"Lutalo, why does the colonel want to take me to Moses?"

"Because he has fallen out of favor with the River Lion," he replied with a smirk.

The colonel was eager to return to headquarters so we departed right away. The pace was extremely fast and sometimes I had to trot to keep up. Lutalo took the colonel's threat to heart. After spending the entire day under Lutalo's watch, there was little room for modesty. I could not so much as relieve myself without him. I was now given food in front of the others. It was as if my status had changed from lowly prisoner to valued prize that needed to be protected at all cost.

By nightfall I was nearly spent. I slept with my back in the warmth of Lutalo's arms, my head resting under his chin. My wrists were tied to his for good measure, but I did not mind at all. It felt good to be close to him as my body warmed within.

In the morning I was sore and soaked to the bone from the rain. By the afternoon I began to worry.

"I'm pleased with the progress we've made so far. We'll reach the Victoria Nile by sunset, where we will cross before nightfall," the colonel said to the men.

"Lutalo," I whispered in the shadows when we had a moment alone. "When are we going to escape?"

"We're not, Matika. It's too dangerous," he said, making sure the others were out of earshot.

"I am leaving with or without you."

"You will do no such thing. It's too risky." I had no time to argue, for we were soon gathered to continue our journey. As we traveled I began to think of ways to escape. In my heart I knew that if I crossed the river, there was no turning back. I decided to come up with a plan. It was risky at best, and downright reckless, but it was my only chance.

I did not bring up the subject again and let him think that I had succumbed to the idea of staying. He would know soon enough and would have to make a decision; either way, his life would be at stake. As I planned my escape, I savored the idea of being free. I slowed down my pace to stall the procession as much as I dared.

It was nearly dark when we reached the Victoria Nile, just as I had hoped. The colonel decided to cross and forged ahead. He told the men to get the canoes. They were not really canoes, but large hollowed-out logs with shaved, flat bottoms. The boats looked dangerous as we all squeezed in, Lutalo and I crouching in the back end. I thought they would tie me up, but for some reason they didn't. We were in the same canoe as the colonel. I reached out to touch the water.

"Don't! There's crocs in the water," Lutalo softly whispered sending chills down my spine. I immediately pulled my hand out of the water.

When we were more than halfway across, my opportunity arrived. I hesitated only a moment, looking back at Lutalo, before sliding off the side of the canoe into the cool black water.

CHAPTER NINE

Taking a deep breath, I dove down into perpetual darkness, as far as my body weight would allow. My adrenaline heightened at the sound of water rushing past my ears. From above, the water had looked calm and inviting, hiding the strong undercurrent that propelled me downstream.

I was thankful my brother Akello taught the village children to swim after three drowned while collecting water from the spring a few years ago. Suda and I would sneak away often to race, swimming upstream.

Opening my eyes underwater in the blackness disoriented me as I conserved energy and air, allowing my body to be pushed by the welcoming current. With my arms at my side, I kicked my feet while undulating my body for additional speed. I held my breath for as long as I could until I became faint from lack of oxygen, though it could not have been more than a minute. Emerging with caution, I scanned the water for the canoe. It was about thirty-five meters away.

"There she is!" one of the men shouted. Lutalo dove into the water and headed in my direction.

Two red eyes glared at me between a long snout. I dove again and swam as far as I could, hoping the croc wouldn't come after me.

"Lutalo, move your arms faster and kick your feet," the colonel said. I was surprised that they could see me in the dark cloudy night.

"Get her, now!" he screamed. I could see Lutalo swimming frantically in my direction. It was apparent that he was not a strong swimmer.

Confident that I could outswim him, I ducked under water and glided downstream. In a fluid motion, I felt something scrape my leg. Was it the croc? I turned around to face my underwater foe, but it was only a sunken log. When I surfaced, the canoes were swiftly heading in my direction. I could hear the colonel raging as he yelled at Lutalo, who had not cut the distance between us. I clutched a small floating log that had poked my side and drifted quietly so the others would not see me.

"Can you see her?" he roared at the closest oarsman.

He might think Lutalo would catch me and swim back to the canoe, but I was one of the few women in my village that could swim.

"Matika," Lutalo panted in the calm night, getting closer. "I can't swim much longer. Please come back."

He was insane. I wouldn't return. I had infuriated the colonel. Lutalo ducked under the water, choking when he came up. "I can't return without you." Panic filled his voice.

"Lutalo," screamed the colonel.

"Then come with me," I answered quietly swimming closer to him against the strong current. He was having trouble staying afloat and it would only be a matter of time before he'd go under permanently. A back eddy carried us a good distance from the canoes. The colonel's lighter flickered briefly in the distance. Lutalo had gone under again and I fought against the current to reach him. He came up a few yards away, thrashing his arms, terror filling his eyes.

"Lutalo, calm down or I can't help you," I said, hesitating to draw closer as the canoes quickly closed in. I was torn. Should I save myself or risk my life to save him? I needed to be in control of the situation and above all, I needed Lutalo calm or he would drown us both.

Exhausted, Lutalo found a small piece of driftwood and clung tightly to it. I could see he had just gathered his breath when a rifle shot pierced the night. The colonel's aim was precise as a spray of blood and flesh filled the water. It immediately became quiet. Lutalo was hit, but I couldn't see where as he drifted silently away from me. He was still alive, a haunted look on his face as he clutched the driftwood.

"Stay where you are or I will kill you too," the colonel snarled at me. "Lutalo should have never trusted a woman." The last statement was directed toward his men but had affected me deeply. He looked at me with deadly hatred. He pushed two more men in the water to go after me. "Because of you, two of my men are dead!"

I drew in a deep breath but I knew Lutalo wasn't dead. The colonel looked utterly demonic, his dark eyes bottomless, cold. His nostrils flared as his lips curled into a sadistic smile. Right now, he was every inch the soldier who brutally slaughtered men, women, and children. "Do you think you're worth it?" Sarcasm dripped from his voice.

I quickly sank deep underwater, trying to get as far away as my breath would allow, for I knew that he would not waste his bullets shooting into the water. I made up my mind. I would rather die trying to escape than be at his mercy. I was all too aware of the fact that women were inferior to men. We were the lesser sex, not good for much more than bedding and breeding. Yes, Lutalo had told me kind things that had boosted my self-worth but it had all been quickly erased by the colonel's comment. I emerged to sounds of distress from the men.

I looked over at the colonel as he raised his rifle and sighted. I knew this was it, my short life story. I waited for the flash of gunpowder that would end my life. "Get away! Crocs!" one cried. "Hurry! Faster!" urged another. I looked back to see the colonel's canoe being rocked as a man's body was being torn apart by two large crocodiles. They were rolling over each other, splashing violently, fighting over his body, slamming against the canoes.

"Shoot her!" the colonel demanded. The crocs had tipped over one of the small canoes, sending half a dozen men into the water. The men began to panic, fleeing the bloodthirsty crocs despite the colonel's command.

A new wave of adrenaline surged through me, as my freedom arrived. I swam as fast as I could above water, disregarding my earlier concerns. More shots rang out and I quickly sank into the water's depths again. I repeated this process again and again until I felt that I could go no more. I wanted to give up when I spotted another piece of deadwood floating close to me. I used my last bit of strength chasing it down. Drifting slowly downstream, catching my breath, I contemplated my next move. I was a safe distance from the colonel and the others. No boats were visible, nor could I hear the men's voices echoing across the water. It was too dark; they couldn't catch me. It was so dark that I could not see shore in any direction. The only option I had was to hang on and drift downstream until daybreak.

I was alone, afraid, as I floated in the oily darkness, not uttering a single sound. The crocodiles were constantly in my thoughts and soon the deadly serpents that were lurking on the surface added to my fears. I pushed these thoughts out of my mind as the water grew colder and colder. Only my kicking legs kept my body warm, but soon they too began to fail, exhausted. My legs ached. I was so tired I could scarcely keep my eyes open, and drifted off.

Sometime in the early morning the shriek of birds awoke me. The river was quiet and surreal. The sun breached the cloudless horizon. I had drifted into a shallow pool of muddy water near the east shoreline covered by water lilies. They were a brilliant white-and-purple, with yellow centers that contrasted against bright green lily pads. The water was brown and murky from recent rains where I rested briefly. Suddenly, I heard feet trudging through the soggy earth coming toward me. They quickly approached, leaving no time to escape. It was the sound of a confident stride that left no doubt in my mind.

"No!" I screamed, sending birds into flight.

"Are you okay?" an older man gently asked. He was carrying a makeshift canoe on his head. He was a little taller than me, with soft brown eyes, and I was taken aback by his genuine look of concern for me. Looking at his slightly concave chest and dangerously pointed elbows, I was astonished that this sixty-something year-old man could carry the canoe.

There were sharp tipped sticks and netting hanging from the canoe's side. He was clad in a dirty tan T-shirt, which may have even been white at one time, with several holes around the midsection. His dark pants, in no better shape, were drawn up to his knees, with cargo pockets hanging by mere treads. Mud covered his shoeless feet up to his knees.

"Where am I?" I asked.

"You do not know that you are in Lake Kyoga?"

"I must have traveled at least forty-five kilometers," I said absently as he helped me stand on my wobbly legs after he had put down his canoe. I remembered that the Victoria Nile flowed into Lake Kyoga on its way to Lake Albert. I squished the excess water from Lutalo's shirt but could do nothing about the mud that covered my arms and legs. My first step brought a sharp pain that radiated from my right thigh. I felt lightheaded and must have swayed a little, for I felt his rough hand grab my arm to steady me.

"You're not well. Come with me. You need a safe place to rest and I will have my wife make you tea." I thought it strange when he began covering his canoe with mud and debris, but before I could ask he said, "There have been many canoes stolen from the fishermen. Nothing is safe." When he took up one of his poles I let him lead me away, because the prospect of having tea overwhelmed my sense of concern.

The lake was more like a swamp and was quite large, with an assortment of green islands in various shapes and sizes. We trudged up the marshy bank that was covered in tall papyrus reeds extending over my head. The reeds littered the water like thousands of floating green and yellow poles. I had never seen anything like it. Even in exhaustion my curiosity got the best of me and I picked a water hyacinth, admiring its thick, glossy, ovate leaves. Masses of the sweet-smelling lavender flowers feathered the spongy earth.

"We must not linger for there are many crocodiles," he said.

"How far is your village?" The exhaustion had suddenly overtaken me. It had been more than twenty-four hours since I last slept, and even then it had been restless at best.

"Not much farther," he replied softly.

The lake soon lost its luster as I swatted at the umpteenth mosquito that annoyingly hovered around my face. The swampy terrain created the perfect haven for millions of insects and parasites that surfaced with every step we took. The papyrus was soon replaced by tall trees thickened by a canopy of leaves. I did my best not to complain, but wished I had a stick to help me walk. My tummy rumbled deeply and my muscles cried out with every step I took.

The old man looked remote and detached as if deep in thought so I avoided conversation. I was thankful that he had not asked me any more questions. I felt guilt wash over me as I recalled what the colonel had said. There was no denying that because of me, two men were dead and perhaps even more if the crocodiles had gotten the men whose canoe had overturned. Still, their deaths were not caused by my hands, though I did not draw much comfort in that thought. I wondered if Lutalo got away, and if so, would he die from the gunshot? I still did not know what it was that I felt for him.

Lutalo was someone who made me feel like his equal and I valued his opinion of me. We could have made the perfect team. He gave me the strength and wisdom I needed to survive in my captivity. He was my shoulder to cry on and my friend to confide in. His gaze made the heat rise to my face and his kiss awakened a desire in me that I didn't know existed. I would forever miss him and mourn for what could have been. If he lived, I hoped that one day I would see him again.

So many new emotions had passed through me in the last several days that I hardly knew myself. I didn't feel like my old self, sheltered and confident. The child in me was slowly being drowned out by this new person who was insecure and uncertain and had to fight for daily survival. Living day to day, moment to moment was an arduous existence. I wasn't sure how much I could take.

The vegetation was thick, choking out any signs of a path, but the old man navigated quickly, weaving through it without pause.

"This is my village," he said proudly when we entered through a hidden opening. It was hard to tell how many huts peppered the small clearing because the vegetation was dense, allowed to grow thick, providing excellent concealment.

"Come this way," he said, breaking my reverie. I wasn't aware that I had stopped. I followed him past several huts. Fresh greenery lined the rooftops. We followed a well-worn path that encircled the village until we reached his hut. There was no door, but an opening covered by a brown burlap sack that hung midway to the ground. The man entered quickly and I hesitated briefly before I crept carefully unto the hut.

CHAPTER TEN

~~~~~~~~~~~~~~~

Stepping inside, I was greeted by the wonderful sweet minty aroma of tea, but my empty stomach churned in complaint. The mud hut was unseasonably hot and humid, but strangely provided a bit of comfort that reminded me of home. I didn't expect the sudden flow of tears and no matter how hard I tried, I could not prevent them.

The old man spoke rapidly to his wife in a tribal dialect I couldn't understand. As he spoke, the plain-faced woman looked at me with wide-eyed concern. She was short and wore a long brown skirt that was tied at the two ends, preventing it from touching the ground. Her orange-and-yellow blouse had sleeves that went midway down her withered arms and was loose on her small, narrow frame.

"Nayanda, my wife, will see to your needs," the old man said, pointing to her as he exited the hut.

"Would you like some tea?" she asked, handing me a warm cup before I could answer. She shuffled around, then set a dish of cold *matoke* before me that was probably left over from breakfast. I sat on the ground and ate quickly, mumblings my thanks. She watched me intently with questioning eyes until every bite was eaten.

The sparsely furnished home was small but cozy. Two bedrolls lay in the corner along with a few dishes and pottery items. Dried herbs and plantains hung with raffia string on the wall above it. Carved wooden spears in various sizes dominated the mud walls. Beside them was a burlap sack that overflowed with personal items and clothing. A small pot was suspended from an iron-and-wood contraption straddling a fire toward the left of the hut.

As I absently scratched my burning legs and arms Nayanda said, "Come. We will get you clean." I was at least a full head taller and weighed a few stones heavier, yet she led me to the bath house as if I were a mere child. I could not imagine how filthy I must have looked with mud caked on my legs and arms like an extra layer of rich brown skin. My matted hair, now a complete solid mass, was unmovable. The true color of my shirt was indistinguishable because of the filth. I was extremely thankful the bath house was nearby and we only came across a few children too engrossed in their soccer game to notice.

The communal bath house was a midsize mud building with bamboo floors. A wet cloth served as a door. Inside, mushy soap stored in small dishes and several large pots filled with water lined the mud-straw walls. Before I had time to hold my breath or undress, Nayanda drenched me with a pot of water. She had removed her clothes and now began scrubbing the dirt from my body with a coarse cloth and slimy soap. She then took off my shirt and began beating it on the bamboo floors.

After using most of the water, I felt like a new person as we returned to the hut. The water not only washed away the mud and filth, it washed away many of my fears, leaving relief in its wake. She gave me a clean, modest cotton dress that fit too snugly about my breasts but reached midway to my calves. I had been cold and wet for so long that I had forgotten what it was like to be clean and dry. My washed shirt hung by the fire. I was thankful when she unrolled a mat for me, as my exhaustion was now overwhelming.

I fell into a deep sleep as soon as my head touched the mat. I slept so soundly that I dreamt I was asleep. Sometime later I heard voices too far away to understand, but I could not awaken. I trembled as I lay freezing, wishing Nayanda would cover me. I dreamt I was floating in an icy sea. The water was calm one moment, undulating me peacefully with its gentle current softly caressing my body, and then it would turn ruthless, pulling me many directions at dizzying speed. I choked on the salty water, unable to keep my head above it.

Time passed slowly in the sea, and then I was alerted by the voices of two women. They were not as far away so I was able to discern some of their words vibrating through my throbbing head. One was speaking of a fever someone in the village had. I wished they would go talk elsewhere and not disturb my much-needed rest, and I would have told them so if my eyes weren't pasted together. I gladly tuned them out and fell into oblivion. I repeated this cycle several times.

Sometime later, how long I couldn't say, there came a point when I wanted to wake up but couldn't. I tried to lift my body off the mat but could not even raise my hand. Something was wrong. Suspended on the cusp of consciousness, I made several attempts to cry out from my parched throat but only managed weak moans of distress. I exhausted myself, succumbing to sleep once again.

"She grows more restless," said a voice I had heard before. My upper body was elevated gently, allowing me to make out shadows around as my eyes opened slightly. Someone mopped my drenched forehead with a cloth. "Her fever has broken."

"You must eat something," said Nayanda, spooning a warm salty broth to my parched lips. I welcomed the fluid, quenching my thirst. "This will help you get your strength back."

Brain clouds began to disperse, enabling me to see clearly. The two women stared at me with undisguised relief.

"What happened?" I mumbled so softly I didn't think anyone had heard.

"You were very sick for a long time, but now you will recover," Nayanda said cheerfully, bringing another spoonful to my lips. After I had consumed as much as my stomach would allow, a thought occurred to me.

"How long?"

"It has been two weeks since you came to us."

No! I screamed in my head. It would be impossible to find Suda again. The longer I stayed here the greater the chances of being found by the colonel or his men. I had to leave now. I attempted to get up but gentle hands held me in place.

"You're not in good health and only time will help you to recover. Do not worry; you may stay here. You are welcome in my hut." Nayanda was sincere in her words. "I will fetch water for you now."

"You're a blessing to Nayanda," said the woman when she left the hut. "She only had one daughter who died when she was only a year old. Her daughter would have been your age. Nayanda has since been cursed with a fruitless womb. She is lucky that her husband is a caring man and has not discarded her or taken another wife."

"But I can't stay. I must find my father."

"Indeed. Though I've never seen Nayanda happier, I understand your need to move on. These are unsafe times, however, and it may be best that you stay here for your own safety." She gave me a cunning look. "Would you at least consider it?"

"Yes," I answered. I was surprised how easily the lie flowed from my lips. I was no longer the naive girl who left the village. I had come too far and had been through too much to stop now. Deep down, the remote prospect of being reunited with my family outweighed the prevailing danger. I would play along until I was well enough to be on my own again because she was right; I was in no condition to leave the mat.

I settled into a routine of sleeping most of the day as Nayanda did the chores and cooked the meals. She anticipated my every need, feeding me when I was hungry and bringing the pot when I needed to use it, although when I requested to use the public latrine she was set against it, fearing for my health if I left the hut. The only thing that was required of me was to rest and regain my health. She gave me morning tea that seemed to make me sleep all day. She said the tea would help me regain my health.

No matter how restless I felt, Nayanda insisted that I remain lying on the mat. I did not complain after all the kindness she and her husband had shown me. I never corrected her when she called me Bahari, which I knew was the name of her daughter. That was okay because I didn't want anyone to know my real name or anything about me, especially when I didn't know whom I could trust.

Her husband was gone from sunup to sundown no matter the weather, and there were days when the storms were extreme. When he was there he said little, spending most of his time sharpening his fishing equipment and repairing the nets. Daily, he brought back few fish, but sometimes returned empty-handed. On those days we all went hungry.

They were extremely poor and relied heavily on fish for food and trade since they grew little in the field beside their hut. Despite what the woman said, the old man could not afford to have another wife, let alone children. I was an added burden to them and tried to eat little, no matter how much Nayanda pushed me with her overly motherly behavior that was downright smothering.

Soon I realized something was off with the couple. Although the old man treated Nayanda with polite kindness, he kept his distance from her, never an embrace, light touch or loving words. He did not even sleep beside her at night, choosing instead to sleep at the far end of the hut next to his fishing gear. He never spoke to me but thankfully looked at me upon entering the hut each night.

Early one morning after the old man had left, I felt truly healthy for the first time in a while. I had stayed up most of the night and was particularly restless, wanting to run and stretch my muscles. I decided to fetch the water to help Nayanda, taking the bucket beside the door. It was still dark, particularly cool, and the brisk air smelled fresh and pure, especially after I had spent more than three weeks inside the hut. My legs were weak and needed to be worked, my joints stiff, causing me to hobble along the muddy path like an old woman. I was not sure where to get the water so I followed a few sleepy-eyed children carrying a bucket and pot to a stream.

Several small huts were conspicuously concealed in the bush. This small village was making a great effort to stay hidden from dangers that I did not want to think about. Perhaps they had been raided before. I hoped that if they had been raided, the assailants would not be back. How far away was the colonel's base camp from here, I wondered. It couldn't be more than a day or two.

"I have never seen you here before," said a boy about ten years old, surrounded by his friends.

I didn't want to be noticed or engage in any conversation, but the children's eyes were on me. There were about nine in all, varying in age and size.

"I am staying with Nayanda," I said as I continued to fill my bucket.

"You're the one staying with crazy Naya!" exclaimed another. "I have heard my mother talking about you. Who are you and where did you come from?"

Crazy? Nayanda was a lot of things, including overly dramatic and extremely controlling, but crazy I did not see. She seemed mildly confused at times, but I had never met a crazy person before and therefore would not know how they act.

"I heard my mom say once that she carried a dead chicken for weeks. She had it wrapped in a blanket like it was a baby. It smelled so bad that some of the kids stole it and buried it by the spring," said the first boy.

"That's nothing! What about the time she took Bacuta's daughter for two days?"

"Really! How did they find out she had her?" I asked.

"The girl cried the whole time and everyone knows she has no children of her own. She swears to this day that Bacuta stole her baby."

"Do you want to know what I heard?" The boys continued their competition of who had the strangest tale of Nayanda. "I heard she drowned her only child because she wouldn't eat her food."

"No, she didn't!" I cried defending her.

"It's true. Why else has she not been blessed with more?" another boy asked when the others grew quiet.

"I will tell you why. Her husband doesn't touch her."

"Do you blame him?" The boys laughed at that. I quickly walked away in shocked silence, not wanting to answer any questions.

"She must be crazy too." The boys laughed as they continued their task.

As I walked away I wondered if she really were crazy. That would explain a few things. I supposed anyone would be after suffering the loss of a child and being unable to bear more. A woman unable to have children was not a woman. Stealing a little time for myself, I went off the path behind a bush to wash my body. Somehow I knew that if I would ask Nayanda, she would not allow me to go to the bath hut. The water was slightly cold but it washed away the sticky sweat.

I used all the water and had to revisit the stream, which was now devoid of children. The sun was beginning to rise and I could see that the water was cloudy from the heavy rains the night before. Seeing the mud, I knew I must be on my way. Too much time was slipping away, making it that much harder to find my father, and possibly even Suda.

Today I would tell Nayanda that I had to leave. Perhaps I may even ask for a few provisions for the journey and I would pay her back one day when I found my father. As I walked back to the hut I tried to think of the best way to tell her. She would surely be heartbroken. I would never replace her daughter and it would be best if I left now than later. I would have to be direct and to the point. I would stay one more night and be on my way at first light.

"Where have you been? I have looked everywhere for you, Bahari!" Nayanda stood behind me with the meanest look I had ever seen on her. Her hands were on her hips and she was shaking with madness.

"I went to fetch water-" she slapped me across the face before I finished and then pushed me to the floor, spilling the fresh water I had collected.

CHAPTER ELEVEN

"How dare you! After all I have done for you and you think you can run off? I gave you life. You must *never* leave this hut without permission. Get inside!"

I scrambled on my hands and knees to the mat where I'd slept. There was nothing I could say to her. In her mind I was running away, although if I were trying to run away I wouldn't have returned to the hut with water. My plan to leave would go untold. After this day I wouldn't tell anyone my plan, but I wouldn't be imprisoned.

"Have you any idea what could have happened to you out there?" She continued to rant and rave, flailing her arms and pacing back and forth. She didn't expect an answer from me and continued shrilly, "There is news not far from here that a violent colonel is tearing apart villages looking for someone who escaped him…we have been at peace with the River Lion, providing them refuge…now it's over…"

My breath caught in my throat at the mention of the colonel; I could barely make out Nayanda's words. My heart seized just thinking of his wrath. Could he be looking for me? Was he that angry that he would scour the countryside to find me? I tried to convince myself that I was being irrational to think that his demonic emotions would propel him to search and ravage villages until he found me. I had to leave at all costs.

"I have to pee," I blurted out.

"Here," she kicked the pot and it landed in front of me. Of course I wouldn't be so lucky to be allowed to use the latrine. She stood glaring, daring me to challenge her, her hands on her hips, her lips tight. She and I locked gazes for what seemed like ten minutes, but was probably closer to ten seconds. I looked away because now was not the time to challenge her. She watched me as I attempted to use the pot but I was too nervous to go. News of the colonel sent chills down my spine.

"I'm hungry," I said, changing the subject, remembering that I had not eaten. Trying to change the subject was the only thing I could think of.

"Are you?"

"Yes, and I feel a little weak."

"You should have thought about it before you tried to run away. And for that you will be given nothing to eat!"

Nayanda waited for me to respond, her chin petulantly thrust upward but her eyes looking down at me. I said nothing. I would not goad her. Satisfied, she went to start a fire to prepare tea, which was usually made by now but was delayed because of my absence. I put the pot aside, hoping she would forget about it. After the tea was prepared she didn't speak to me the rest of the day, making me extremely uncomfortable.

She worked around the hut, not once asking for my help. I waited for my opportunity to get away. She made several quick trips outside but was careful to never stay away too long. As the day passed by at a tortoise's pace, I pondered my next move and how soon it would be before the colonel came here.

"Do you have any idea what they do to children? You should be more careful…" At first I thought she was talking to me, since I was the only one in the hut. But when she continued to talk even as she walked in and out of the hut and directed her comments to no one in particular, I knew she was seeing ghosts.

"Why do you say that?" She paused a minute before she said, "Very clever. You are a smart girl, but you must not be too smart for your husband." Her conversation with her ghost continued most of the day.

Nayanda's broth simmered over the fire all day. When she finally ladled the thick liquid into with a wooden bowl, I was famished and my mouth watered at the wonderful aroma that wafted through the air. True to her word, she did not offer me any as she slowly sipped the broth and occasionally made slurping noises.

I didn't beg her for food like she may have wanted, because I didn't want to play a part in her game. She again continued to talk to her ghost and ignored me. This was not the first time I had gone hungry and it wouldn't be the last. After she had eaten, her husband entered the hut.

"We have already eaten," Nayanda said without precursor as soon as the old man sat down. He had returned much earlier than usual and Nayanda attempted to act as if nothing had happened, but her statement was out of place. The old man glanced at me with questioning eyes. I said nothing and looked down at my hands.

"Why have you come back so soon?" she suddenly asked.

"One of the fishermen told us about a raid in the Simi village." He put his hand up to stop Nayanda from interrupting as he continued. "No one was taken, but there were some injuries and food and supplies were stolen."

He looked at me as if uncomfortable, then he began to speak to Nayanda in a local dialect that I couldn't understand. She listened to him with unsuppressed interest as she shared information of her own. It seemed as though she was talking about me with her gestures, but once they switched back to Swahili they said nothing to me.

The old man was more than a little concerned, which was disconcerting because he rarely showed emotion. His thin body was tense, with his shoulders down and his head lower than usual. He was more alert, which was a huge difference from his daily lackadaisical demeanor. Something was eating him and I was tempted to ask, but at the same time I was afraid to find out.

"I'm sure there is no need to worry. They have been here many times in the past." It was like he was trying to convince himself more so than us as he stared blankly into space. His voice was barely above a whisper.

"Yes, I agree. There is no need to concern ourselves. Come now and eat." Nayanda didn't seem to notice the fear in his eyes as she prepared his meal. She didn't notice anything out of the ordinary and responded without any emotion.

That night I waited patiently for them to fall asleep, dozing off several times in the process. When I heard the rhythmic breathing from the old man and Nayanda's steady snore, I quietly rose from the mat. I had nothing to gather, since I came with nothing but the torn shirt on my back. I would have to take Nayanda's dress, but one day when I found my family and everything was back to normal, Baba would buy her a new dress to thank her.

I crept toward the makeshift door as quietly as I could. Although it was a small hut, it took forever to get there.

"I wouldn't do that if I were you," said the old man as he came toward me. I let out a sigh of relief, thankful that it wasn't Nayanda who had caught me. His sleepy voice was low, with an underlying kindness that would have normally put me at ease. It was clear that he didn't want to wake his wife.

"I must leave," I whispered.

"It's not safe." He grasped my arm desperately. Then he paused as if contemplating something. "They say that the colonel is looking for a girl. Not just any girl, but a beautiful one who escaped him."

"Please," I begged, "let me go." Now panting, my voice was barely above a whisper because I couldn't catch my breath.

"You are the one they are looking for; the one that drove the colonel mad. No one has ever escaped the colonel. It makes him look weak in the eyes of his men."

I could not see his face but could hear the admiration in his voice. "You are as beautiful as they say."

"I must go now, before they take me again."

"You may go at first light. My wife will get you what need for your journey."

"No, she will not. She tries to keep me here. She said that I can never leave this hut."

"I will tell her to let you go."

"You don't understand. I went to fetch water today and she thought I was running away. She struck me and wouldn't allow me to eat. She calls me Bahari." I paused to gauge his reaction this.

He seemed sadden by the news and let go of my arm.

When he didn't say anything, I continued. "I know that Bahari was the name of your child that died. She must know that I am not her child."

Nayanda stirred on her mat. The old man motioned for me to follow him outside. We went to the tree line, not far from the edge of the sleeping village. It was a clear, warm night with a partial moon and bright stars.

"She has her own way of dealing with things."

"How do you deal with the madness? Most men would have put her out," I said. "I'm sorry. I shouldn't have said that."

"I have heard that for years, but I will tell you something. When I was a small boy, my family was killed in a village raid. They were murdered like animals. There was no one to take care of me so I lived by the river in fear of returning to my village. A fisherman found me half-starved and afraid. He took me in his hut and he and his wife raised me like the son they never had. He was my new father. His wife's mother had been cursed with a barren womb after she angered the *sangoma* when she refused to pay her debt. At that time she had one daughter and could not have any more children. When his wife could not have children, all believed that the curse was passed on to her as well."

"Did she ever have children?"

"Yes, many years later she had Nayanda and nearly died in the childbed. Everyone knew about the curse and no man would take her as a wife, not even in neighboring villages. There was not a single offer for her hand. What good is a woman who cannot bear children?"

"So you married her."

"Her father became very ill. I made a promise to him on his deathbed that I would always take care of her. He was a father to me and I owed him my life. I would not let her be humiliated, even though I had no means to take care of a wife. I thought that it was the least I could do. Her mother died soon after."

"I'm sorry. You're a good man."

"It was a good thing her mother died before she could see what happened to Nayanda. After years of trying she was only able to have but one daughter, Bahari."

"How did Bahari die?" I felt a guilty asking but I had to know if what the boys said was true.

He lowered his head, recollecting the past. Nearly a full minute passed as I waited in silence.

"The fever took her at a young age." The pain in his voice staggered him as though he was remembering the worst day of his life. He sighed. He carried the weight of the world on his shoulders. I wanted to comfort him, but didn't dare encroach on his space. "That drove her mad to a point where I did not think her capable of caring for another child. Our marriage was not right and was cursed from the beginning, and I knew it then as I know now. I feel that it was my fault and should not have put her through it. I have not lay with her since the death of Bahari and will never share my mat with her again."

That explained why he never joined her or touched her in any way. Their relationship was no longer that of a man and wife, and perhaps never should have been. They had grown up as brother and sister and he could not accept her as anything else. I wondered how Nayanda felt about the sudden separation.

"What of Nayanda?"

"She never even noticed," he said shaking his head in frustration. I didn't know what to say. The pain he must have felt, I could only imagine. His loyalty to her father was deep and he had given that loyalty to Nayanda. I was curious whether he loved her, but I dared not ask such a personal question.

"Since you have been here, Nayanda has been almost normal." He paused briefly and it seemed as though he were regaining his composure. "I wanted you to stay with us, but now I see that it is not possible. Where will you go?"

"I will go to Kenya to join my Baba." I started to walk away.

"Wait! You have a long way to go. Stay here while I gather a few things for you."

"Thank you, but you have done more than enough."

"No, I insist. I am helping you like a fisherman once helped me. You brought me peace since you have been here." With that he walked back toward the hut.

He had barely walked away when I had a sinking feeling that something terrible was going to happen. I stood absolutely still, listening. I was nervous. The old man was taking forever. Many minutes passed and my worry tripled. I needed to go before morning, which was quickly approaching.

Something was wrong. The hair on the back of my neck stood up. Hurried steps echoed through the bush. Someone was coming fast. My legs refused to move and I stayed rooted in place. I was a terrified, like a small animal waiting for a lioness to pounce from the bush. It had to be the colonel and his child soldiers.

Too afraid to move, let alone breathe, I stood frozen as the footsteps stopped behind me. I felt a strong hand on my shoulder and I squeezed my eyes shut, wishing myself out of there, not wanting the slightest glimpse of his demonic face before I died.

CHAPTER TWELVE

This was the end. Thoughts of my family filled my mind. Why did it have to end like this? I cringed thinking of what the colonel would do to me, which kept me from opening my eyes.

"Are you all right? You're still too weak to travel." I opened my eyes to see the kind old man's face looking extremely concerned. I was so relieved to hear his voice that I hugged him tightly.

"I was scared. I thought you were the colonel."

"The colonel? I brought you fresh water. I'm sorry I frightened you."

I stepped back and he handed me an old rusted tin of water and two smoked fish wrapped in banana leaves. He covered it with a frayed cloth that he tied around my back.

"Go around the perimeter of the village." He pointed a crooked finger toward the left. "There's a game trail beside a recently cut stump. Stay on that path. Avoid the main roads. It should lead you in the direction of Namalu in the Nakapiripirit district. From there you will be a day and a half, or about one-hundred kilometers, from the Kenyan border."

"Is it safe?" I asked, wanting as much information as I could get.

"They say there are few villages but watch out for lions in the savannah. There is a pride roaming the area. They come near the river. "

More fear descended upon me.

"How long will it take to reach Namalu?"

"It's less than two hundred kilometers. It'll take two weeks traveling by foot. I'm not sure because I've never left the river since I came here as a boy. A fisherman who hunted at Murchison Falls told me that it is the safest way to go to avoid attention. He often did business in Kenya."

I knew his kind. I'd heard many stories about poachers who would sell hands and teeth of gorillas or rhino horns to wealthy people around the world. It was against the law and carried a high penalty for those who were caught.

"Once you pass the city, travel southeast to the border. There's plenty of fresh water, along with plantains and wild fruit on the way. Use the mud from the water's edge to protect you from the sun and, more importantly, malaria mosquitoes that fester this time of year," he said, and with a quick hug we parted ways forever.

By the time I found the path, the moon had faded as the predawn light torched the sky. I walked quickly, leaving the sleepy village behind. Sweat formed on my brow as the sun moved to its apex. I stopped in the heat of the day from pure exhaustion and hunger. My feet were sore. I deviated a little off the path and tore a few plants to note my direction. The jungle foliage all looked the same and I didn't want to get disoriented and mistakenly travel back to the village. Going without food for nearly thirty-six hours because Nayanda wouldn't feed me was taking its toll. I thought it was best to eat now.

I ate all the smoked fish and drank plenty of water. It tasted wonderful and I chuckled, thinking about the words Mama often said to me: "Matika, you have enough on your bottom to last you many days without food."

It was not funny then, but thinking about her words lightened my heart. I was never one to miss a meal or eat lightly. What would Mama say if she could see me now, devouring all my food rations? I couldn't help it. I was so hungry and the salty fish was spiced to perfection.

After eating I decided to take a nap. I was tired from the night before and rationalized that it was better to travel in the cool of the evening and on rested legs. The dense vegetation provided an illusion of safety. I felt almost lost as I lay down with the green leaves closing in on me, like a comforting cocoon with the perfect amount of shade. The ground was covered with soft plants that were spongy and inviting. Within minutes I was sound asleep.

Raindrops bouncing off my cheeks awakened me. The ground got muddy, making travel much more difficult. Pushing hard, there seemed to be no end in sight, leaving me discouraged and disoriented. I was determined to cover as much ground as possible, stopping only to eat and collect fruit along the way, but in the back of my mind I knew I was lost and was no longer sure if I was even traveling in the right direction. When the rain finally stopped, it was sundown on the second day. It was humid and hot and the starving gnats were eating me alive, but I was thankful to be out of the rain.

At dusk I reached a river and crossed it because I wanted to take a quick dip and wash away the sweat and mud. Entering the river fully clothed, I relished the cool water that caressed my fevered body. I reached the other side with little effort, letting the gentle current take me downstream. The view of the water was breathtaking, even in the evening glow.

I topped off the water tin before finding an open field of tall elephant grass nearby. As I lay on my back and gazed at the starry sky, thoughts of my family and loneliness snuck up on me. I was frightened and didn't want to be alone for another second, but I had no choice. I rewrapped my belongings, tying them snugly so that they rested across my midsection, cuddling it to assuage my loneliness. I wondered if there were a road or a village nearby. Despite what the old man had said, I hadn't seen a single person or any form of civilization, which led me to believe that I was hopelessly lost. Finally, I drifted off to sleep.

A swishing noise woke me. I froze. I thought of sweeping the ground in a dusty hut. I couldn't believe that I had fallen asleep so quickly. It was still night. I lay there listening, concealed by the tall grass, the sky illuminated by the bright stars and a harvest moon.

Suddenly a deep grunt rumbled through the grass. What was that? It didn't sound human. I heard it again. Too close. Another deep grunt like an oversized African bush pig sounded again. Quickly, I sat up. Danger lurked. I looked everywhere but couldn't see a thing. The menacing animal grunted again and fear seized my heart like hot pincers squeezing the life out of me. I couldn't breathe.

Then another snort was emitted, but this time from behind me. I was surrounded. What was out there? I couldn't move. I had to get away. I knew that whatever was out there was getting closer and closer. I hoped I hadn't been spotted.

Slowly and quietly, I exhaled and drew in a swallow of air. I panicked, wondering whether they could hear my breathing. Quietly, I got down on my hands and knees, afraid to rise up and expose myself to whatever was out there. It had to be a herd of large beasts. I wondered how many. Where had they come from?

Parting the grass ever so slightly, I couldn't believe my eyes. Big, menacing black Cape buffalo were grazing in the tall elephant grass. Slowly, I let go of the grass. I rose but still couldn't see the ten-thousand-kilogram monsters. Memories of my village flooded my mind about the time a herd of "Black Death" thundered through and gored an old man who had sacrificed himself to distract the beasts from the children. He'd tried to outrun the buffalo, but was slammed against a tree and speared with a horn. I wished there were someone who could help me. I had to move. Cape buffalo had poor eyesight but their mean, aggressive behavior made them killers.

Quietly, I stood up. They were everywhere. I was surrounded by a large herd, but still they hadn't detected me. I was so close to one that I could see claw marks on his back and rear quarters.

Looking around, I spotted an opening. Too afraid to stand and run, I ducked and quietly separated the elephant grass and began to crawl.

One of the buffalo snorted. I froze. My heart beat so hard I thought they would easily hear its pounding. I cinched my belongings even tighter around my waist and waited. Had they heard me? Should I move forward? Should I get up and run for it?

I closed my eyes and wondered whether spearing horns awaited me. Had I come so far only to be gored to death? I listened but heard nothing. I didn't move. Finally, I started moving again, determined to escape these massive beasts. No matter how hard I tried to mentally block their noisy breathing and fearsome grunts, my body trembled. I clenched my jaw to stop my teeth from chattering and crawled forward.

But it was too late. Angry red eyes spotted me, and charged. I instantly jumped to my feet. Like an angry storm, he came at me from five meters away. I couldn't outrun him. At the last moment, I dodged to the right, then left, feeling his tail swat me as he rumbled by. Before he turned around, I ran for the only tree nearby. I didn't know if I'd make it, but I ran as fast as my legs could carry me.

To the right, another buffalo reared his black head and ran straight at me. The distance between us was shrinking as I silently begged the tree to come closer. Running as fast as I could, I tripped on an exposed root, falling flat on my stomach as the buffalo roared by. Getting up, I jumped into the tree like a spider monkey, hugging it tightly. I felt a tug on my body as a Cape buffalo had my bag in his horn as he slammed the tree trunk. My bag and his poor eyesight had saved my life. With my adrenaline spiked, I climbed higher as the angry buffalo snorted again and reared up as though he could climb the tree. Swinging his horns to impale me and pull me out of the tree, I felt his moist breath on my legs. Scrambling even higher, I finally escaped.

The big buffalo suddenly dropped down, shaking the ground angrily. Snorting, he hammered the tree with his head again. It shook, but I grabbed it with my arms and legs. Then another buffalo charged and slammed into the other like thunder crashing in the night.

Snorting loudly, they each walked off in a mutual stalemate to eat more grass. My heart pounded for a long time, the adrenaline becoming a familiar sensation. I sat in the tree for at least three hours until the buffalo headed toward the river and I couldn't see them anymore.

It was dawn before I got down from the tree. My scratched legs were stiff and cold, my body sore, but most off all, I felt such a profound exhaustion since the adrenaline had long since worn off. Hastily I forced myself to overcome my pain. I looked back often, hoping not to see the black monsters.

A deafening silence compelled me to stop and look at my surroundings. Like an invisible force that made my head swivel, I craned my neck, afraid to commit my body. I saw them in the distance. There they were. There was no mistake. They had lost many, which led me to believe that the missing ones were gone forever, killed in the water that day I escaped or gunned down by their leader in a fit of rage. They were roughly three kilometers away and I just knew they had seen me as I saw them.

I felt the colonel's commanding spiritual presence before he crested the hill behind his men. With his shoulders back and chin tilted up, his mere essence towered over them, looking down at the world. I thought I could see a sinister smile shaping his lips, or his beady eyes narrowed slightly, straining to view his quarry in the bright sunlight.

He had found my trail and I hoped the old man and his crazed wife hadn't suffered. I shuddered at the thought of their lifeless bodies lying on the floor of their hut. What did it take for all to be told to the colonel? Torture? I could only hope that maybe the fatherly man was out fishing before the colonel tracked him down.

I'd have to travel swiftly to never find out, because I was sure that the colonel was more than eager to tell me in great detail what he had done. At most, I was an hour's trek ahead of them. Considering that they were men in the utmost shape and under the colonel's grueling command, they could reach me in less than forty-five minutes. I'd gotten stronger and tougher over the last few weeks. My only hope was to keep moving as the adrenaline kicked in. I had already lost precious time because of the buffalo.

I didn't know whether I could escape from them again, but I was going to try. I was determined to move quickly, not even stopping for the night, traveling through darkness. Sleeping in the night would be impossible knowing how close they were and the thought of waking to their lust for brutality was unimaginable.

My first instinct was to run, but that would only tire me so I continued the brisk pace. I could only go so fast without an all-out run. Looking back at them would add to the stress and jeopardize what little advantage I had.

A few hours later, it began to rain heavily. I welcomed it. The rain allowed me to take water in my open mouth and container without breaking stride. Large puddles filled the terrain and slippery mud was like silt on my bare feet, squishing with every step I took. When I realized I was leaving footprints, I slipped to higher ground.

Much of the area was recently flooded from the heavy rains and had not recovered from the rainy season. I approached a village in a shallow valley where water went to the knees of the few people who muddled about, collecting what few goods were still usable. Other villagers looked like they were fishing with nets, but it was hard to be sure. Some huts were clearly destroyed and their scattered debris floated in the tepid water. Other buildings remained steadfast, as if they had seen more than one flood in their day and welcomed the flowing water with an open door.

I looked back for the first time in hours and was relieved that the colonel and his men were not in sight. Then it dawned on me. They could have gone another route, a shorter one, and I would be caught in a trap. Or, they might have split up and were flanking me on both sides. Either scenario had me trapped. I should have kept an eye on them.

I wanted to stop and ask the handful of people in the village if I was at least headed in the right direction, but I didn't want to put anyone else in danger. I knew the colonel and his men were close. He would expect me to go to the villagers for help. In the end, I decided to do a little maneuvering of my own. I changed course and headed up a difficult trail, not dropping into the valley at all. If the colonel's men split up, I would only encounter half of them. If they all went in the other direction or waited in the village, I wouldn't encounter them at all.

My worry subsided as the sun began to set and there was no sight of the colonel or his men. I sat down beside a thick brush to rest. I just needed a little rest to recover and then would continue to travel through the night. It would be my only chance of losing them. The bush was full and provided enough of a shelter for me to stay hidden. My feet throbbed badly and it felt wonderful to sit down. With knees to chest, I hugged my legs and wiggled my toes to get the blood going.

Ten minutes, I kept telling myself. What's ten minutes when facing hours and hours of traveling? That's all I need, just a short rest. Nine minutes to go. That seemed about right. How much time could have passed? I would be able to travel even further through the night. It felt so good to curl my toes and flex my arches. Eight minutes to go… I awoke with a start.

"I know she's in this area," the baritone voice said.

CHAPTER THIRTEEN

Footsteps. Someone was coming quickly.

Please, just be a lonely hunter, I thought. Frozen in terror with my mouth agape, I was on the verge of screaming. Too many footsteps to be one person. Men were suddenly surrounding me. Once again, my body had betrayed me and I had fallen asleep. I wasn't sure how long I'd slept but the sounds of night insects told me it was at least a few hours. Too long.

"Keep your voice down or I'll cut out your tongue."

The colonel! There was no mistaking the acid in his quiet tone. The others chuckled but stopped when the colonel silenced them with a deadly look.

The harvest moon was full, partially covered by a blanketing cloud, casting an eerie yellow glow that could expose me to my assailants. They had traveled nonstop to catch me while I slept as if I hadn't a care in the world.

A booted foot casually walked forward and was only inches away from my face where I was hiding in the bush. The boot wasn't large like Baba's or my older brothers', but it wasn't small either.

"Spread out," commanded the colonel curtly. Footfalls rapidly dispersed.

All except one. I could see so clearly through the bush. He lingered for what seemed like hours, but could have been a minute or two. Utterly silent we were locked in a game to see who could be the most quiet. Without warning, the pair of boots stalked off, gradually receding.

Slowly gathering my sore body into a crouching position, I waited in the silence. I couldn't hear anyone. I had made it through another night. I decided to wait a little longer to be sure the men believed that they had lost me. Closing my eyes to concentrate, I listened for any sound, such as a twig breaking, a movement in the brush, or a bird scared into flight. Nothing. Not a sound.

Still I stayed put. There was no mistaking the feeling that something wasn't right. It was too silent. I was at war with my body's need to flee and my mind's desire to stay hidden until the danger had completely passed.

Just as I was about to run in the opposite direction, my head snapped back as if struck by a buffalo horn.

Hitting the ground hard, my eyes flew open. Before I could even blink, I was struck in the jaw, a metallic taste pooling in my mouth. Dazed, I bit my tongue to fight off unconsciousness as limpness crept over my muscles and threatened to overtake me.

Trapped beneath his hard body, I looked directly into his cold eyes. Eyes that told me exactly what sick death he had planned, one that would leave me begging for a swift demise. I cringed as I recognized the face of the evil – the colonel.

"Please, no," I sobbed through trembling lips, which was like telling a coiled snake not to strike, or a hungry lion not to chew the captured prey in his jaws.

Panic set in as I fought against him. I couldn't move no matter how hard I struggled. Both my hands were trapped beneath his body, a knife or pistol stabbed at my hip.

"For the first time, I'm at a loss. I don't know if I should pound your head until I crush your skull to powder, or to take my time and peel off every inch of your skin from your body, starting with your tits, using my dull knife," he said ripping my shirt open.

His piercing gaze promised that and more. His eyes glistened with a reddish glow. A conduit had opened between us that I could not close or resist. I was looking into the dark abyss, devoid of any humanity, filled with utter misery and pain. My soul was slipping out of my body and being sucked into a malevolent void. It was a deep sensory cocoon where nothing intruded. There were blackened thoughts, and feelings so profound they left me paralyzed in agony.

Every limp muscle was worthless. I struggled to breathe. I could sense all the people he'd killed. In my mind I heard their screams and pleas for mercy while he showed no emotion. He didn't care whom he hurt or killed or even why. All that mattered was the supreme power he felt over his victims as he made them suffer.

"Baba! Help me, please," I tried to cry out, but fear stole my words. Then, I shook so badly that the vibrations poured into his body, causing him to pulsate with the tempo.

This is it. *I'm going to die*, intrinsically I knew it. No one would ever know what had happened to me. The colonel would dissect my body and the animals would devour what remained.

"As much as I wanted to redeem myself in Moses' eyes…" he said, features softening a bit as he pulled up short and reached with a rough hand, turning my face away from him, exposing my neck. My veins were pumping fiercely to supply oxygen, "…such a perfect piece for Moses' collection."

I felt another shift and the rounded edge of a pistol implanted at the base of my throat, working its way down to the cleft of my breast, scraping my delicate skin.

His movements had freed my left hand. A newfound energy coursed through me and with it came a ray of hope. With my left hand free to roam the ground around me, I tried to grasp any weapon I could get. I wouldn't give up without a last-ditch effort to get free. I had nothing to lose. I was doomed to die. Yet not a single stick or pebble was within arm's reach. Getting desperate, I swiftly felt the colonel's body for a weapon that I was certain he had in his cargo pockets.

"Too bad. You are so worthy. A beauty like you would please the River Lion, but…I will have to find another gift worthy of him."

His words changed quickly from slight admiration to pure hatred. "I own your mind and body and I will spend days torturing you in so many ways that you will know the ultimate suffering for the rest of eternity. You have been an embarrassment to me, a curse that will end this night…"

I couldn't see anything but the bush with my head turned so sharply, the cords straining, threatening to disconnect. When he shifted his body weight, I grabbed ahold of an object from his pocket and struck him across the face with my left hand. Grabbing the bloody gash that extended from lip to chin, he let go of my face but didn't get up. Blood poured out like from a slaughtered goat.

It was some sort of handheld tool with a small sharp edge no bigger than a thumbnail. I attacked again with increased confidence, aiming for his eyes, but he struck me, sending my small weapon flying into oblivion. His blow was deflected by my attempt at his eyes. I was lucky to escape the full impact of it, but the weapon was lost.

For a moment, I hesitated. With no weapon to rely on I bared my teeth, sinking them into his throat. Wildly, he howled and cursed, pulling away from me. With just enough room, I bucked my knees, sending him stumbling backward. The instant he was off, I got up and ran like never before.

"You filthy whore! I'm going fillet you alive!"

I weaved in and out of the terrain, not taking a straight path. His yells echoed in the night sky, calling his men. Hearing one nearby, I dove behind a bush. My head was throbbing, my vision blurred. I watched the world through a small tunnel. The man must have been so eager to answer the colonel that he ran right past me.

As soon as he left I continued on and didn't stop. I had had nothing to eat all day, but fear stole my appetite and my sanity. My heart leapt at every movement in the grass or bushes, at every noise or animal cry. I was constantly looking over my shoulder, my neck throbbing in concert with my swollen jaw. I traveled the remainder of the night and throughout the next day. The colonel and his men were out of sight.

By afternoon I was so exhausted that I started to hallucinate. I kept seeing trees waver as if the world were underwater. A flock of birds took flight from a sudden movement that had me in tears, gasping for breath. The feeling of profound fear was constant and all-consuming. If I didn't change gears soon I would be youngest healthy person to die of a heart attack, yet still I ran on.

When night came again, I was filled with a sense of dread. During the last few kilometers, the terrain had changed gradually to a savannah that was dryer, with no place to hide and only a few acacia trees in view. I was exhausted, but knew the colonel and his men had to be as well. They had traveled non-stop looking for me while I slept for a few hours.

I continued until my legs gave out and couldn't carry me anymore. I had no choice but to stop. Keeping my belongings tightly secured to me, I slept restlessly with my ears on alert, listening for the next assault.

Waking up well before dawn I continued to trek at a rapid pace, my muscles aching in constant complaint. Not wanting to be caught out in the open like the day before, I felt that if I kept moving I'd be safe. By the time the sun began to rise I had added several valuable kilometers, and I should have been pleased, but I felt a strange sensation, as if I were still being tracked.

CHAPTER FOURTEEN

Scanning the area and its breathtaking view, I saw that I was alone. "Stop looking for him. He's hasn't found you," I said sharply, chiding myself vocally. At this point, I had resorted to talking openly to myself to deal with the loneliness. I tried to put away my paranoia.

As the day wore on, I stopped in my tracks and the sense that I was being followed increased tenfold. Baba once told the girls during one of his stays that a sixth sense was the one that affects your soul. "You may not hear, smell, taste, touch, or see it, but you will know it is there. I know when someone is lying or telling the truth even before interrogations because it is my sixth sense that tells me. When things do not seem right or if all other senses are not clear, trust your sixth to make good decisions."

I wanted to shout at the top of my lungs, "I *know* you are watching me. Just come out and be done with it," but refrained after remembering an important lesson Mama taught me. I could still feel the beating I got when I wouldn't tell Mama where Suda was. Suda had gone to the village to meet a young man. Although I wouldn't lie to Mama, my loyalty to

Suda was great and I had stupidly boasted of it after being pushed and slapped repeatedly. I said to Mama, "You can do whatever you want to me, but I will not tell you where Suda is." Mama had responded with, "Be careful what you ask for."

How could I have missed it? There before me, less than twenty meters away, was a Thompson's gazelle that blended perfectly against the tall grass and bushes. It should have been afraid of me and never allowed me to get that close to it. It was lying with its legs tucked beneath it, alone, perhaps sick or wounded. When it spotted me, it made a feeble attempt at stotting, trying to show its strength or scare me off, but it failed miserably and within seconds went back on its belly.

Why I decided not to just walk around the gazelle was a mystery. I was drawn to it knowing that I couldn't help it. I wasn't afraid because one of my mother's families had maintained Thompson's gazelles for meat. They didn't pull up the grass by its roots when they grazed like other livestock. Overall, they were a good animal to have.

The animal didn't even attempt to run when I approached, as if its energy was truly spent. I knelt down in front of the gazelle, but not quite close enough to reach out to touch it. It felt good not being alone and my fear subsided. The animal looked as defeated as I felt, yet unafraid, like it had accepted its fate.

For several long minutes I sat there in silence, at peace, reluctant to move. Then I sensed it again. Someone was watching. I had no doubt in my mind. The constant hum of the insects ceased and the chirping birds went silent. All noise stopped. I turned and saw a wavering movement in the grass.

CHAPTER FIFTEEN

Paralyzed, I looked over at the frightened gazelle. Fear gripped its heart and it was trembling. I looked around to see if I could spot something, someone, in the eerie silence. I trembled alongside the gazelle, feeling that the lion was stalking its prey, me. Where could I run to? Where could I hide? There were no trees to climb. I wondered if a tree would do any good. Lions could climb. I looked again to see if the grass was moving. Where was he? My throat was parched and I wanted to grab a drink of water, but I couldn't move, not even to get the water tin. I covered my ears, closed my eyes, and awaited the gruesome death that would claim my life.

Birds took flight from the grass nearby. When nothing more happened I released a relieved breath. Someone up above was watching over me, although I'd never considered myself a religious person. Mama made Suda and I stay home and do chores while my other mamas and siblings went to the village church. It felt like a greater being from the spirit world wanted to see me reunited with my family. I was comforted knowing that, and it eased my anxiety.

I was careful in my trekking and didn't encounter any more dangerous animals over the next week. Food and water were scarce. I consumed as much water as possible at the seasonal ponds and streams, trying to keep the fluids in my body and stay cool. I bathed whenever the opportunity was available. The climate was dry and the terrain rugged, making traveling challenging.

I was lucky to find a small abandoned farm where several dehydrated potatoes were left behind, or, more than likely, grew in after the owner's departure. A lean-to with a corrugated side provided shelter for one night and I had the best sleep since I'd left the old man's hut. I felt as safe as one could be alone in the unforgiving wilderness.

After weeks of trekking through the hot and dry days, I reached the edges of a city that I hoped was in the direction of Namalu. It was the largest city I'd ever been to, the only true city I'd ever seen. My father often stayed in Kampala and traveled to other parts of the country for the military. I had visited only my mother's village that was a day's walk from our home, unlike some of my brothers, whom Baba occasionally took to Kampala for short stays. They bragged about our capital being larger than life itself.

The sun was low overhead, casting a reddish glow on the partly cloudy sky. I walked along a paved road filled with potholes and ridges with the other travelers and was surprised by the searing heat that radiated from the black asphalt, creating heat waves like a hot brick oven. An endless stream of cars and trucks flowed slowly to and from the city, honking horns at pedestrians and other vehicles on the narrow road. To my delight, I overheard a woman with a basket on her head and a child strapped to her back speaking to another about her family who were moving back to Namalu from Kapchorwa. I was giddy with the news, grinning from ear to ear, bubbling with excitement. I had finally made it.

The white-washed flat-top buildings were clustered together like rows of teeth in a crocodile's mouth. The multitude of people walking quickly in and out of buildings and up and down the streets to their unknown destinations was intriguing. Children zigzagged through the masses in high-speed chases as irritated women swatted them with bamboo and straw brooms. Everyone was in a hurry.

I was drawn to the city like a mosquito to blood despite the old man's warning about avoiding the villages. Darkness descended swiftly as building lights and signs were turned on. I was amazed to the point that I forgot my purpose and my objective. Trash littering the streets, women sweeping plumes of red dust from concrete paths uncaring about the passersby, and the intoxicating smells - a mixture of garbage, cooking, smoke and unwashed bodies that merged into a hot vapor - did nothing to dilute the beauty of the city. It was at least five degrees hotter and much more humid inside the city, but I didn't care.

My attention was snagged by a middle-aged woman who sat on a dirty brown mat singing an eerie song.

> *"Jesus paid much too high a price*
> *For us to pick and choose who should come*
> *And we are the body of Christ."*

She sang louder and louder, her voice rising to higher notes, sending chilling waves though my body and caressing my ears like a sweet summer breeze. Some people dropped coins in her clay pot that clicked against more coins, while others gave small fruit as they walked by. She wore a blue headcover that draped over her shoulder to the floor and a faded dress of the same color.

As I approached the woman, I saw that her legs were amputated from the mid-thigh and her dress was shamefully pulled up to reveal the shortened limbs. Her teary eyes were a silvery blue staring into space.

"That was beautiful," I said when she'd finished her song. She rummaged through the coins, feeling its weight or perhaps counting them but didn't look up.

"You think so?" she said after some time.

"Yes, and if I had money I'd give it to you."

She laughed loudly as if I had told a funny joke, taking out a pipe from a small cloth bag and lighting it. "Silly girl! You would give your money to someone who has more than you?" She took a long drag from her pipe then blew the smoke out her nostrils.

"If I had it, I would."

"I don't need your money. What are you doing here? Have you run away from home to come to the big city? If you have, I suggest you return because there's no work here."

"I'm just passing through. How did you know that I'm not from here?"

"I may be blind with no legs, but I'm not stupid."

"You're blind?" I said more to myself. It was so obvious and I didn't even notice. I made a mental note to myself that I needed to be more aware of things. She laughed again.

"What happened to your legs?"

"It is a long story that happened many years ago. Go on your way little girl; my son will be here soon. Yes, I have a family and a house to live in."

I was astonished and started to walk away.

"Wait! It's been a good day and since you have made me laugh, take this for your journey." She handed me several coins from her dirty hands.

"Do not give it away because nothing is what it seems." Just as she said that, an old white car pulled up; her son had come for her. He collected his mother, lifting her carefully and putting her in the passenger's seat.

Her kindness was astounding. I would have gladly offered her what I had but instead it was she who provided to me when I had nothing. At that moment, as the tears burned my eyes, I looked up at the sky, knowing that I was being watched over. With renewed hope I continued down the street.

The crowed thinned considerably as people went home for their evening meal. With the coins burning in my hand, I could taste the *matoke* they would buy. I hadn't eaten a warm meal in a long time and the prospect of good food caused my mouth to water and my spirit to soar. I wandered around looking for street vendors, but the roads were almost empty. There were so many when I first arrived but now there were none to be found.

After searching, I came upon a part of the city where the rough unpaved streets were littered with broken bottles. A large drainage ditch, with water as black as night, ran through it with plastic containers collecting on its banks. I crinkled my nose as the smell of raw sewage and decay assaulted me, even though I was breathing through my mouth to avoid the stench. Piles of garbage were dumped in a large pit and I was shocked to see people foraging through them for food that was so vile and unrecognizable that I didn't think even the poorest would eat it.

Makeshift cardboard and tin huts were set up throughout the area, broken up by an occasional run-down building devoid of windows and doors. Women were moaning, babies were crying, and men were yelling at each other. It was frightening and depressing at the same time. This was a horrid place that I didn't want to see in daylight, so I ran. I ran and ran, giving up any hope of finding food. Finally, I stopped after reaching the edge of town.

Music was playing and I saw a small structure with several electric ball lights and cars parked next to it. Cautiously drawing closer, I saw an outdoor feast in full swing. The area was covered with a tin roof balancing on wooden beams and no walls. It was roped off except for a small opening where two large men stood with expressionless faces.

This wasn't the kind of feast I'd ever seen. People were moving their bodies in sync to Western music coming from a loudspeaker. Women were dancing seductively close to their male partners, brushing up against them and allowing them bold liberties that would make even Suda blush. At the table the partiers were drinking and eating merrily, enjoying the festivities. They were served by young women in short shirts tied in a knot at the back and even shorter skirts that barely covered their butt cheeks.

"Do you have the cover charge?" the younger of the two men who stood by the opening asked, startling me. I hadn't realized I had ventured that close to the roped-off area. He looked bored and a little tired, as if he didn't want to be there at all.

"Let her go in. It's late anyway, and we close in less than an hour," the other said. Their expressions were like yin and yang. His pleasant smile reached his eyes, with crinkles on the side as if he smiled often. The other was completely emotionless with cool eyes, not adverse, but not friendly either. "Don't mind him; he takes his job too seriously. Go on in, you can pay later."

I hesitated for only a moment before quickly walking to the only empty table at the far end, sitting in a broken folding chair with a seat that leaned steeply downward. I was hungry, thirsty, and my famine overruled every thought.

"What are you having?" a serving lady asked rudely, holding a pad of paper and a pencil, standing aloof with her weight shifted on one leg. She was a heavy lady with a shirt cut low, exposing an overflowing bosom the size of melons that made mine look minute in comparison. Her makeup was vibrant, with dark green eye shadow and eyelashes thickly covered by mascara, causing the lashes to clump together. With lips painted blood-red and pink blush on her cheeks she looked like an overstuffed doll, save for the annoyed expression on her face. "I don't have all day, little girl."

"Sorry," I responded, reaching in my wrap for the coins the old lady gave me. "What can I get with this?"

She scoffed. "Are you joking?" She looked at me awaiting a response, but when none came she replied, "Nuts. You only have enough for nuts." She took the coins from my outstretched hand and walked languidly to another table.

The music was upbeat and everyone was having the time of their lives, laughing, dancing, and singing along to the tune. The men wore collared shirts, some with buttons, pants made of expensive material, and dress shoes or nice sandals. Most of the women wore high heels that elongated their legs, making them as tall as the men, while others were less formal and wore decorated sandals. With an array of bright colors and patterns, the women's clothes were assorted like a box of colored silks. Hairstyles varied from straight, to wavy, to natural curls.

All the men and women wore Western clothing, making me look homely with my plain dress and braided hair that needed to be redone. My hair grew so quickly that I needed to re-braid it often. Subconsciously, I reached for my hair but realized that it wouldn't make a difference, so I returned my hands to my lap. At least I was clean, as I had bathed and washed my dress yesterday.

I was the only one, except for a young boy who was dashing back and forth cleaning tables and collecting dishes, who had no shoes, showing dirty feet and dusty ankles, but no one seemed to notice. I felt like a thorn bush in the midst of a flower field, completely out of place among the beautifully colored hues.

The chubby lady returned to my table carrying a small drink and sat it in front of me. "*Auntie*, I didn't order this."

"This is from the man over there," she said pointing to a man three tables to my left sitting alone, staring right at me. "I'll be right back with the food he ordered for you." She hesitated briefly before she added, "You need to go back home to your mama, little girl, before you get in trouble."

I looked over at the older man, who was still staring at me, gave a quick nod of acknowledgement before taking a large gulp of a bitter brown drink in a not-so-clean cup that tasted like a cross between urine and sweat. Why would anyone order such a drink for me when simple bush tea would have suited me well enough? Out of politeness I sipped the horrid beverage that was despicable at room temperature, thinking that perhaps it just needed to be served hot. But I was thirsty.

The chubby lady returned with a bowl of beef stew and a small plate of piping hot chapati cut in small triangles. It smelled heavenly. Dipping the soft chapati in the thick stew like a spoon, I relished the first cooked meal in weeks. It was mouth-wateringly delicious and filled my stomach with warmth and comfort that went straight to my core, making me giddy. Even the bitter drink started to taste better, causing my lips to tingle.

It was after I finished the drink and sat content in the broken chair, casually tapping my foot to the catchy tune, that the man finally approached and smoothly pulled up a chair, conveniently blocking my view. I was disappointed because I enjoyed watching the people dance.

"Well, hello," he drawled in a singsong voice that I found quite irritating. He was by no means handsome, but he wasn't too poor on the eyes either. In his late twenties or early thirties, his hair was closely cropped and his face cleanly shaven. He wore an orange-brown collared shirt with sweat stains on the armpits and dark brown pants. "I've been watching you. You're not from around here. What's your name?"

"Matika," I answered shortly, not wanting to encourage conversation, especially about myself.

"A beautiful name for an even more beautiful girl. Let me introduce myself. I am Mark, here to serve you. I see that you are finished with your beer. Would you like another?"

"No. What I meant to say was thank you for the food and drink, but I don't need anything else."

"Would you like to dance?"

"No, thank you."

"Good, so let's just cut to the chase. How much for the night?"

"*Wangie!*" I exclaimed out of respect a little louder than I should have over the music. Had I heard him correctly? I hoped he didn't buy me food to get a place to stay for the night. "I don't have a place to stay myself so I cannot help you, but maybe you could ask the server."

He laughed, "I'm not looking for a place to sleep."

"What do you want?" I asked innocently.

"You don't have to play hard to get with me, but if you like the game, I know how to play too."

I sensed a bit of anger in his voice.

"I don't know what you are talking about, Mark." I was confused and didn't know what he wanted. "I really must be on my way."

"Not to worry your pretty little head," he smiled like a hyena with sleepy eyes. "Would you like go for a little walk?"

"No, thank you."

"Come now. Humor the lonely man who fed you and keep him company. It's a good night to view the stars."

"I suppose I could go on a short walk, but then I really must be on my way."

I had a sinking feeling as I began to walk away from the party that I shouldn't be doing this. I kept looking behind me as the party drew farther away. Then something clicked in my head. This was not right and I needed to return right away. I didn't trust him and once again I was led away like a sheep for slaughter, like Wandera had done. I was about to turn and run back toward the party, when Mark grabbed me roughly around the waist.

CHAPTER SIXTEEN

It felt as though the blood had drained from my body, leaving me icy cold and numb. I didn't fight him, at least not right away. My heart was beating so hard I could barely swallow past my pulse.

"Now, let me see what's under your dress," he whispered from behind, so close to my neck that I could smell the bitter drink he'd consumed earlier and feel the heat of his breath.

"No! Stop! Let me go!" My pleas fell against a stone wall. I struggled to no avail as Mark put his hand under my dress. Although just a little taller, he was much stronger, with a solid build and wide shoulders. Holding my waist in a vice grip, his seeking hand attempted to reach the junction between my legs as I kicked and squirmed in his arms.

"You're the girl the colonel is looking for. You're worth your weight in gold. I like a girl who is aggressive."

I felt his hardness against my bottom and slammed my head against his face.

"Ow, what's this?" he asked bewildered, rubbing his bloody nose with the back of his hand. I was shocked that I'd made him bleed, causing me to hesitate for a moment too long. He pounced on me like a lion, sending me to the ground, knocking the air out of my lungs. I was pinned beneath him. My lungs ached as I gasped for air. Recovering quickly, I let out a piercing scream that was so loud it reverberated through my head.

"Shut up! I will get what I paid for!" he shouted over me as he put his hand over my mouth to stifle my cries. I bit his hand hard and he quickly pulled it away. I refused to be an easy conquest for him. He lifted his body, just a little, in reaction to the bite, creating just enough space for me to reach my hand between his legs and grab his *makende*. He yelped. Suda once said that this was the most sensitive part of a man's body. She told me that you could control a man if you held the *makende*; I didn't know if she meant it literally.

"You touch me again and I will pull them off!"

He jerked his hand away from me as if it had been burned. He looked outraged, shocked and turned on all at the same time.

"You would not dare." When he reached for my hand that held his manhood I squeezed harder. His face contorted in pain. He struck out at me.

I turned my face, avoiding most of the blows. I squeezed it even tighter and turned my hand, putting my nails into play. Like a dog he howled in pain.

"Get up!" I shouted, my confidence rising.

"Oh!" He cringed, looking sick with pain. "Okay, okay!" He panted, lifting up on all fours. I followed him with my hand firmly in place.

"Please, be careful," he pleaded, his voiced strained with agony as he tottered backward. "I won't touch you, just let go."

I heard deep laughter and approaching footsteps. I didn't turn around because I wouldn't dare take my eyes off Mark. For now, he was my immediate threat.

"To think that I came here to rescue you," he chuckled. His voice sounded familiar. Yes. It was the man who let me in the party for free.

"Please, make her stop Kumowo," Mark gasped but didn't move a muscle, afraid.

"He will not harm you. You can let go," Kumowo said with authority.

Suddenly, I felt silly with my hand gripping Mark's *makende*. Still, I needed assurance that I was safe, not from Mark, he was clearly done with me, but from Kumowo. Holding Mark wouldn't do me any good. I let go and he stumbled forward and curled into a ball on the ground, moaning.

"Come," Kumowo said as he started walking toward the party. I followed him at a safe distance, looking back cautiously to make sure Mark was where I left him. I was comforted that Kumowo came to help me. "Are you all right?"

"Yes, I am."

"You are lucky. Mark is not an honorable man. He comes here often but the ladies don't care for him."

"I can see why," I said. He laughed musically.

"I seem to find myself in situations like this a little too often."

He didn't comment on that. After a long pause, I asked, "Why did you come after me?"

"It is as I said before. He is not a good man."

"I know what you said, but why did you come for me?"

"You are not from here. You seemed lost to me and alone. I knew what Mark was after when he took you away." His smile faded and he looked rather uncomfortable, losing his carefree spirit for a moment.

He rubbed his arms as if he was cold, but the night was warm. His gaze was directed straight ahead and he wouldn't make eye contact with me.

"You said earlier that I could pay you back later," I said changing the awkward subject.

"No, you owe me nothing and by the looks of it, you have no money," he said, his smile returning.

"That's true." My shoulders slumped with relief. "Thank you, for everything." We had reached the party where only a few scattered people remained, some piling in the remaining cars while others walked, presumably home.

Kumowo touched my arm gently, "Do you have somewhere to go for the night?" He seemed genuinely concerned and I found I couldn't lie to such an honest face. It just felt wrong to even consider it.

"No, but I will be fine."

"Are you sure? Namalu is not safe for a young girl. One of the barmaids can take you home with them for the night." He started toward the chubby server and I quickly grabbed his heavily muscular arm with both my hands. There was no way I'd stay with her; my pride wouldn't allow it. I was humiliated enough knowing that she was right and I was naive.

"No, please, I'll be fine. I wouldn't feel comfortable staying with anyone tonight."

"Are you sure?" he asked, turning around.

I nodded, thankful that he listened to me. "I'll not be here long, anyway."

"Where are you headed?"

"I am going to Kenya." I felt like I could trust him, and at this point it really didn't matter if he knew where I was headed. "I am meeting my father there."

"Do you have papers to cross?"

"No, but there must be another way to cross undetected. They could not possibly watch the entire border," I thought out loud. I had nothing but the clothes on my back. I was going to cross the border if it was the last thing I did.

"There is, but it's very dangerous. Since the fighting began, many refugees and former soldiers have flocked to Kenya, and now they have tightened security with militia gunman. They are posted around the border and are there allegedly for protection and security, but their real agenda is to detour illegals with any means necessary. The refugee camps that were designed to hold up to sixty thousand now hold triple that number and growing with people from Sudan, Somalia and Rwanda. Refugees are on top of each other and there are not enough resources to go around. It's a fight for survival."

"What is this camp? Where is it? Is it near the border?" I just knew in my heart that I would find my father there.

"So many questions!" He laughed heartily. It was contagious and produced a smile of my own. I couldn't help it, but I had to be a little pushy. My life depended on finding my father. There was nothing else for me, and I had no one.

"There are two major camps that I know of, Kakuma and Dadaab. I am not sure where they are, but they are not near the border. It would be too risky."

"How will I ever find my father?"

"You should not go to the camps. They are worse than prisons. If your father is not there, you will be stuck because of the tight restrictions that are enforced to control refugee populations. You must seek help from the UN Refugee Agency. They have an office in Nairobi and should have a record if your father applied for asylum."

"Do you know the best way to get across the border?"

"I do not, but…" He scanned the area, now deserted, except for the busboy who cleaned the tables and the chubby waitress who was collecting the last of the dishes.

"Kiki," he called. She came bustling over with a wide grin meant only for Kumowo. She didn't glance in my direction but came intimately close to him, thrusting out her breasts, though did not touch him.

"What can I do for you?" she drawled slowly, putting emphasis on every syllable.

"I need a favor."

"Anything," she purred, moving closer to him.

"Does your brother still sell the *cassavas* across the border?"

"Of course, he goes there almost every morning. If you want I can get them for you after I close and have them before morning."

"No, thank you. Could your brother take her across the border?" She turned to look at me. Kiki could not have looked more shocked if she'd been slapped in the face. Her face quickly changed from shock to anger, then calmness washed away her emotions, but I could still feel them.

"Why would you want to do that?" She directed her question to Kumowo but never took her eyes off me. I was being torn apart with her calm gaze.

"A favor. She needs to go to her family."

"And what did she do for you in return for this favor?" she demanded, seething with anger, yet the only indication of this were the twitches in the muscles around her jaw. Kumowo noticed and immediately worked his magic.

"Nothing at all. She is just a girl. You know I only have eyes for the full and beautiful." He gave her a smile that made me blush, like she was the only woman in the world for him. "Unfortunately, I am married and can only handle one woman at a time."

"If you married someone like me, you'd have no problem."

"Not everyone can be as good as you are Kiki," he said as he put his hand against her cheek. She seemed to melt in his touch and I was uncomfortable, but thankfully forgotten. Kumowo must have felt my unease and looked at me briefly before returning his attention to Kiki. "Do you think you can get your brother to do this favor? I will buy him a round of beer when he comes again."

"Honey, I can get him to do anything. Besides he owes me."

"I knew you could."

"Just have her here and ready before dawn and my brother will come with his load." She continued to ignore my presence, talking to Kumowo as if I were invisible. I didn't say a word as long as I had safe passage across the border. I didn't care what Kiki said or how she treated me. She was willing to help me just to please Kumowo.

"Thank you, Kiki. I owe you."

"You owe me big. See you tomorrow, Kumowo," she said walking away, her hips swaying in her wake. Her stride was confident, as if she'd won a great challenge. I watched her collect her small red handbag and put on a pair of worn sandals, replacing her high heels. The young boy was nowhere to be found.

"Thank you," I said turning back to Kumowo.

"It's my pleasure. Are you sure about tonight?"

"Yes, but I will be close by." I didn't want to even think about missing Kiki's brother. That was my only ticket out of Uganda.

"You may come to my house for the night; I am not far from here."

"No, you have done enough for me." I didn't even consider going to his house. It's not that I didn't trust him – he'd done enough to prove that I could rely on him – but if Kiki's brother came, I couldn't risk it. I would stay awake, vigilant, all night if that's what it took.

"At least stay the night here. Kiki's brother is a good man deep down inside, but he is also the best salesman I've ever met. He'll do anything to make money. Do not let him talk you into doing anything illegal. Make sure you tell him that you are my cousin. Have a safe journey."

I was glad that he didn't push the issue of my staying with him. He must have seen the reluctance on my face. With a slight nod, he took his leave, whistling lightheartedly as he walked away, shutting off the electric bulbs.

"Thank you!" I called out to him.

"Anytime, cousin," he replied with a smile and continued on his way.

I found a comfortable spot behind the bar that smelled of sweat and stale beer. It was out of view from anyone who might approach the outdoor club. I sat with my back against the bar, holding my knees against my chest, waiting for the arrival of Kiki's brother, not wanting to fall asleep. I thought of the stories my family told as we enjoyed tea while sitting on our mats before bed. It was the most comforting time of day, when nothing was expected of us. Our daily chores were done and we indulged in our amusement. Up until this point, I hadn't allowed myself to dwell on the past because it hurt my heart to think of everything I had lost. This night I found comfort in the very thing I kept myself from doing, remembering stories of the past.

I imagined my family sitting in front of me as I told a story about a cattle herder who wanted many children to make his friends jealous. He could only afford one wife while his friends had many and boasted of their fertility. He grew impatient waiting for his wife to recover after the delivery of his firstborn son, just a few days old. He went to the village *sangoma* for help. "I want many children, many more than all my friends have. I want them to be as strong as a bull and as smart as a fox. I only have one wife and cannot take another until I have more cattle."

He stressed the urgency of his need and complained about the length of time it had taken for his wife's pregnancy. "Let nature do what it's intended to do and your wife will have more than a dozen children." The man refused to listen to reason and grew angry at the *sangoma* for not wanting to interfere with nature. "You mean to tell me that your magic is not strong enough? The gods no longer see you in their favor?" He continued to question the *sangoma's* influence with the gods and insult her magic until she grew angry.

"Bring me three of your cattle at midnight," she said slowly, but the man saw it as defeat and smiled inside at his cleverness.

Pleased with his work, he left the *sangoma's* hut and headed for home. He didn't tell his wife about his visit and near midnight he left the hut with three cattle in tow. He gave the animals to the *sangoma* and in exchange she gave him three red yams to feed to his wife right away. He headed home, excited, and immediately cooked the bright red yams. He saw the confused look in his wife's eyes when she saw him cooking so he told her that the yams would make her strong and recover fast so that she may have many more children. She ate the yams and did not question why he didn't share them with her.

Suddenly, she felt better than ever before. Within a week she was pregnant and gave birth to triplets three months later. Several women from the village had to help feed the babies because their appetites were insatiable. It was a blessing that offered much attention. The man paid no attention to his firstborn son but focused his love on the others. For two years, his wife gave birth to triplets every three months – with or without his seed.

When they had twenty-four children, the man wanted no more. The children grew three times faster than other children, overflowing their hut and consuming large amounts of food, forcing him to slaughter most of his cattle. The man went back to the *sangoma* and begged for her to make his wife stop having children.

"For three years you will have three children every three months. It is beyond my control."

"Please!" he begged her, dropping to his knees at her feet. "They have eaten almost everything." The *sangoma*, feeling a little sorry for him, said there was only one thing he could do. "You must bring the all children born of the yams to the old tree and return them to the gods at midnight tonight."

The man thanked the *sangoma* and returned to his hut. He didn't tell his wife, because she had just given birth to another set of triplets. At midnight he gathered up the children, but his wife woke up. "What are you doing?" She didn't like the look in his eyes. "I must return the children to the gods at midnight. They were never ours to have. I'm sorry to have this happen. It was my mistake." He returned all the children. He had lost most of his cattle and could never afford another wife, but from that day forward, he never complained about the one child he had. Although he never had more children, he was the happiest man in the village.

I awoke to the sound of tires crunching the earth and the irregular gasps and moans from a tired engine. I wished I'd lain down because now my butt was sore, my neck was stiff and my left leg was asleep. Awkwardly, I arose and was blinded by headlights. A man was getting out of the vehicle but he appeared as a dark shadow against the bright light.

CHAPTER SEVENTEEN

"We must go. I don't have all day," he called, motioning for me to follow. "Come on, girl." A heavy load rose above the truck bed, covered with a dark canvas and tightly secured with rope. When I approached the idling truck, for a moment he just stood there. Something flickered through his dark eyes; interest, curiosity, amusement? The look was gone before I could hope to figure it out.

"You can ride up front with me until we reach the border. As you can see, I have a full load and cannot risk the damage." He opened the driver's side door. "The other door is jammed," he said curtly.

I climbed in over the bench seat to the far end, pressing myself against the passenger door. The truck was cramped, littered with rags, blankets and plastic bottles, and smelled of diesel exhaust and oil. He did some adjusting of his load before he climbed behind the wheel.

Although my father had a vehicle, I had never ridden in one. The road was rough and we bounced along. When we were children, Suda and I would sit in the parked car and pretend we were driving until

Mama would yell at us to get out. When I see Suda again, I thought, I am going to tell her all about it.

I was excited as he backed away from the club and shifted the gears. We were on our way. My face was so close to the window that I could feel its coolness against my nose. I couldn't wait for the sun to come up so I could see the landscape passing by.

"My sister said you are going to meet your family in Kenya and you lost your papers."

I was startled when he broke the silence. There are times when a person just wants to enjoy an experience without someone talking about something they did not wish to discuss. That was how I felt. I wanted to say, "May I enjoy the drive to Kenya without you talking?"

"Yes, that is true. We have been apart for some time." My voice was surprisingly calm, as if discussing the weather over afternoon tea, when deep inside there was a whirlwind of excitement bubbling just beneath the surface.

"My name is Sam. And you are?"

"Matika."

"That's a very pretty name. How fitting. You are going back so your family can take care of you?"

"Why do you ask such a question? That's what families do; they take care of their children."

"You're not a child anymore. My sister was married with two children by the time she was your age. You're going back to Kenya so they can take care of you again. What if they don't want you to come back?"

I was close to correcting him, but I didn't. If he wanted to believe that I was from Kenya, so be it. He had a tone is his voice that made me angry, like scraping wood with your fingernails. He brought up a point that I never thought about. What if my father didn't want me to show up in his life right now? What if he had no means to take care of me?

"Your family would be really proud if you had a job and could help out financially."

Why couldn't he just stop talking for once? I felt guilty thinking that I might be a burden to my father. "Yes, I suppose I'll find a job when I get there."

"Do you speak English?"

When I didn't answer, he went on.

"There is a little problem. Any good job you would hope to get will require you to speak English, at least if you want to make enough money to help your family. What kind of job do you hope to get?"

"I don't know right now, but I'll think about it later."

"Think about it now, because I could get you a job to make lots of money."

"Doing what?"

"I know people who could get you a good job." Sam was clearly avoiding the question.

"Why do you care if I have a good job?"

"I am a caring person. Besides, I want to do this favor for Kiki and, of course, Kumowo. He's a good friend. I want to help you help yourself. Your employer will teach you English and give you a place to stay. They will also get you papers so you can travel anywhere in the world. Do you like to travel?

Of course I'd always dreamed of traveling the world and having grand adventures like the next person, but now that I was traveling, I wanted nothing more than to go home. I was thrust into this unbelievable adventure, certainly not fun, but an adventure nonetheless. At this point, staying in my village, getting married and having children was exactly what I wanted, especially if it meant I could have my family back. But I knew everything had changed forever and there was no turning back to my war-torn village.

"I don't care much for traveling."

"Really? You are traveling now, *alone*."

A chill went down my spine as he spoke. I looked at him cautiously and he was staring right at me, his dark eyes brooding. I felt like I needed to explain my current state without revealing anything. I thought of the first lie that came to mind. They were starting to flow much easier and it made me feel strange.

"My family moved to Kenya and I had to stay behind to take care of a sick grandmother who has just passed away."

"Or maybe you are running away from a husband. I see that a lot too."

"I'm not married. I am sorry but I don't want a job right now. You can meet with my cousin Kumowo and see if he thinks it is a good idea for me to get a job." I threw in the last statement in hopes that he would back off, yet continuing to be polite and not anger him.

"Funny, he didn't mention to me that you were a cousin."

"I'm a distant cousin," I said, tensing up.

"Right," he replied.

The sun was beginning to rise, showing breathtaking scenery. Zebras were grazing on a hillside beneath a Shea butter tree and springbucks were off to the right. I didn't care. The road was full of potholes and I was constantly being bounced from side to side, but Sam didn't slow down. I don't know if it was because I was looking out the window or because I hadn't eaten, but I felt nauseous and wanted the ride to be over. Putting my head on the dashboard and my palms against my temples, I fought to keep my stomach out of my throat. The saliva was rushing to my mouth, causing me to gag. I clamped my hands over my mouth as my stomach pumped last night's meal up my throat and through my nostrils.

"Not in my truck!" He slammed on the breaks and the truck slid for some time before it screeched to a halt, sending some of the *cassavas* tumbling down the windshield. He jerked the door open and pulled me over his lap, and I went head first on the dusty road. Luckily I put my hands out and saved my face from the pavement as I heaved yellowy bile. With my legs over Sam's lap, I lay there waiting for more.

"Sorry to throw you so hard, but you look heavier than you really are."

I continued to pant as he lifted me into a sitting position on his lap once I'd stopped vomiting. Dark spots danced across my eyes. I felt weak but my nausea was passing. I stiffened. My fatigue vanished. Sam's hand, resting on my knee, was now slowly creeping higher and higher, caressing my thighs. His hardened manhood stiffly poked me.

"I don't feel well at all," I said quickly, hoping to distract him. No, not again!

"You're just carsick. It'll pass."

I glanced at him surreptitiously and was greeted by the unmistakable sexual hunger in his eyes. They were at half-mast and looked like he was daydreaming. A hint of a smile shaped his mouth that many women would call handsome. He was a man used to getting what he wanted from the ladies and was probably never told "no." I attempted to move but he held fast.

"Please, I'm going to throw up in your truck. I know cousin Kumowo would be disappointed if I told him."

The look he gave me was akin to embarrassment. He quickly let go. I got out of the truck and went round to the back while Sam adjusted the load and gathered the fallen *cassavas*. I heaved again, until nothing came up. "I can't ride in the truck without making a mess," I called out to him between gasps of air.

He handed me a dirty plastic bottle of water that was half-full and smelled of mold. I drank the stale water slowly and its coolness soothed my sour throat. A little food might calm my stomach, but even if I had something the thought of eating wasn't appealing at the moment.

"We are almost to the border so you can ride in the back."

Looking at the bed of the truck I thought that there couldn't possibly be any room for a person. I was wrong. He went around back, lifted a section of the tarp, pulled out a large basket of yams and sat it on the ground. The basket concealed a wooden crate secured with a latch.

"Get in," he said after opening the door. The crate was filled with rifles and replacement parts. "Don't worry; none of them work. I trade the broken ones for better weapons in Kenya. You just need to stay very quiet and I'll let you out as soon as we are safely across the border. It should take about forty minutes."

I didn't feel good about his plan. Being locked up in a crate in the back of a truck was just too frightening to contemplate. I would be lying on weapons that were obviously part of an illegal trade. I could go to jail and who knows what would happen then? If all went well across the border, there could also be other issues. What if he decided to sell me to a rebel camp? What if he didn't let me out and just forgot about me?

"Don't worry, but you do need to hurry because I have a schedule to maintain," he said, jerking me back into focus. I didn't know if this was going to be the best decision, but what could I do? I could think of no better option. I had come too far to stop now. Risking capture on my own could prove to have more dire consequences.

Against my better judgment, I climbed in, taking the water bottle with me. With rifles digging into my ribs I tried to find a comfortable spot. It was impossible, so I settled on my side, wiggling against the barrels. Sam smiled down at me in a failed attempt to be reassuring.

"It's safe. There are a few holes near your head for air. Don't move a muscle when we stop at the border, no matter what."

When he closed the crate, my heart tightened in a moment of panic that intensified further at the click of the lock. Why did he have to lock it? If I needed to get out in a hurry, I'd be in bad shape. I refused to dwell on that nightmare.

The basket felt like it was on my chest instead of the crate and seemed to drain air from my lungs. The small holes near my head provided some airflow, but not much. It was like I was breathing in my own hot air again and again. For now, I was trapped and I had to trust that everything would be okay.

I tested the crate by pushing on it with my hands and feet and learned that it was as sturdy as a house. I also discovered that it was pretty large, which was deceiving because the small hatch opening made it seem like a narrow crate. It was almost as long as I was and about as wide.

Finally, the truck began to roll forward, but the movement brought back the familiar nausea. I clutched the water bottle tightly with both hands and the crunching sound it made temporarily distracted me from my bubbly abdomen. "Thirty minutes," I chanted, willing the time away. The minutes stretched into a small eternity. Finally, the truck rumbled to a stop.

Music from a radio mixed with muffled voices in the background. My heart beat in my ears and I strained to hear the dialogue. The music was turned down and I heard footsteps approaching.

"I'll handle this one. Let me see your papers." The man's voice was clear as running water. I was glad that the compartment was on the driver's side so I could hear the exchange. There was a long pause. Everything was quiet, tense. I could no longer hear the distant hum of the music or any other voices. Silence. "I shouldn't let you cross," the man said firmly.

"Why?" Sam asked.

"Your papers are about to expire."

"Yes, I will be renewing them shortly," Sam replied.

"Where are you headed?"

"Nairobi."

"Why are you going all the way to Nairobi to sell vegetables? It will cost you more gas than it's worth."

The man had a point. There wouldn't be much to gain from a trip like this. Locally grown produce is much cheaper. I thought he did this regularly. Sam said nothing to this. More silence. Then to my horror, the man began rummaging through the truck. I felt him lift the basket off the crate and for a moment I panicked. It was like he knew exactly where to look.

I know Sam told me not to move, but I couldn't just stay still when the trap door was opened. As quietly as possible, I shifted myself to the far end of the compartment and pulled my dress tightly around my legs. I was sweating so much it was like someone poured a bucket of water over me. I pressed my body so close to the edge of the crate that not even a hair could pass through the space between. I bit my tongue to keep silent and held my breath for what I knew was coming.

"The key," he said too confidently. I felt the truck shift while Sam must have been foraging for the key. I knew he carried it in his pocket, so he must have been buying time. I don't know what would be worse for him, the agents finding the weapons, finding me, or both. I was filled with dread as I took in a deep, calming breath.

"Here," Sam said. His voice was close as he got out of the truck to watch the agent. I hoped that they couldn't see me and I wished I were invisible, like a spirit. A quick click sounded and the door opened, letting in a cool breeze on my fevered skin.

CHAPTER EIGHTEEN

There was no time to prepare. I wanted to squeeze my eyes shut but couldn't. I felt vulnerable, helpless and exposed at the same time, like an ant trapped in a child's hand. I could clearly see the man staring down at me and we locked eyes.

"You have less than usual," the man said, using the tip of his rifle to sift through the broken ones. As he pushed the parts around to gauge the depth, his rifle came very close to my face and at one point pushed up against my breast. Although his gaze was cast in my direction, he wasn't looking directly at me.

"Business has been slow."

"You got a light?"

"Of course," Sam said. I heard him fumbling through his pocket.

"You got a cigarette, too?" the man asked.

"Yes." Sam gave him a cigarette and lit it for him once it was in his mouth.

"We have been looking for a girl that may cross the border," he said after taking a long drag. I just knew it had to be me they were looking for. There seemed to be no end to the colonel's madness.

"A colonel has put up a high price for her safe return. It must be his daughter or something. Still, she's worth a lot of money." He let out a ring of smoke directly into Sam's face. His free hand rested on the crate opening just a short distance from me. Did he see me and was playing with Sam's mind? I wanted to cry. I willed my body not to shake.

"Interesting," Sam said, absently rubbing his hairless jaw.

"Have you seen a girl on your drive out here?"

"No, no girl."

"What is this?" The man reached into the crate, his hand only a few scant centimeters from my forehead, and pulled out the water bottle. No! I had forgotten about it. I gritted my teeth angrily at my stupidity, wishing to rewind time. How could I miss that?

"Oh! There it is. I was looking everywhere for that. Let us get to business," he said, quickly changing the subject. "How much today?"

"Fifty."

"As you see, this is a very small load so I will not be getting much. It would cost me that much just to make this trip."

"Forty-five."

"That's what I paid you yesterday for a much bigger load. Twenty-five."

"Okay, thirty and make it quick before the others come near."

"It's a pleasure doing business with you." I didn't see Sam give him the money but it must have been done cleverly.

"Tell your sister I said hi."

"You tell her yourself."

The man just laughed and walked away. Sam looked though the crate opening curiously in my direction, pausing a moment before securing it once more. What I would've given to know what he was thinking just then.

I let out a deep breath when the truck started to meander down the road again. I was shaking and despite my best effort to control my emotions, I started crying hysterically. That was such a close call that I could practically smell my freedom flying away and it still wasn't over. Sam must have known that I was the girl the colonel was looking for. What did he plan to do with me? It was told he would do anything for money. I was also told that he was a good man deep down inside.

Fifteen minutes passed, though I'm not quite sure how long it was because I had lost all concept of time. I started to lose what little control I had over my mind. The compartment started getting smaller and began closing in on me like a fitted glove.

The air was stifling and I started to hyperventilate. Sweat dripped from my body like rain falling off leaves from a banana tree. I started kicking and screaming and clawing at the box, but to no avail. To my alarm, the music was turned on full blast, drowning out any chance of anyone hearing me. I was in full panic now. I called out to Sam repeatedly but the truck continued on its way.

I no longer cared about being captured. I just wanted out because I knew for sure that I would die in this box. It was suffocating. My life was slowly being choked out. My head was beginning to enter a fog. There was no world anymore; nothing existed but me and the top of the box. No family, no life, just the four wooden walls.

The truck ground to a halt. I stopped banging on the box. The crate was thrown open.

"Are you all right?" Sam's strong arms pulled me from the beneath its surface and held me.

"Let go of me!" Wrenching out of his grip, I stumbled away from the truck. My body was drenched and my threadbare dress was almost transparent and clung to me like an extra skin. I needed to get away from his hot, smothering hands. Open space and freedom were all I could think of. I wanted to run but my legs were too shaky. Then I was angry at Sam. "Why did you not stop when I called for you? I was screaming at the top of my lungs and what did you do? You turned the radio on full blast!" I was panting, doubled over with my hands on my knees. I couldn't think straight.

"Matika, you could have gotten us both killed!" he shot back and was at my side immediately, roughly grasping my arm, forcing me to look at him. His dark eyes were wild with fury. "I had to turn up the music so no one could hear you."

"I didn't know," I conceded, clearly surprised that there could be rational explanation for what he did.

"I know who you are."

"What do you mean?" My heart was beating violently in my chest. I knew he knew but I was not going to offer any information.

"No more games! The River Lion is looking for you. Is he your husband?"

"No! He isn't my husband," I said with more venom than I wanted. I didn't want to display so much emotion; it would give Sam more information than he needed.

"You must be something to him if he is willing to pay a high price for you. Who are you, really?"

"I am no one. I was abducted by the colonel and escaped. He will kill me if he finds me again. Look, Sam, all I want is to be with my family," I pleaded.

"What will you give me if I let you go free?" he said, undressing me with his eyes, making it clear what he wanted in return.

It seemed like it was the only thing men ever thought about around me. I'd only met a few men, not from my immediate family, who wanted nothing sexual from me. Kumowo was a good man who helped me unconditionally. If he did feel differently he hid it well, which was just as good.

"I know this colonel and I can tell you that you do not want to do business with him. You will not only condemn me to death but you will also lose your life, as well. Not only will he not pay you, he will kill you. I've seen him kill his own men without blinking an eye."

Sam was clearly reconsidering his options as his eyes lost focus on me briefly. Taking me back to the colonel was not in his best interest. It could be a deathtrap.

"I still should have payment from you."

"Why? You said you were doing a favor for your sister and my cousin Kumowo. I owe you nothing."

"I could easily take you back across the border or better yet, sell you to a brothel. Kumowo would never know if I told him I dropped you off at a bus stop."

I bolted into a full sprint off the road in the direction we were headed.

"Matika!" he called after me and was in full pursuit. "I was only kidding. I would never do that to Kumowo." Although I had a head start he was upon me quickly. He grabbed me around the waist and lifted me up over his shoulders, kicking and screaming.

"Why are you doing this? I've done nothing to you!"

He forced me into the driver's side and got in behind me.

"I'm not leaving you here. As promised, I'll take you to a bus stop."

There was nothing I could do and fighting him was useless; the passenger door was jammed. He started the truck and drove on. I didn't know where he was driving or how long it would take, but for now there wasn't anything I could do.

We drove in a thick uncomfortable silence. I wanted to know what he was thinking, but couldn't bring myself to look at him. Instead I kept my eyes fixed ahead as I sat rigidly, waiting for any indication of our destination. The radio played softly in the background and he hummed to it every now and then.

I was glad I wasn't sick anymore and it seemed to help looking straight ahead instead of out the side window. We drove for hours in silence until we reached the city of Eldoret, which Sam said was a good place to catch a bus to Nairobi.

"You can use the toilet here but make it quick. I have a schedule to meet," he said as he pulled into a petrol station. "Of course you can ride with me to Nairobi and save your money." Not waiting for a reply, he got out of the truck and disappeared into a small store.

I went to the toilet because at that point I really needed to go. I wanted to save money and maybe buy food with what little I had. It was already midafternoon and the city was bustling with activity, but I had no idea when the buses left for Nairobi.

Honestly, I was more afraid of the condition I was in and was horrified after looking in the small metal mirror. I was dirty, my hair was a mess, and my dress…well, to say it was indecent was an understatement. The thought of being in a crowd didn't appeal to me in the least. At the same time, I knew I couldn't trust Sam. I used the toilet and scrubbed my hair and body as best I could with the small bar of soap before I returned to the truck.

Sam emerged from the store all too quickly, carrying a brown paper bag, looking around constantly before he returned to the truck. He handed me a cold aluminum can and fried sweet buns sprinkled with granulated sugar.

"Cola," he said reaching over and popping the top. He then opened his and took a heavy swig, his Adam's apple moving up and down with each swallow.

I stood there, leaning against his truck as he pumped gas, not committing to his offer just yet. If he was trying to bribe me with food, he made a good choice because I rarely turned down food. I don't know what I expected the cola to taste like but I was surprised to find it sweet with a fizzy bite that pleasantly foamed in my mouth, biting my teeth and tickling my tongue. The bread was warm and sticky and the combination of the two was amazing.

Sam watched me intently as he pumped gas, breaking his gaze only to look around for an unknown assailant. His paranoid act was making me weary.

"I would like to catch a bus," I said after I'd finished, which didn't take me long.

"Do you have enough money?"

"I think so," I pulled out the money Kumowo had given me. Sam looked surprised.

"That is not the right currency used in Kenya. Give me what you have and I will exchange it with some of mine."

I watched him carefully as he exchanged my money with some of his, as though I knew the exchange rate. I could only hope that he didn't cheat me. I didn't know much about money and I knew even less about an "exchange rate."

Within twenty minutes I was at the small station waiting for a bus that was scheduled to leave in two hours, and Sam was out of my life and mind, despite his repeated offers and proposals. I sat on the dusty ground, knees to my chest, willing the time away, surrounded by mostly women and children who were also waiting.

I was glad I came early because when we finally boarded, the crowd was thick and the seats were limited. The bus was filled beyond capacity and many passengers had to stand or sit in the aisles. I couldn't even give up my seat to an old woman who could barely stand because I was sandwiched between two women whose bodies took up far more than their share of the bench seat. Their filthy bags covered the floor, including my feet.

Although the trip was long, the bus stuffy and smelly, it was invigorating to finally be so close to seeing Baba again. I had such a good feeling in my heart that things were going to look up for me from now on. My journey would soon be over and I would be able to put this nightmare behind me.

The bus meandered up and down hills at a dangerous pace. The woman sitting next to the window covered it with a small blanket, not allowing in sunlight or fresh air. After six hours of driving, stopping two times to somehow add more passengers along the way, the bus finally arrived in Nairobi.

It was night; I had to find a safe place to rest until morning. Finding a secluded place was impossible given the multitudes of people in the city that was lit up like torches in a festival. They were everywhere and there was no avoiding them. I finally settled in an area where a few young teenage boys were rolling cubes. In the dimly lit area between two tall buildings, the boys' laughter echoed against the concrete slabs.

I crept beside a trash bin out of view. I was exhausted and fell asleep quickly.

When I awoke I set out to find the UN Refugee Agency. I asked directions from a local cab driver who offered to take me there for a "small fee" that I politely refused. The building was not far from where I was and it stood out like a beacon in a sea of huts and seemed to reach the sky. Its sheer size and beauty were intimidating and fascinating. A guard stood at the door and checked people's identification cards as they came into the building. Once inside they were also frisked for weapons.

"ID," said the first guard as I approached. He was short with a slight receding hairline. His eyes were intense and suspicious. He had a look that made you feel like you did something very bad. I wanted to confess to some unknown crime to break his stare. "Do you have papers?"

"No, but I need to see someone with the UN Refugee Agency."

"Okay, the line is over there," he said, pointing to a large cluster of people that looked no better than I. They were in a small roped-off area and were not permitted to go any farther into the building.

I learned from the others that people had been waiting for days and didn't seem to move any further on the list. If you could not read or write it took even longer for someone to help fill out the application just to be seen. This was going to be a long, long day, or several days. I had to stand with many others because all the seats were taken and the guard didn't allow anyone to sit on the ground. I wished I had come earlier; as it was, people who came later than me were not able to wait in the area.

The hot afternoon sun arrived when it was finally my turn to get an application. The woman behind the counter was curt but had kind eyes. It was as if she had heard too many sad stories that had hardened her heart.

"Young lady, your parents have to be present to fill out the application. Where are your parents?" she said, scanning the crowd.

"*Auntie*, I am alone. I have traveled from Uganda alone and I am here because I need to find my father."

"You came alone?" Her eyes were filled with disbelief but after a quick assessment of my person, it quickly changed. "Are you okay? Do you need to see a doctor?"

At that I began to cry, my legs shaking from standing so long without any food or water. I didn't realize how badly I wanted someone to care about me. I felt so lonely. The lady rushed from around the counter and ushered me to the back. She sat me down in a wooden chair. She spoke rapidly to another woman who ran to the back.

From this point things moved quickly. I told my story to the agency representative while leaving out the parts that made me blush, although I think she knew I was leaving out information as she gave me encouraging pats on my shoulder. I was given food and water and a long wrap to cover my upper body. I know the woman wanted to cover my dress that hugged my breasts tightly.

"We have record of your father and I will send you to him straight away."

With that I was ushered onto another crowded bus, on my way to a refugee camp where I was told my father was living. I hoped she was right because I couldn't live through the disappointment. Not after everything I had been through. I was so weak emotionally and my family would be the only thing that could make it better.

CHAPTER NINETEEN

As the bus slowly pulled up to the barbed-wire fence of the camp, I had mixed feelings. There were only a few buildings surrounded by a sea of tents and some shacks. On one hand I was elated that soon I would see my father again and I wouldn't be alone in the world anymore. On the other hand I was filled with anxiety about how he would react to my coming. I didn't know whether he would be angry or embrace me. My father would know that I had risked my life to get here. Regardless of the outcome, I was here and was not going back.

My legs trembled as the passengers gathered their belongings and began to file off the bus. I wished I'd sat in the front because now I would be one of the last off the bus. Old ladies were taking entirely too long and it took every ounce of patience I had not to plow through them. Inside I screamed with impatience, irritated to the core with the crowd. Outwardly, I displayed the customary respect, keeping a modest distance befitting a young girl of my station.

Finally, I was off the bus and I bolted through the crowd to the front of the line for check-in. I heard muffled complaints but nothing too loud as the travelers were wary and much too tired. Many had lost their loved ones and homes for one reason or another.

"Your name?" asked a man sitting at a white folding table just inside the gate. He didn't bother to look up, but continued to scribble in a green logbook, his thick glasses hanging dangerously low on his pointed nose. He was wearing a button-up white-collared shirt with long sleeves folded up to just below the elbows. Although his pants were hidden from view, a pair of expensive shoes peered from beneath the table.

Two guards stood like statues on each side of him. They looked sinister in their uniforms and dark sunglasses, but most intimidating was the automatic rifles they carried across their chests. Although I could not see their eyes, I felt them boring into my skin, sending chills down my spine. A wave of fear passed over me and I wondered whether I'd always feel that way about soldiers or men with guns. I held tightly to my oversize shawl, thankful for the lady's kindness.

When I didn't respond right away, the man repeated his question slowly, as if I didn't understand him the first time, while looking above the rim of his glasses with an expression I could only describe as being irritated at my "stupidity."

"Matika Okello Naminiha," I replied, using my full name. The man looked at me curiously along with the guard, and one of them even lowered his glasses to stare at me openly. I didn't think I would get that response, but it filled my heart to know they recognized the name.

"Are you related to Batalo Okello Naminiha?"

"Yes, he is my father. Do you know where he is?"

"I do," he said looking over his shoulder. He called for a young man to cover his post. "Follow me and I will take you to him."

I was so excited that my earlier apprehensions were forgotten. The man walked at a decent pace but I wanted him to run. We passed rows and rows of tents and makeshift huts with laundry hanging on strings spanning from tent to hut. People walked everywhere while others sat outside their dwellings with blank expressions. Although it was extremely crowed, next to impossible not to bump into them, they made plenty of room for the official and closed in as soon as he walked by, swallowing me in the midst. I quickly learned to stay on his heels, damning respectability.

The size of the camp was astounding and seemed to go on and on. It was a city but with no stores or shops, at least none that I could recognize. After about fifteen minutes of meandering through tents, we stopped suddenly.

"Batalo," he called from outside a tent that was much larger than the others we'd passed.

"He's asleep," a women's voice called though the hut. At this point I wanted to run through the draped cloth used as a door and wake my father.

"Wake him. It's urgent," demanded the man with such finality that I knew the woman would do as she was told.

The ruffled movement of canvas followed by hushed voices, one of which was the unmistakable baritone of my father, perked my ears. I waited what seemed like hours for him to respond.

"This better be important," Baba said in anger before charging out of the hut. "It has been a long-" he stopped mid-sentence and stared at me.

Everything stopped. I no longer heard the throng of people. Baba had changed so much since I'd seen him last. Gone was the man who was muscular, vibrant and full of life as this shell of a man before me was sad, depleted, and hungry for life. The father I knew stood ramrod straight, pristine is his uniform that he wore proudly, letting others know his status and superior rank, but this man was dressed in a dirty T-shirt, loose trousers that hung low across his waist, and was hiding from the world. His once proud stance was now slumped.

"This girl claims to be your daughter," the man said, breaking the ice that froze my father and me in place.

"Baba!" I rushed to my father ,wrapping my hands around his waist tightly. I was beginning to worry when he didn't respond.

"Matika, is that really you?"

Pushing me back and looking into my eyes, I saw so much pain and fear that it broke my heart. It looked like he wanted to believe it was me, but for some reason was afraid to hope.

"Baba, it's Matika," I said pulling the shawl from my head and letting it fall to the ground.

"You were taken by our enemies."

"Baba, I got away and I came here to be with you."

"Matika!" At last I broke through to him. He embraced me so tightly that I lost my breath, but didn't care. It felt so good to be in his arms. I made a promise then that nothing would ever keep me from him again. Tears flowed down my checks and I cried, wailed, and laughed at the same time. His body shook as warm water slid down his cheeks, yet he made no sound.

I don't know when the man discreetly disappeared, but we were so caught up in the moment that a bomb could have exploded and we wouldn't have heard it. Baba led me into the tent, which was stuffy, but not hot. No light was let in so it took a while for my eyes to adjust to the darkness.

The floor was lined with mats that smelled of soiled linen. No ground was visible. Several baskets lined the left and there was a large cloth, slashed in the middle for an entrance, spread across the hut, making another room.

A woman sat weaving a basket, which was incredible considering the lack of sunlight. She was wearing a dark dress, but I couldn't see its color, nor could I make out her features. She looked up at me with interest, then watched my father as he reached up and opened the flaps to let in light.

"This is my precious daughter, Matika. The Lord has blessed us with her presence once again."

"Matika, this is your mama, Evelyn."

I was shocked. Surprised, she dropped her basket. I turned to my father and then back to Evelyn. How could my father marry again so quickly? Our family was torn apart and he had the audacity to marry yet again to start another one. It was a slap in the face.

"Stay here and I will return shortly with some tea for us all." Father left the hut and, in turn, left me alone with his new wife.

"Matika, I've heard so much about you."

"Well, I've heard nothing about you."

Either she chose to ignore my sarcasm or just completely missed it and continued politely.

"This is the first time your father has opened the folds of the tent since he heard about what happened to you. He has been mourning ever since, sleeping most of the days and kept up by his nightmares during the evenings."

"How did my father know what happened to me?" Then it hit me. Suda! Where was she? Just then, someone came charging into the tent as swift as the wind.

"Matika!"

"Suda!"

We held each other, not wanting to let go. I was overwhelmed with emotion. If it was a dream, I didn't want to wake up. Deep down I knew it was real, my journey was finally over. My heart floated to the sky with relief. Suda was my dearest friend and favorite sister and I knew that I couldn't go on without her in my life.

"Are you okay?" she whispered into my ear as we continued to hold each other.

"I've never felt better."

"You've lost your baby fat. You've turned into a woman."

I smiled shyly, looking at my feet.

"What took you so long?" She started to cry. I had never seen Suda cry, even when Mama was giving her the worst beatings. "For weeks, I waited for you to come to Kenya until I lost all hope. I thought I'd never see you again. I just knew that you were suffering a fate worse than death and it was all my fault."

Suda was the same as I remembered, unlike our father who, although it had only been a couple of months, had changed dramatically. Suda was thinner, clothed in rags, but her hair was neatly braided. She was clean and most importantly, still possessed the strong spirit that blazed from her eyes.

"It killed me to see that you were taken and I couldn't do anything about it. I tried to follow you, but Walyam didn't let me. He said it was too dangerous and I could get you killed."

"What happened to Walyam?"

"He's here. He shares a tent not far from here. Baba favors him for saving our lives." She was blushing and broke eye contact with me, her feelings for Walyam clearly visible.

"You must tell me everything," she said routing the discussion back to me.

"I'm glad you didn't come after me, because those soldiers were dangerous, but most of all, the colonel was the devil. He didn't hesitate to shoot anyone who got in his way. Walyam was right to stop you. We could've both been killed."

"I know, but you can't imagine the guilt I felt in my heart that I've carried ever since. I am the one to blame…"

"No, you're not to blame. I walked away from you. It's over and I'm here now." Evelyn chose that moment to leave the hut, mumbling about needing to get water.

For the first time, I told my story to the one person I trusted more than anyone. I told Suda about the ransacking of the village we traveled through. Unburdening my soul, I didn't leave out a single detail of the soldiers' massacre of the remaining living children. She was shocked to hear how cruel the colonel was and appalled that he would kill his own men. When she learned about the hunt for me even through the border crossing, raw fear was in her eyes.

"Did they rape you?" she finally asked, and I knew that the question hung in the air between us since the minute of our reunion and I was glad she waited until my father's new wife left.

"One of the soldiers tried to, but I was saved by Lutalo." She was interested in hearing all about Lutalo. Now it was my turn to blush as I told her about my first kiss with him and how he made me feel. Then I was sad thinking about the possibility that he might be dead.

"What happened to him?"

"The colonel shot him when I escaped the boat."

"I'm sorry that he was killed because he seemed like good man."

"I don't know if he died for sure, but I hope he is okay."

"Please do not tell Baba about me and Walyam. Baba thinks highly of him. I believe he's considering offering me to him in marriage. I really hope so because I love him, but Baba must not know about us."

"Of course I would never tell Baba," I said hugging her again. Walyam was the reason that her spirits were so high. She really cared for him and for some reason after all this time it still bothered me, but this time I was going to give him a chance. "I am so happy for you." I truly was happy, not about Walyam, but simply for her happiness.

She started to say something more but Father returned to the hut with tea, followed by his wife with fresh water. That night we rejoiced in our reunion with hot tea, dried meat and millet bread. I shared my escape with Baba, leaving out many details but he didn't seem to notice. His admiration showed as I told him about my daring swim in the cold river.

Suda took out my old braids combed out my matted curls. She then put my hair in two thick braids, wrapping them around my head like a crown as Baba told me about learning English with Suda. He had applied for asylum with the United States, United Kingdom, Spain, and France.

"It may take a while before a country accepts us but no matter where we live, English is a language that will be beneficial. Evelyn, give Matika one of your dresses," he said addressing his wife. She was not happy with the order but complied with no complaint. "Your dress is indecent and a girl should not be walking around like that."

I felt really self-conscience but there was nothing I could do. I looked around for my wrap but couldn't see it. Sensing my concern, Suda made a daring comment. With Mother not here, there was no stopping her.

"Baba, it is not like she picked out that dress."

"Bah!" He waved his hand, dismissing her comment and I wanted to laugh but didn't dare.

That night Suda and I told our favorite stories to each other while Baba and his wife slept in the back of the hut. It was so great being with my family again that nothing could bring me down. I was so excited that I was afraid to go to sleep and find out that this was all a dream. I was always a light sleeper so when someone entered the hut I immediately knew it.

CHAPTER TWENTY

I looked up and saw the outline of a man in the darkness. He knew exactly where Suda slept and went straight to her, waking her up gently with a kiss. She woke up promptly and although she slept beside me I couldn't hear what she whispered. When Walyam looked over at me I knew she had told him I was here.

"Matika," Suda whispered to me. "I'll be right back. Cover for me."

"What should I say if Father asks about you?"

"Tell him I'm at the latrine." I was extremely uncomfortable with lying and she knew it. "Don't worry, Matika. Baba sleeps like the dead. I'll be back in less than an hour."

Anxiously, I waited up for her, constantly watching out for Baba. At first I was upset at Suda for leaving me and putting me in a situation where I might have to lie to Baba, but then I thought about how happy Walyam made her. I thought about Lutalo and whether I would do the same thing if he were here. Soon I couldn't keep my eyes open any longer and I let sleep overtake me.

When I awoke, it was morning and Suda slept soundly beside me. Evelyn was moving about the hut, preparing a light repast for Baba.

"Suda, get up," Evelyn said nudging her. Suda moaned then sat up, stretching out like a cat.

Evelyn gave me another dress that fit well and wasn't too tight across my breasts. I didn't want to attract unwanted looks in the refugee camp. Suda had warned me about the frequent rapes. We quickly left the hut hungry. When I asked Suda about it she told me that the missionaries would feed us at school. That was one of the main incentives for going to school.

It took us a half-hour to reach the school, which was within a small collection of buildings, all of which had long lines of people waiting to get in. The buildings were painted drab yellow, like egg yolks, with putrid-green doors. In the center was a cement courtyard with three water pumps. It swarmed with women and children collecting water.

"Over there," Suda said pointing to the farthest building that had a line stretching from its entrance to about three hundred people deep, "is the clinic. Try not to get sick because as you can see, it is impossible to be seen, and it is barely dawn. Some people try to wait in the lines overnight but the guards will not let them break curfew."

"Oh," I said shocked that one would have to wait so long for medical care. Furthermore, Suda had gone out last night and I hope she didn't one day get caught for breaking curfew. The camp was depressing.

After we each collected bowls that were stacked in a neat pile, we waited in a line outside the schoolroom where the missionaries ladled out oatmeal from a large pot and gave us a piece of stale bread. We ate outside the classroom, sitting cross-legged on the ground. The bread was strange and it crumbled at the slightest touch. The oatmeal was delicious, warm and a little sweet with a creamy and, at the same time, lumpy texture. After putting our dishes in a bucket we all filed into the classroom.

"Come sit up here," Suda said pulling me to the front row on the left side. There were four rows of three wooden bench-desk combos that stretched from one end of the classroom to the other. Each bench fit three large children or four small ones, as there was clearly no age limit. The walls in the classroom were covered in off-white plaster except for the front wall, which was red brick. There were three cutout windows, but no glass. The dark-brown cement floor was free of dust until we came in.

Now I understood why Suda was quick to pick a front-row seat in the center, because the classroom filled up quickly and some children were sitting on the floor or standing. The girls were on the left and boys on the right. Most of the children were boys and Suda and I were among the few girls older than ten.

Our teacher came in and silence descended in the classroom. He was kind but strict and didn't tolerate distractions, saying that what he taught us was a precious gift from God that could help us overcome our struggles. There were a few books that we all had to share, huddling together for a glance at them.

English was hard. There were so many exceptions to the rules, but it was fascinating. Like a sponge I soaked it up and spent my free time studying and practicing pronunciations. We were lucky that Baba was fluent and quizzed us regularly. He would smack us across the head for mispronouncing a word that he thought we should have known at this point.

Although Suda had a head start, with my drive I not only caught up with her but surpassed her, earning frequent praises from Baba. She practiced some, but most of her time was spent with Walyam, and she continued to sneak out almost every night. When they were together, I sometimes thought about what it would have been like to be with Lutalo, to have him hold me close and kiss me the way I saw Walyam kiss Suda. Then Walyam's naked body would appear in my mind and the heat would rise to my face. I couldn't look him in the eyes because of it and only spoke to him out of necessity.

I developed a routine that was both comforting and mundane. I woke up before dawn to go to school and then returned to our hut for light chores. The chores were limited to collecting water and washing clothes and dishes. Then I would study, eat, and study more until nightfall.

My new mama was kind and though she took a backseat for Baba's attention when we were around, she harbored no resentment toward us – at least none that was obvious. Eight months mercifully slipped by in this hellhole.

One day after class, Suda asked me to wait at the school for a short while until she returned. She said she wouldn't be more than an hour. After a while I got tired of waiting and decided to walk around a bit. Getting hungry, I found myself walking toward a delicious aroma wafting through the air. Meat was cooking over open flames, which was a rare and costly item in this godforsaken camp.

Walking toward another run-down building with peeling paint, I followed the smoke. Many children were gathered around, watching the game rotate on a spit, the juices sizzling and crackling in the fire below. Two men with rifles at their sides watched the food while another darted back and forth from the building to turn the meat or to add rich seasoning water to it.

There was something familiar about the boy cooking the food but I couldn't get close enough to see. The other children closed in like a swarm of bees, some crying from hunger. Wading through them, I forced myself forward just as the man entered the building once more. When he emerged I immediately recognized him.

"Lutalo," I called out waving my hands so he would see me among the mass.

He looked up as I pushed forward, breaking away from the others. He was as handsome as ever, wearing a striped linen shirt and a pair of creased pants with leather shoes that looked brand-new. Lutalo looked like a man from the Kenyan city, not from the ravaged villages in Uganda.

"Get back," a guard yelled pushing me with the butt of his rifle like I was vermin at his feet.

"Don't touch her! She's with me," Lutalo growled at the guard. He was always the protector. He had filled out much since I saw him last, and was also a lot taller.

The guard stood down but glared at him in return. To be corrected in public was an insult in my village. The guard must have been waiting to eat and didn't argue.

"Matika, I have been looking for you for so long. How did you get here?" Pulling me into his newly developed chest, he embraced me tightly.

"How can you be alive? You were dead, Lutalo. You were shot," I pulled away and scanned his body for the "fatal" wound.

"In the shoulder," he said reaching up and patting his left shoulder lightly, "but as you can see, I have healed."

"But you drifted away and the crocodiles…"

"…were busy with the other men. I let the colonel think he'd killed me because I was a dead man for letting you get away. How did you escape him?"

"There is so much to tell."

"Can you wait fifteen minutes? I have to finish this before I can be dismissed," he said pointing to the succulent meal.

"I will wait by the school, but I don't know how long I can stay." We were drawing some interest from the guards.

"Please, just wait. I'll be right there," he said as he hugged me again before hurrying off into the building.

Seeing Lutalo brought back strange feelings again. I blushed remembering the kiss we shared; my first kiss. I didn't know what had come over me. With my emotions going crazy and living through a nightmare, I still didn't know what the kisses we shared meant. I latched on to him and he to me; maybe we needed each other. Lutalo could have been killed for even touching me the wrong way. He had risked so much.

But I felt special with him. He always made me feel that way, like I was more than just a woman; I was his equal. Did he feel the same way about me? If he didn't, would it affect me? It was impossible to know whether my feelings for him were a desperate attempt to get away from the situation I was in or something more.

"Sorry I kept you waiting," he said. "I can't believe I found you. I had to leave. There was nothing left for me there. How long have you been here?"

"Eight months," I said, exhaling and closing my eyes briefly. "That demon colonel tracked me everywhere and would not stop. I barely escaped him with my life. There were many close calls."

I told Lutalo most of what happened to me. It felt like nothing had changed between us but everything had changed. He was no longer my captor taking me to Moses as a prize, yet he had captured my heart all over again.

He was impressed with my resolve to make it to Kenya and to find Baba. After traveling to many of the camps looking for my father, he had finally made it here about a week earlier and gotten a job as a junior enlisted security trainee. He had sold valuable weapons to get the job and he was literate in English.

"It was very difficult to find your father because he's listed under a different name for security purposes. Even under a different name his exact location is not listed. I'm so glad I found you," he said moving closer to me, only centimeters away from touching.

"I'm so glad you came here. I've been thinking a lot about you," I said looking up at him. He looked so good and much happier than I remembered him.

"Matika, ever since we've parted, you're constantly on my mind. For a while I didn't look for you, thinking that you would just fade away. I was wrong; thoughts of you just wouldn't go away. I had to know what this was," he said putting his hands on my shoulders. "I've never felt this feeling before. I had nothing to lose because I have nothing, no one back there."

"Lutalo, you've never left my thoughts. I grieved for you thinking you were dead. I was certain that I'd never see you again."

"Oh, Matika," his voice was like a gentle caress as he stroked my back. He longingly looked at me. "I thought that I would never see you again. I've often wondered what I'd say or do if I did see you. Now that we're standing face to face, nothing seems good enough for a moment like this."

"You could kiss me." Did I just say that? The blood instantly rushed to me face. Yes, I wanted to feel his lips against mine again. I wanted to know if what I felt before was real. To say it so openly, however, was much too bold and wanton.

"Matika, you always surprise me. I love your spirit," he was smiling down at me as he pulled me into his arms, so beautiful the moment was that it made me weak at the knees. Slowly he drew closer until our lips barely touched.

His kiss was just how I remembered it, soft and sweet and no deeper than before. I was a little disappointed that he didn't kiss me the way Walyam kissed Suda, long and thirsty. Still, it felt wonderful to be kissed by him again. With his hands resting gently on the small of my back, he made no move to touch me inappropriately. Again, I found my body wanting more but he pulled away far too soon.

"I can't stay long; they'll be looking for me. How often do you come here?" Again, he was looking over his shoulder. His superior must have been mean for him to be so cautious. It was on the border of paranoia.

"Every day for school except Sunday," I responded sheepishly.

"Good. Maybe I'll get a chance to see you tomorrow," he said looking toward the building. A couple kissing was not out of place in the camp so there was no need to be wary. One didn't have to look far to find much more disturbing public displays.

"Yes, I can try. I'll be here tomorrow."

"Perhaps one day I'll have the honor of being introduced to your Baba."

"I don't know. Baba doesn't like us to bring any visitors. He's very watchful of our hut."

"Matika, I want to give you more than a kiss if you'd have me. I want to ask for your hand in marriage. I would only have you the right way because you deserve that and much more."

"Lutalo…I don't know what to say…," I began. "I'm extremely…"

"Matika!"

CHAPTER TWENTY-ONE

"I must go!" I called, running off without a goodbye. Suda had called at an inconvenient time, but I was very thankful. Honestly, I don't know what I was going to say to Lutalo. He had caught me completely off guard. On one hand, I felt I knew him to be the perfect husband, and on the other, I felt I didn't know him at all. I knew I owed him something for his kindness to me, for risking his life, and what better way to show my gratitude than a lifelong partnership devoted to be his loving wife?

With conflicting feelings, it was hard to know what to say when approached with such a question. One thing I knew was that Lutalo valued and respected my feelings. He wouldn't want me to make a decision under obligation or duress, but he wanted me to come to him freely and honestly. Was I ready for that?

"Where were you?" Suda asked impatiently.

"Just around the corner," I stammered. "Why, what's happened?"

"Come, we must go before Mama notices that we're late."

We ran home. Suda, stressed and perturbed, didn't speak the whole way. When we arrived home, Mama was waiting for us.

"You're late," she said sternly, handing us water buckets. "Get the water and hurry back because I need to start the evening meal."

How I wished for the game roasting over the fire that Lutalo was attending. It was a much better option than the gruel Mama made, which was nothing more than spices, grain, vegetables and animal fat that created the illusion of meat. I wondered whether Lutalo was able to eat the meat he prepared.

I didn't tell Suda about Lutalo, afraid she might be jealous because of his intent on marrying me, thinking it best to wait until Baba approved of Walyam.

Over the next few months I saw Lutalo about once a week for an hour or so. We always spoke of a future that we would one day share together. He brought me little things to eat, such as pieces of fruit or bread. Every now and then we would share a kiss but nothing more.

I was uncomfortable every time he asked to see Baba. He always pressed me for the location of our hut but I stood fast. I wasn't ready. So much had changed in my life and I didn't know how best to respond. Besides, I couldn't get married before Suda, and Baba had not mentioned a proposal for her at all.

"I see you've been speaking to a boy," Walyam whispered hotly in my ear.

I was behind the hut, sanding the pots to get them clean, while Suda and Mama were at her friend's place helping with chores. Walyam always had a way of sneaking up on me, finding every opportunity to touch me where he shouldn't.

"Why are you watching me? It's none of your business who I speak to," I said shrugging him off my shoulders, turning to face him. He knew I hated it when he spoke in my ear; the chills that ran down my spine when he did that were insufferable. It was because I told him this that he made sure he did it.

"I'm making sure that you don't give yourself to him. Baba wouldn't be pleased," he said giving me that sly smile I despised.

"I'm not giving myself to him, but I could if I wanted to. I know what you do with Suda so you have no grounds to tell Baba."

"I remember the way you looked me that day. I know you want me," he said rubbing his hand up my arm.

"Stop it!" I slapped his hand away.

"You're a fighter just like your sister. One day you will stop fighting the feelings you have for me. When that day comes, I'll show you what a real man can do for you, unlike that boy you have been speaking with."

"Lutalo is more a man then you'll ever be."

He grabbed my throat, squeezed, and pulled me to his face, nearly touching mine. "He is your father's enemy. Don't forget it," Walyam pushed me away and marched off. Good thing, because I was seconds away from hitting him with the cast-iron pot I held. Things would have gone from bad to worse if that had happened. Suda would be mad at me.

What did Walyam mean by Lutalo being Baba's enemy? Did he know something that I didn't? We were in hiding because Baba had many enemies but he had nothing to fear from Lutalo. He was a good man and would make a great husband.

Yes, he was part of the Lord's Liberation Army in Uganda but he must have been forced into it like Walyam. Baba trusted Walyam like his son so I was sure he would feel the same way about Lutalo. Soon, but not yet, I was going to work up the courage to tell Baba and Suda. I did love him and wanted to spend the rest of my life with him, but the time was not now and timing was everything with such a delicate matter.

"Are you ashamed of me, Matika?" Lutalo asked after I had politely refused his request to meet Baba once again.

"Why would you say that?" I asked staring at my bare feet, not able to look at the hurt etched in his big brown eyes.

"For one, you never asked me to meet your family. Not even your sister who goes to the school with you," he said pointing to the schoolhouse.

"I know Lutalo, but it's not that easy," I began. "You don't understand…"

"…I understand you're ashamed of me. Don't you know that I can take care of you? I have means and I'm probably doing a lot better than your Baba. I'm sure your precious Father is living in some hovel and yet I'm not good enough to meet him."

"That's not true." I did not like the tone he had taken. "I have to go." Turning from him, I started to walk away.

"Matika, wait," he said pulling me gently to him and holding me tightly. "I'm sorry. I didn't mean to upset you. I don't want to waste another moment without you as my wife. I love you with all my heart."

That was the first time he had ever said those words to me. A man rarely says those words to anyone other than his mother. It makes him vulnerable and may be perceived as a weakness.

"I love you too, but it's too soon. I still feel that we need to learn each other more. We don't have to be married right away."

Lutalo had opened up so much to me since we first met but I needed to know more.

"There is a reason why I want to get married to you before I touch you," he started, dropping his hands from me and looking into the distance. "I never told you about my family. They were from a small village near Gula in the far north. Mama was restless and ran off to Kampala alone to seek a better life. She fell in love with a military man and got pregnant.

"My Baba never married my mother but cared for us, sending me to the best schools money could buy. I only met him a handful of times. One day, about five years ago, when I was thirteen, Baba caught Mama with another man. Not just any man, but with one of his fellow officers.

"My Baba was humiliated and could barely show his face. He beat her to death right before my eyes in a drunken fit of rage. He then made me help him cut off her arms and threatened to do them same to me when I begged him not to make me touch her." His eyes showed him reliving the horror of that moment and I regretted taking him back to that memory. "He said to me, 'This is what you do with whores like your mama.' I don't understand how he expected her to be faithful to him. He was never around. I was left on my own and had to return to Mama's village humiliated and devastated. That was the last I saw of my Baba."

"I'm so sorry," I said reaching up and cupping his handsome face in my hands.

"I would never pour my seed into anyone and risk making a bastard. That's why I want to marry you. I refuse to take you as my whore."

"I will take you to meet my Baba. Just give me time to prepare him."

Lutalo was very excited. He spun me around and hugged me tightly like I had just given him the world. He loved me and would never be Baba's enemy. Walyam was wrong.

For the next week I tried to find the perfect opportunity to tell Baba about Lutalo. Though there were fewer people in our dwelling compared to our old village hut, there was still no time alone with Baba. He always returned after everyone was present. Once I came really close, but I just couldn't bring myself to tell him because Baba looked at me with so much hope in his eyes and I felt I would only betray him.

Avoiding Lutalo was easy to do because he couldn't leave work until about an hour after I got out of school. I knew that he would be upset with me because I hadn't spoken to my family since I spoke to him last. I loved him much but he didn't understand my plight.

One day I went to collect water as usual while Suda had stolen more time to be with Walyam. I saw a few soldiers with rifles. Two were white and the other was black but they were European, speaking English fluently. They were laughing merrily but I couldn't hear what they were saying.

My breath caught when I locked eyes with the tall one and everything ceased to exist. His dark hair accented his light eyes, but I wasn't able to make out the color. It wasn't his looks that caught my attention; most would describe him as cute with his boyish face, but the energy that raged between us was like lightning in a tropical storm. I was drawn to him and when I caught myself walking toward him I stumbled over my feet, spilling the water I'd collected. I was mortified.

"I'll be there in a bit," he said to the other soldiers.

I wanted to scurry away, but my body betrayed me. I was frozen in place, hoping to sink through the ground. There was no option.

"Are you okay?" he asked kindly. His voice was like a liquid caress that flowed over me, touching my soul. When I didn't answer right away he said, "You don't know English,"

"Yes. I'm okay," I managed to murmur through a mouth suddenly gone dry. I struggled to get up but my knees wouldn't corporate.

He reached out to me and our hands touched. "Let me help you." He pulled me to my feet with a strength I didn't expect. His camouflage suit of various shades of brown hid a muscular body. He wasn't as thin as he looked from a distance.

"What's your name?"

Green! His eyes were so deep I got lost in them. His handprint still felt warm on my arm, then I realized he hadn't let go.

"Helloooo? What's your name?"

"Matika. What's yours?" I really had to snap out of this trance he had me in or else he would think me slow. English was a third language for me so I had to think quickly. I was never one to be outgoing and my newfound boldness startled me.

"Maytika?"

"Ma-tee-kah."

"Matika. I'm Chaz. Well, that's the name I go by anyway." His eyes swept over me briefly but not undressing me, just a simple look of appreciation. His mere glace had me blushing.

"Do you come here often?"

"Every time to get water."

"You mean every day to get water."

"Sorry, my English is not so good yet. I'm still teaching."

"You mean learning. Hey, how about practicing with me? There's not much to do around here and I'm bored out of my mind…"

He started speaking too fast for me understand. When he saw my confusion he slowed down.

"If you come here tomorrow at this time, I'll meet you here," he said.

"That will be good. It would help to practice with English."

"Well, I better go to chow or they'd miss me. See you tomorrow?" he asked with a hopeful look in his eyes, his smile revealing a gorgeous dimple in his left cheek. He gave my arm a polite squeeze.

"Yes, I'll see you tomorrow."

Chaz followed in the same direction the others had gone, looking back at me twice as I stared dumbly at him. Sighing, I got more water and headed for our makeshift tent.

I spent the rest of the evening with my head in the sky, thinking about my Chaz. How would I make it until tomorrow? Staring blankly at the English book, I knew there was no fooling Suda. We were alone while Mama was helping a neighbor with a baby and Baba was "networking," as he called it.

"Where are your thoughts?"

"On nothing important."

"Come on Matika, you know you can tell me anything. Besides, you know more secrets about me than anyone," she coaxed, looking at me knowingly. Suda could always get me to talk.

"How did you know you loved Walyam?"

"Are you in love with someone?"

"No, at least I don't think so. I barely know him. I mean, we just met."

"Then it is lust. I knew right away that I wanted Walyam. Now, I can't imagine life without him. He is so handsome and so good to me. I hope that we can get married soon."

"I hope so, too," I said, but deep down inside I just didn't know about Walyam.

"What does he look like? Is he from school?"

"No, not school." I didn't want her to know he was white. What would she say? How would Baba feel about that? Although it was never really discussed in our household, many people around me spoke badly of different races, especially whites. For now, it would have to be a secret. "He is just a boy I met." I avoided the question like cholera. "You want to practice English with me?" That should take my mind off Chaz and Suda's mind off questioning me.

We practiced until she grew bored, which wasn't long. Mama returned and made us a light meal of bread and bush tea. Our rations were getting low, but no one spoke of it. It was a subject that was too frightening to bring up.

I was up long after everyone fell asleep thinking of Chaz. His name hovered in my mind, along with a vivid image of his green eyes.

A strong hand slid over the bare skin of my stomach, gliding down over my hips. I turned, seeking the warmth of his body. I rolled onto my back and he covered me with his body, the contact making my skin burn under him. I felt every ripple his muscled body had to offer as his shoulders flexed under my hands.

"Matika, you are so beautiful." His face was devilish, frightening me, taking my breath away and exciting me at the same time. He smiled down at me before capturing my lips. His kiss was fierce and hot, but tender and moist.

He dove into my mouth with his tongue, creating a rhythm that he matched with his pelvis as I felt his hardened root against my center, seeking entrance. He pulled back, staring down at me with a raw hunger igniting a flame in me that begged to be fed, and then quenched.

"Matika, I will have you…"

I awoke with a start and sat up, feeling intense heat between my legs. When I touched my most intimate center, I found it wet and swollen with a heartbeat of its own. A wave of pleasure shot through my body. Quickly I pulled my hand away. I was afraid of my body that was begging for something that puzzled me. My need was so great that I was trembling from the force of it. This had never happened before. I didn't know what was wrong.

Walyam entered the hut. He came to me thinking I was Suda and touched my breast, grazing his hand across my hardened nipple. Immediately, I swatted his hand away but I gasped as he added more fuel to my intimate heat. I was appalled at my body's response to him, a body that clearly didn't want him to stop.

"Matika?" he quietly whispered and then made a deep sound in his chest; he was much too close to me. I inhaled the alluring scent of his manly body. He paused for a minute and we stared at each other in the darkness. I held my breath against the tension. What was wrong with me? I wasn't sure if I would wake the household if he tried something, but I didn't want to hurt my sister. Instead I reached over, awaking Suda, saving us both from the humiliation and Baba's wrath.

CHAPTER TWENTY-TWO

After a sleepless night I was glad to go to school. That was the only place where Chaz stayed in the back of my mind. These lessons helped me better communicate with him. There was so much I wanted to learn about him and his culture. For one, I really wanted to know what it was like where he was from and how he spent his time. Was he married? How many wives did he have? Maybe I didn't want to know that just yet, because thoughts of sharing him didn't sit well.

When Suda tugged at my arm to leave, I realized Chaz had stolen into my mind again. I couldn't remember anything that was said in the last hour of school. Lutalo had been a distant memory that I pushed away for more than two weeks now. I felt too guilty about him to even bring it up.

"Matika, Walyam and I are going to see someone. Do you mind walking back to the hut without me? Just tell Mama I went to work for rations."

"Suda, you know I don't like lying."

"I won't be long. Why don't you get water now and I'll be back before you return to the tent for chores. I'll help this time, I promise."

That didn't sound like a bad idea. I could go to the makeshift bath house and get cleaned up before I saw Chaz later. I had washed my dress the night before, volunteering to wash all the laundry to not look suspicious.

"Okay, but promise me you will do my hair for this favor," I knew Suda couldn't pass up a bargain. She never wanted to take anything for free except from me. I rarely asked her for favors, so when I did, she always agreed.

"I'll make you hair so pretty that I will be jealous."

"Just hurry," I exclaimed playfully as she ran out of the classroom without a backward glance.

There were a couple of familiar faces at the bath house, where I hadn't visited in a while because it was always crowded, choosing instead to normally wash in an area outside our tent. The bath house was about ten minutes from our tent, near a major cooking area where only women were allowed. Laundry and cooking were done here by any woman who wished to use the facilities. This was one of the few places at the camp with running water.

"Where is your mama?" Mama's friend Mayahna asked. She had a newborn strapped to her front. She looked weak and moved around slowly, in obvious discomfort. Two bare-bottomed children, no older than two and three, ran around her skirt. She clearly had her hands full.

"I think she's in the tent." The lady looked disappointed.

"Do you have soap for your bath?"

"No."

"I will give you soap if you take them with you to the bath house," she said indicating her children. "I have cakes that smell of lavender that I got from a missionary. I think it's from America."

She was trying to interest me but I was already sold. "Sure," I said reaching for the soap that was melted in a plastic bag. There wasn't much left but it would be enough to bathe me and the kids. After rounding up the little ones, who chose that moment to run in separate directions, I went into the bath house.

It was more like an area than a house. There were three concrete walls and a floor with four raised taps that came to an average woman's chest. Women and children huddled around, sharing the water as they took turns at the pump. This would take all day if I waited politely for our turn. The children were already getting out of hand, splashing in the tepid water that collected at our feet because of the slow drain. Above all, I had to make it in time to see Chaz.

After I undressed, I shouldered my way through the ladies, pretending like I was pursuing the now-naked children but in reality was pushing them into the fray. Soon I was under the water and quickly bathed the kids in record time, but spent more effort making sure I was clean. It was no small feat considering that I had to hold our clothes without getting them too wet. They would be stolen if I set them down.

Before I returned to our tent, I helped Mama's friend wash her laundry and carry it back to hers which wasn't far. Suda was waiting for me, grinning as I entered our tent.

"I told you I would be back before you," she said smiling at me, true to her word.

"Where is Mama?"

"I think she went to wait in line for rations, but will be back soon. She was leaving as I came."

"Now do my hair like you said." I needed to be out of the house getting water before she returned seeing me with my hair done and clean.

Suda came over and began unbraiding my hair, which had been plaited for more than a month. I helped to make the process quicker, getting nervous that at any minute Mama would return. Although she probably wouldn't have said anything to me, I had no doubt she would bring it up to Baba.

"You should wear your hair down. It's very pretty."

My hair reached past my shoulders and was wavy from the braids, giving it a different look from its normally tight curls.

"It would get knotted and frizzy."

"I have an idea," she said smiling down at me. Suda braided the front part of my hair in a crown that looked more like a bridal headband and left the rest of it down. "You look so beautiful and smell really good. Now, go before Mama comes back. I'll stay here and cover for you and no matter when she comes back, I will say that you just left."

"Thank you," I said, almost forgetting to get the bucket before I left. Suda knew all along that I was going to see the boy I met and I was just glad that she didn't follow me or tease me about him. She was very observant and there wasn't much I could get by her.

I wasn't sure how much Walyam told her about Lutalo but I wanted to keep the details to myself. He may not have told her anything in order to keep it hanging over my head, but there was no way to be certain except by asking her directly. Still, if she believed that I was meeting Lutalo, then that was definitely for the better.

When the hut was safely behind me, I made my way to the water pump, relieved that I didn't encounter Mama but nervous and excited to see Chaz again. My heart skipped a beat. There he stood with his arms flexed across his chest, looking in my direction. His face lit up with a broad smile that nearly sent me to my knees.

"I almost thought you weren't going to make it. I'm really glad you came," he said.

"I'm sorry. I couldn't get away sooner." He was taller than I remembered. Standing on the tips of my toes, I would still be too short to reach his lips.

"You look really nice."

I thought the muscles in my jaw would cramp from my inability to stop smiling. I felt like a bubbling fool, filled with happiness at that simple comment that, if given by another man, would have made me uncomfortable, but instead sent my spirits higher than the clouds.

"Thank you," I responded, more than willing to accept the compliment.

"We can go somewhere to sit for a while." In a gesture that was both intimate and polite, Chaz put his hand on the small of my back as he led me to a remote area near two abandoned lean-tos. There was little privacy but we were at least out of the water traffic. We sat cross-legged beside each other, idly watching the people pass.

"So, I thought we can start your lessons by learning about each other. Like where are you from and what you like to do for fun."

"Okay."

"I'll go first. My name is Chaz and I'm from California, which is in the United States."

"I thought you were from England, because you don't talk like our teacher."

"That's because he's from somewhere in the South. He's got a thick country accent that people in the South have. Just ask him where he's from. I bet he's from someplace like Alabama or Mississippi."

"I see. I shouldn't have assumed that all Americans have the same accent. We do not have the same accent here, either."

"Yes, the U.S. is a pretty big country. Where are you from?"

"I'm from a little village in central Uganda, outside Kampala." I told him briefly about how part of my family ended up here but I really wanted to know more about him.

"You have to be the prettiest girl I've ever seen." He scooted closer to me and I could feel his body heat and smell an exhilarating fragrance that was unfamiliar to me. I wondered what soap he used.

"Really?" I asked, dropping my eyes to my lap. "You have seen many women from all over the world, how could I be the prettiest?"

"To me you are definitely the hottest."

"I don't understand? What is hottest?" I was truly puzzled.

"Okay, I'm going to teach you how we talk in the U.S., and it won't be anything you'll learn in any class. When a person says you're hot, that means you're sexy...Let me put it another way. You're very beautiful."

"What is sexy?" I asked looking into the windows of his world that captivated my soul. He was gorgeous. I wondered what it would be like to feel his lips on mine.

"It's the kind of look someone has that attracts them to the opposite gender or the same gender, but we won't go there. Like a person you would want to have sex with."

"Oh...Oh!" I said, finally understanding. I was positive that we would never cover this in class. My throat went dry as I felt the heat creep to my face.

"It doesn't mean that I would try to do that to you. It's just that I am attracted to you."

I smiled. I was extremely attracted to him but I was not going to admit it. I just wished he would kiss me even out here because I was willing to risk being seen just for one kiss from him.

He spent a great deal of time teaching common American expressions and slang. It was a lot to learn and I absorbed as much as I could. I wanted to be able to talk to him and to understand everything he said to me.

I learned a lot more about him, too. He was in the Marine Corps and didn't know how long he was going to be here. It was supposed to be a small detail that served as an escort to some medical staff on health assessment for one week. That was two weeks ago and his detail had been bored out of their minds ever since. He was not married and that surprised me.

"I'm too young to get married. I'm only eighteen."

"My sister is already married. She's sixteen."

"Your younger sister was married so young?"

"She is my older sister." He was shocked by my statement. Chaz's jaw almost hit the floor. He moved away from me like I had bitten him. "What's wrong?" I was so worried that I had offended him in some way.

"How old are you?"

"I'm fourteen. Have I upset you?" I was nearly fourteen, close enough anyway.

"You don't look fourteen. I mean, look at you. You have the body like a…look, in my country I could go to jail for being with you. I'd like to see you again but I don't think that's possible. I'm having thoughts that I shouldn't be having."

He started to get up and I seized his arm as my panic set in. I wouldn't let him leave like this. I might never see him again. My world was changing so much that I didn't know who I was. My body was controlling my mind.

"In my country I could be married and with child by now."

"Maybe, but it's not right."

"Not to me. Look at me. I'm a woman," I said putting my chin up. I felt like I was selling myself. I wanted him more than I had ever wanted anyone. Not waiting another minute, I pulled his head down to mine for a kiss. As soon as our lips touched there was a jolt of energy that flowed between us that couldn't be denied. He returned the kiss that I'd started.

It began gentle as we relished the taste of each other. His mouth tasted like warm honey, sweet and smooth. When his tongue glided into my mouth I thought I would explode as he took my breath away. A low moan escaped my throat as our kiss deepened and his hands came down from my shoulders slowly and found my willing breast.

They were so sensitive to his touch, begging for more as his gentle hands sent chills down my back. He made circles around my nipples, pulling at them gently. He growled so deeply that I felt it more than I heard it as it vibrated his chest. My body burned with a need so fierce that it paled in comparison to last night. As Chaz trailed hot kisses down my neck his breath was soothing, pausing as he sucked at the hollow of my throat. As he teased me with his tongue, I let my head roll back with abandonment as he pressed his firm body tightly against mine.

I didn't care where this was going nor did I care how we got here, as my earlier shyness was a distant memory. Gone were the thoughts of modesty; they were replaced by the pure joy of his lips on me and his soothing hands. I was amazed at how my mind and body were in sync and openly welcomed his touch that was denied to so many others. My heart was racing and my breath was short. In that moment I was crippled by a need so wanton nothing could bring me back.

CHAPTER TWENTY-THREE

I didn't hear the children laughing until Chaz pulled away, leaving me breathless and confused. Everything propelled into focus as the openness of our surroundings came into view. Groups of snickering children quickly ran off when I glared daggers at them. I was more concerned with how Chaz would react than my own feelings.

"I have to go," he said looking around, his face an even shade of red on his tawny skin. He ran a hand through his closely cropped hair.

"When will I see you again?"

"Tomorrow," he said reaching up to cup my face. "Let's just practice your English. We got to take it easy. I don't know what you do to me, but I can't seem to control myself. You can't ever tell any one of my guys how old you are because I would be fried for sure." Again, he had to explain his expression to me.

"I won't," I said elated that I could see him again.

Chaz bolted so quickly that the air didn't have time to part. When he left, he took a part of me with him and I knew I wouldn't be whole until I saw him again. How would I make it until then? At least I could see him in my dreams.

As I hurried back, I wondered what it was about him that set my body on fire. There was no denying it, not even for him. He wasn't the most handsome man I'd ever seen, but the attraction I felt toward him was primal, far surpassing what I'd felt for any man, even Lutalo.

Lutalo. Thinking of him washed me with guilt, effectively killing my blissful state. He was shot because of me yet had traveled to Kenya to find me. He loved me so much and wanted to marry me but I couldn't even commit to telling Baba about him. I had to stop torturing myself. If it meant having an opportunity to be with Chaz, I would never see Lutalo again.

Someone came up from behind me and held me close. Wishfully thinking it was Chaz I almost leaned back into him, but instantly knew it wasn't. Chaz was not that forward.

"Looks like you had a good time," Walyam purred.

"What are you doing?" I tore out of his grip and faced him.

"I thought I'd escort you back to the tent but I saw that American touching you," he hissed, spitting on the ground like the very word disgusted him.

"It's not decent," he said between clenched teeth.

Stepping back, nearly tripping over my feet, I was stunned by his words. This couldn't have been worse. Well, at least Baba hadn't seen.

"Don't pretend like you're shy. There was nothing shy about you when you were with him. First it was the boy by the school called Lutalo, and now this. How could you let that white man touch you like that?"

"That's not your business," I said breathlessly, my heart hammering. I started to walk away and he painfully grabbed my shoulders, pulling me around so I could look into his face.

"It may not be my business, Matika, but it will be Baba's!" With that he pushed me from him and stormed in the opposite direction.

I was horrified with his threat. Would he tell Baba? What would he tell him? He could make up anything. I should have been more careful. I wanted to cry, but even my tears were too afraid to fall. What was supposed to be a promising evening was ending as a terrible nightmare.

This was the most time I had ever spent with Baba and he was proud to have Suda and me as his daughters. He told us this more than once and we were all he had now. If Baba discovered what Chaz and I had done in public, thereby disgracing him, well...I just didn't know what he would do. Everything about Baba was his reputation and he took great pride in keeping it perfect.

I returned to the tent dazed.

"How did it go?" Suda asked after everyone had fallen asleep. She was itching to ask me all evening and kept giving me the "look" she often gave when she wanted to share or inquire about something private. I had been quietly sitting on eggshells all evening, listening to Baba's latest progress report on our immigration, which we found was moving right along. Due to his rank and status in the military, we were high on the priority list.

"It was okay," I said.

"Just...okay? Matika, you have to tell me everything. No more secrets."

I really wanted to tell her everything because I didn't want to be alone in this, but I was just as afraid of Suda finding out as I was Baba. What my sister thought of me was more important than what Baba thought. Baba could beat me and could do things to hurt me physically, but Suda could hurt me emotionally, and that emotional scar would stay with me forever.

"He's a very nice man, but won't be here long. I'm afraid of getting too close to him so I may not want to see him again. It would make things easier." I could just end it now and never see him again.

"No, that's not a good thing. You will not be happy if you did that. One thing I've learned is that you must take what you can now because you never know when it will be ripped away from you. That's why I cherish every moment I spend with Walyam."

The mention of his name made me sick to my stomach and I fought hard not to react to it. I couldn't tell Suda that her sweet Walyam had threatened to tell Baba about Chaz. If only she knew. Then I thought about Suda's words. I could live my whole life sorry that I'd never spent the time I could have with Chaz because of Walyam's threats.

"I'm really tired, Suda, because I didn't sleep at all last night."

"Me, too. It seems I hardly sleep anymore. That is the price for love," she said as she rolled over and fell asleep.

The next day there was no school. It was Sunday, the only day of the week off. We had the option of going to church that was held in the same building and would receive food for attending the service.

My heart wasn't into going so I stayed back to help Mama, who was very appreciative. Suda, on the other hand, had said she would attend, but was likely spending the day with Walyam. Mama and I made the rounds of collecting food rations, doing chores and helping her friend, who was always so needy. When we returned later that morning, Baba was waiting.

"Where is Suda?" he asked Mama.

"She went to the service," Mama responded.

"Okay, when she returns, have her stay here until I return. Matika, come with me," he said to me sternly.

"Yes, Baba," I said and followed him out of the hut. Had Walyam told Baba about Chaz? I mentally prepared myself for the worst. Wanting so badly to ask where we were going, I didn't dare question him but hurried after him in silence. This was it and I would have to face him once and for all. Walyam had made good on his threat. The suspense was killing me and it felt like hours had passed.

"I wanted to get you both together but I'll take Suda later today," Baba said switching to English as he always did now when not addressing Mama. She didn't speak it and he didn't seem to care whether she learned.

"Wangie, Baba?"

"I'm taking you for identification. We've been accepted into the United States. It wasn't my first choice, but we can make a good life there."

I was so happy about this unexpected surprise that it took everything in my power to keep from crying out. Maybe I could have a future with Chaz.

"When do we leave?"

"It could be a few weeks to months, depending on the paperwork. You don't need to worry about that. It'll be just the three of us. Your mama will not be coming."

"Why not?" I asked before I could stop myself. I bit my tongue at my error. As a woman you never questioned a man, especially your father.

"It'll be us for now." Thankfully, he didn't comment on my questioning him. "I need you to be on your best behavior and study hard in school. I have heard only good things about you, Matika, and your efforts will be rewarded soon. There will be many opportunities for you to go to school and even a university. I know you have it in you. Your sister, on the other hand, may not go to college, but that doesn't mean she won't have opportunities. She is strong-willed, like your mother, and won't take no for an answer."

Baba took me to get fingerprinted and my picture taken, then we returned to the tent. Suda and Mama were waiting for us and it felt awkward as they sat in silence.

"Come with me, Suda," Baba said and he left the tent. She looked at me with questioning eyes.

"I'll get water," I said, leaving the hut as well. I knew Mama was wondering what was going on. Did she know that she was not coming with us or that we were leaving soon?

This time it was my turn to wait for Chaz because I was early. Relief washed over me when he showed. His long strides were smooth as he all but glided toward me. I couldn't wait to tell him the news but I would hold it until just the right moment.

"You look happy."

"I am. Did you have a good day?"

"Same old, same old. I brought you something." It was a green bag that he handed to me sheepishly. "Let's go somewhere that's a little more private."

We walked to the edge of the camp to a group of camouflaged tents. There were a few soldiers standing watch and another with a woman whom he led to a nearby tent. We went inside one as well. It was a nice set-up with organized compartments accommodating multiple soldiers.

"Welcome to my home," he said as he led me past a canvas curtain where a cot and sleeping bag was set up. "This is where I sleep."

"It's nice." It really was, and there was three times as much space as we had in our little tent.

"You can sit here." We both sat on his cot, that squeaked under our weight. I opened up the bag he gave me and looked inside.

"Just gathered some odds and ends here that I thought maybe you would be interested in. These are some things that will help you understand our culture. If you don't like any of it you could give it to someone else."

There was a pair of furry socks and a shirt that he pulled out. "This is my favorite T-shirt and socks that I want you to have." The shirt was a cotton pullover with a picture of a man holding a surfboard.

"I love surfing," he sighed, holding the shirt like it was his most prized possession.

He pulled out a small plastic bag that contained toothbrushes, toothpaste, deodorant, a bar of soap and shampoo. There was a brush and also some things that Chaz called "feminine items" but didn't elaborate on their use. "Don't asked how I got them," was all he said.

That was one thing about Chaz that I had to get used to. He spoke so fast, especially when he was nervous or excited. At least I thought so, but it was hard to know for sure.

"Are you hungry? I got some MREs."

"Yes. What are MREs?" I was hungry since I missed the service and we had nothing to eat until evening.

"They are meals in a bag. It's food rations that we use the military. We eat these a lot when we are out in the field. Lately, that's all we've been eating because our supplies are running low. I've got pasta!" he exclaimed in mock happiness.

He warmed up the contents of the pouch with an internal heating bag that required only water to work. The food was a chalky red sauce mixed with some sort of noodle. There was also a packet of cheese spread thick as mud and the driest crackers I'd ever had, the *only* crackers I'd ever had.

"How do you like it?"

"It's different," I said and started to choke on the thick cheese that stuck to my throat like *kuweka*, or paste. He handed me some water and patted me on my back. It was also salty and made me so thirsty that I drank the entire canteen.

"Oh, you're just being too nice, Matika." He was laughing at me. "Okay, if you like them so much, I'm going to give you a couple to take back with you." He put three pouches in the bag. "If we were back in the States, I'd make you a proper dinner. I can cook really well – at least breakfast food."

"You can cook?" I was impressed.

"Sure can. I can make all kinds of things. I got kind of tired of cereal and sandwiches."

"Only the women cook here. What does your father say about that?"

"My dad cooks better than I do and taught me everything I know. My mother, on the other hand, could burn water." It was my turn to laugh. Chaz loved his parents and it was obvious as his eyes lit up talking about them.

"My mom may not cook…or keep house, among other things, but she can find a sale on any rainy day. She loves shopping."

"Why does your dad stay with her if she doesn't cook or clean?" In order to get married, a woman had to make certain dishes to perfection for her prospective family, wooing them with her cooking.

"Love. It's just different there," he grew quiet as his expression turned serious. His green eyes shone with a desire that was bold and hot, like he wanted only me.

I held my breath in expectation of his kiss as he gently laid his hand against my cheek. His hands were large and his fingers long and graceful with calluses that were both smooth and thick. He took possession of my mouth and I melted at the sensation of his tongue sweeping against mine. Reaching up, I touched his face that was smooth and soft, the scent of his skin intoxicating. I wanted to stay like this forever, kissing him.

Wrapping his arms around me, he held me close. "You feel so good to me. It's been a long time since I've been with someone."

Instantly, I went rigid in his arms. The thought of him being with another woman bothered me more than it should.

"I haven't had a girlfriend in a year, so you have nothing to worry about." He looked at me with such sincerity that I was ashamed for my earlier feeling.

Relieved, I lay back on the cot, gently pulling Chaz on top of me as we resumed our kiss. I felt the bulge of his manhood against my thigh but it didn't scare me. I wondered what it would be like to have him naked, feeling his warm body pulsing against mine.

"Am I too heavy for you?" He attempted to shift his weight and lie beside me but the cot was too small causing it to collapse and fall, sending us crashing to the ground. "Okay, that was embarrassing." We were both laughing so hard that we fell again when we attempted to get back up.

"I don't think this was made for more than one person."

"I think you're right." He gave me a dazzling wink that warmed me inside.

He helped me up and then fixed his cot, arranging the sleeping bag. We both heard other soldiers enter the tent.

"It's getting late and my family will be wondering where I am."

"The guys won't do anything, but remember what we talked about. I won't be able to see you tomorrow because we are meeting up for a supply run, but I will meet you the day after. I'll walk you home."

"Don't worry. I know my way from here."

"No girl of mine is going to walk alone in a place like this. It's not safe, especially for a girl – no offense."

"Fine, but hurry." I was getting nervous about the other soldier being so close by. I had no doubt that Chaz would not let anything happen to me, but still…I was uncomfortable.

"You're the one who got me like this," he said laughing, indicating his bulge that refused to go down. "I'm going to be in pain for a while." His smile was infectious, his dimple was adorable, and so I couldn't help but join him.

Chaz worked at adjusting himself while I got my bag ready to go. True to his word the other soldiers didn't say anything, but I felt their hungry gazes on me as we left. When we were nearing the water pump, I felt like we were being followed.

CHAPTER TWENTY-FOUR

"I don't live far from here. Thank you for walking me."

"Okay, I'll see you in a couple of days, Matika."

"Bye, Chaz." I walked away before he could kiss me to avoid what happened yesterday.

Returning to the tent as quickly as possible, I was glad that Baba hadn't yet returned. Mama was gone so I practiced math, which was my favorite subject next to English. With math there was always a right answer, and one could spend hours exploring different ways to get that answer.

Still, I couldn't get Chaz out of my mind; his taste and scent were branded in my very being. So badly I wanted to share it with Suda so she could help me understand these new feelings, but I couldn't dare risk her asking any questions about him. I only hoped Walyam wouldn't tell her or Baba, yet I felt that it was only a matter of time.

Suda rushed into the tent, falling on the blankets in front of me. On her hands and knees, she pounded her fists on the ground, letting out a scream of frustration. Her anger and pain was so thick it was tangible.

"How could he not listen to anything I say! I love Walyam and I cannot just leave him," she cried, choking on unspent tears.

I'd been so selfish in my own happiness that I failed to see what was happening to Suda. I sat back as the guilt washed over me like a gushing river over rocks. Putting my hands in front of my face, I was ashamed to look at her.

"Baba said that Walyam isn't good enough for me!" she cried pulling my hands from my face, demanding my full attention. "He saved our lives, what more could he want?"

"Suda, Walyam is not family. I don't think Baba can take him with us," I offered, trying to see things through Baba's eyes.

She let out a huff in protest. "Matika, he promised that he would try. I would rather stay here with him then never see him again. It would be better to stay here and be happy than leave and be miserable without him." The tears flowed freely from her big brown eyes.

I was riveted by the panic in her voice. The saddest thing was that I couldn't blame her. The trade-off for a new life seemed too unfair because there was no way for her to be with Walyam. Baba wouldn't be contradicted or go back on what he said no matter how wrong he might be. He was our father, our lord, at least until marriage – then our husbands would assume the role.

"But I will miss you." I held her now as she sobbed in my arms. It was the first time I'd seen her cry in a very long time, so long, I couldn't recall the occasion.

She inhaled sharply and looked up at me with such anguish my heart nearly broke. "Matika, please, please make him understand that I cannot live without Walyam."

"I will talk to him." I didn't know what I was going to say but I was committed. The thought of talking to Baba about Suda frightened me. I was asking for big trouble.

"I can't be here right now. I must see Walyam," she said rushing out of the tent as quickly as she'd entered.

I let out a deep breath to calm my nerves. It had been a long day, a continuous seesaw of emotion and it wasn't over. More than anything, I hoped Suda wouldn't try anything foolish. She was so headstrong that I didn't put anything past her.

"Where is Suda?" Baba asked as he stepped into the tent, squinting to adjust to its dimness. He was angry and spoke in Swahili.

"She's not here," I answered in English. "Baba, may I speak with you?" I got up and walked toward him on shaky legs.

"Speak," he said curtly, giving me a hard stare, his large body and commanding presence filling the entrance to the tent. The sun at his back gave him a majestic glow.

My courage faltered. This was hopeless. "Suda is very upset. Walyam did save our lives," I blurted out before I lost the courage.

"She's just a girl who doesn't know what's good for her, and it isn't him."

"Is there some way that he could come with us?" I couldn't suggest her staying here because the thought sickened me.

"I can only take family and he's not family," he looked like he was thinking as his eyes wondered off. "I've been in contact with Akello in Uganda."

I was elated with the news. He was such a good brother and I missed him dearly. Why hadn't Baba mentioned it before now?

"He has Namazzi under his care. He's not coming. Akello will stay and find our family before he joins us in the States."

Namazzi was supposed to be married. Had her husband died? Whatever the reason, Baba was not forthcoming and I didn't question him.

"I suppose I could have him arrange an exchange of money for Walyam to come with us by marrying Namazzi. Namazzi is of age."

What have I done? Suda would be mortified. She'd kill me. Instead of helping her...I couldn't think. I wanted to shout at Baba and tell him not to do this but I bit my tongue, cursing my stupidity. Baba had to know that Suda was in love with Walyam, but he chose to ignore it. If Suda ever found out that I was the reason why Walyam would marry Namazzi, she would hate me forever.

"I can't even take Mama because I don't have the proper marriage documents that are required. I'll pay to get her over as my sister at best, if that works." Only a man's first wife was his true legal wife. The first wife was protected should anything happen to her husband. The other wives had to rely on the first wife's good graces or return to their families in hopes of finding another husband.

"This is a time of survival. Suda doesn't see it. She's too stubborn, like her mama," sadness darkened his eyes after mentioning Mama. He looked away. "Go find Suda," he barked, dismissing me with a wave of his hand.

Leaving the tent, I paused outside, gathering my courage to face Suda. Sorting through my thoughts was like sorting through the fibers of an acacia tree, completely overwhelming. Heading in the direction of Walyam's tent consumed me with dread.

That area of the camp was filled with single men and boys. Few women were brave enough to go near there, let alone venture alone. Increasing instances of rape were a constant topic among the women because the men and older boys grew bored from lack of work. Women were encouraged to cover their breasts by wearing shirts or tying scarves around them, no matter how hot and sticky it was, but few listened.

The camp's population had doubled since I'd arrived, taxing the already-strained resources. We were lucky that Baba was able to get extra rations, yet it was still not enough to fill our bellies at night. There were others who were close to starvation; they bartered stolen goods or sold their bodies. Then there were the dirty children, some with babies strapped to their backs, pulling at your skirt, begging for food that you didn't have.

I slipped through the shadows, trying to avoid anything that might expose me. I had only been near Walyam's tent months ago, so I didn't remember exactly where it was. These shanties were more run-down than ours and the area was filthy, smelling of urine and feces. Holding my breath didn't combat the stench that attacked my nose. There was waste in the most unlikely places, such as in front of a dwelling or by cooking fires. This part of camp was a living nightmare where not everyone had shelter to lie under at night or to protect them from the unforgiving sun during the day.

Young men hung out playing cards, stopping their game to stare at me with hungry faces. I couldn't pass without notice. I was more out of place than a gazelle in a pride of lions. Ready to bolt at any moment, I spotted a route for a fast escape because this was no place for a girl to be. How could Suda come here? I was angry that I had to come and fetch her. Baba had no idea where she spent her days as he had forbidden us to go here and rightly so.

Walking quickly, I stayed vigilant to avoid notice or stepping on the sleeping bodies as there was nothing to do here but sleep.

"You come here to play?" a *kijana,* or young boy, asked, stepping in front of me, suggestively thrusting out his pelvis. He was about my age, maybe a year older, yet he seemed so young, like a younger brother. There was an audience of boys – some older and some younger – watching us, egging him on with their cheers.

"Go home to your mom, little boy!" I said with more confidence than I felt, trying to step around him.

He slapped me across the face so hard that I stumbled back. I was more shocked than outraged. His bully squad roared their approval as he tackled me to the ground. He tried to pull up my dress but I fought him. The *kijana* was strong, but there was no way this boy was going to take me against my will. I fought hard to not have my most valuable asset taken from me by a boy trying to be a showoff in front of his friends.

Finding the opening I needed, I landed a solid stroke with my knee to the juncture between his legs. He let out a howl so high-pitched I almost felt sorry for him. The others backed away as I got to my feet, ready for the next attacker who maybe closing in, but they were afraid of me now. I hid a satisfied smile.

"What's going on?" Walyam said from behind me.

I was disappointed to hear his voice. "He tried to attack me," I pointed toward the boy who was still clutching himself.

"This is Suda's sister. She's off-limits!" Walyam yelled for all to hear. He kicked the boy on the ground with a solid blow. I heard the boy's rib crack. Then he repeatedly kicked him like a crazed animal, with a feral look in his eyes that frightened the others.

"That's enough!" I yelled, but he didn't seem to hear me. The other boys stepped back significantly, while some ran away. No one tried to stop his madness. I tried to pull Walyam away from the poor boy who had stopped moving, but he knocked me to the ground with a sharp backhand across my face.

Walyam gave the boy an unsympathetic sneer but stopped kicking him. Stalking forward, he pulled me up by arm to my feet and then held the back of my neck so tightly it felt like it would snap under the pressure. At that moment I knew without a doubt that he could kill me with his bare hands.

The tic in his jaw muscles was intense. "Don't ever embarrass me like that again!" his tone was acerbic, cold with a deadly undertone as he breathed down my neck. He was filled with so much anger that it seeped through his pores, burning my skin with its venom.

"You could have killed him," I ground out through clenched teeth, ignoring the pain of his death grip. He couldn't know that he truly scared me, so I did everything I could not to gouge his eyes to get him away. His closeness was suffocating, making my breath come out in short rasps.

"Better he dies and they all listen. You have no idea what it is like to be gang raped. If not for your sister, I would have let them have you and even joined in, especially after you let that white man touch you." He pushed me toward his tent.

I stumbled to compose myself before I was forced inside.

Suda, who was making tea, looked up at me in surprise. "What are you doing here?"

"Baba told me to get you," I responded, letting out a nervous half-laugh. My nerves were completely raw but I did my best to act as if nothing had happened.

The hut was well-illuminated with flashlights hanging from the ceiling. Although Walyam shared a tent with others, it was suspiciously filled to capacity. There wasn't food but there were several cooking pots and utensils, batteries, radios, clothes, shoes, homemade knives and soap. Brown bottles were arranged neatly in a corner that Walyam quickly covered with a blanket.

Suda followed my eyes and when I looked back at her guilty face she said, "Let's go back to the tent." She quickly led me outside and Walyam followed. I looked for the boy and was relieved he was gone. Once we were near our area, they kissed goodbye before he left.

"Did you talk to Baba? What did he say?" Suda asked eagerly.

I tried to swallow the lump that formed in my throat but it wouldn't budge. What was I going to say? I could tell her the half-truth but she might have seen right through it.

"Yes. Baba said that he would do what he can."

"What did he mean by that?"

"He will do his best, Suda. Please don't fight him. You will only make him angry and he may change his mind," I pleaded with her desperately.

She was happy with my answer and her whole demeanor changed as her shoulders dropped in relief. With brightened eyes she squeezed my hand.

"Thank you so much for talking to Baba. I knew I could count on you." She walked inside the tent before I could contradict her.

Even though I was edgy, Baba and Suda were both in better moods that night. When Baba told us that we were only allowed out to go to school and do chores, I thought Suda would argue with him but she didn't. He told us to always stay together and to be in the hut before evening meal from now on.

Chaz popped in my head and I began scheming how I was going to get a chance to see him the day after tomorrow. Suda was probably thinking the same thing about Walyam.

"Yes, Baba," we responded together lowering our heads in submission.

Long after my family was asleep, I stayed awake worrying about what was going to happen. Suda would never talk to me again if Walyam married Namazzi. I couldn't imagine Walyam saying "no" to Baba if given the opportunity to go to America and leave this hellhole.

Walyam. He could be a thorn in my side for years to come. If Suda didn't love him so much, I'd hate him. As it was, I forced myself to see the good things about him that Suda loved. He treated her well. He saved our lives and no matter how hard I tried, I couldn't ignore how handsome and "sexy" he was.

Walyam was very tall and had filled out significantly over the year. His hairless face was clear and smooth with a strong jaw and soft brown eyes. To Suda, his smile filled her with joy, but to me that same smile was sinister, sending chills down my spine, making my skin crawl.

She only saw the good things about him, or maybe just what he wanted her to see, but I knew his cruelty firsthand. I could still hear the thud of the blows he repeatedly dealt to that poor boy long after he'd stopped moving. My neck was sore from the bruises he'd caused with his powerful hands.

Walyam had at least two personalities, one reserved for Suda and Baba, and one for me and others who crossed him. I had to wonder what he was like when he and Suda were alone. On top of all else, Walyam had a massive weight over my head and he had no problem wielding it.

CHAPTER TWENTY-FIVE

The day I was supposed to meet Chaz I was extremely nervous with butterflies churning in my stomach. Though I'd washed up, I did nothing special to indicate I was going to see him. Suda didn't even notice, which was a miracle.

"Matika, do you think we can do the wash today? I want to see Walyam," she said as we walked toward the area after school.

"I'll ask Mama if we can." Great! I was going to suggest the same thing but she beat me to it.

We hurried inside and got permission from Mama to do the laundry. Suda quickly deserted me as we left, saying she'd meet me at the wash area in an hour. I was stuck with the basket that I had to carry to our meeting spot. The clothes would have to wait.

I missed Chaz so much and it hit me like a brick when I saw him. I dropped the basket and rushed into his open arms. He twirled me around then held me close for an earth-shattering kiss. It felt so natural to be in his embrace. I wanted to stay forever and feel the strength of his chest against me.

"I don't have long today. Baba's being really strict," I said once the kiss ended.

"Who's Baba?"

"My father. Baba means father. We'll be leaving soon. We were granted asylum in the U.S."

"That's awesome! We can see each other again no matter where you live. You will always be a plane ride away. Come on, we better make it quick," he said leading me to a hidden area that was completely out of view. He must have found this place while waiting for me.

His hand gently caressed the small of my back. His light touch cast delightful shivers down my spine. He had such an effect on me that I lost all sense of reality around him. My body awoke to his every touch and it took all my willpower not to beg him to make me his forever. Relishing our time together, I didn't want to bring up anything that would cause a dark shadow to loom over the feelings we shared.

"Come here," he said pulling me onto his lap. There was no mistaking the bulge that sat firmly against my hip. "I missed you." He picked up my hand and nibbled my fingers. "Mmm. You taste so good."

"I want you too, but I'm limited on time," I said looking nervously around, expecting Walyam or Baba to burst around the corner at any moment. At least Walyam was with Suda right now so it wasn't likely he would surprise me. Chaz started licking the side of my neck, dispelling any reservations I had. I was lost to him once again.

"I want to make love to you so badly I can taste it."

"I want you too," I said, boldly sliding my hips against him.

"Mmm," he groaned deeply. "Matika, if you don't stop I will lose myself right here." He reached for me then, guiding his hand up my dress.

My legs parted on their own accord, allowing him access to my womanhood. I gasped when his long finger stroked my most sensitive bud, unable to believe the searing pleasure as he kissed me in rhythm with his exploring hands.

It was getting harder to inhale as my breath became ragged. I wanted more but I couldn't explain to him what I needed, because I didn't know myself. "Chaz…" I cried in his mouth. He read my mind, quickening his pace. I felt like I was on top of the highest mountain about to fall to an unknown abyss. When his fingers entered me I nearly lost my last ounce of sanity.

"You're still a virgin?" he asked breaking our kiss for just a moment.

I wanted to tell him that I was but instead I cried out as he sent me over the edge. Just when I thought I could take no more, he brought me higher than the clouds, riding the waves of the wind currents. Chaz showed no mercy as he stroked me until every spasm that rocked through my body had ceased.

"Oh Chaz, what just happened to me?" I was both shocked and baffled, my head still in the unknown. I could feel the primal wetness soaking between my legs.

"That's normal and nothing to be afraid of. It's your body's way of telling you it enjoyed what I did."

"Did you feel it too?" I'd hoped that he felt at least half the pleasure I did.

"I almost came just watching you."

"I want to please you, too," I said reaching for his belt.

"You don't have to do that, Matika."

"I want to, Chaz," I insisted, reaching down between our bodies. He helped me free his hardened member.

Holding it for the first time I was in awe. I didn't know what I'd expected a man to feel like, but I wasn't prepared for this. It was smooth and yet hard like pristine marble, or limestone sanded to perfection. Slowly, he showed me how to please him, guiding my hand to stroke him. Closing his eyes in enjoyment, he spilled his warm seed in my hands within minutes.

We sat there dazed for a few moments, completely sated. I sat on his lap as he held me to him. "I have to go," I said reluctantly getting up.

"No, no, please. Stay just a little while longer," he begged, pulling me close to him, resting his chin on the top of my head. "There is something I want to tell you. We went for the supply run yesterday but nothing came. I don't know how much longer we're going to be staying here if we don't get supplies."

"Please, Chaz, don't think about that now. Let's enjoy what time we do have." I didn't want to think about him leaving. My goal was to see him every chance I got while he was here.

"I almost forgot." Shifting me in his lap, he reached into his cargo pocket on the side of his pants. "You got to try this. It's my favorite chocolate bar. 'Snickers really satisfies,'" he said sarcastically with an exaggerated impish smile that drew me to his heart.

He looked so cute I wanted to stare at him forever and get lost in his vibrant green eyes. His face was blemish-free without hair and it didn't look like he had ever shaved. But there was nothing boyish about him.

"Here you are, my dear," he said handing me half the candy bar that he'd unwrapped. It was melted and looked more like something from a latrine.

Trusting him completely, I took my first bite and delicious sweetness flooded my mouth. Never tasting chocolate in this form, it was very rich and decadent and I wanted to share some with Suda. She loved sweet things. Then again, she would ask where I'd gotten it; at least it was an excuse for eating the rest of the candy.

"It's good," he said with his mouth full.

"I love it," I said licking the melted chocolate from my fingers.

"Let me get that." He took each of my fingers into his mouth, taking his sweet time. "You made me hard again just watching you eat."

As much as I would have given anything to stay with him longer, I knew where this was headed and I didn't have the time to spare. "Chaz, I really have to go. I'm supposed to meet my sister," I said getting to my feet.

"Okay," he said getting up more slowly. "Can I come with you?"

"Not this time."

"Can I see you tomorrow?"

"Yes, I'll find a way to see you. Just meet me at the same place and time." Giving him a quick kiss I picked up the basket and headed to the wash area.

"I can't believe you, Matika," a voice sounded from behind a tent flap.

"Lutalo!" I cried surprised by his unexpected appearance. "I'm sorry." Sinking into the floor would have been a better idea than confronting him right now. I was caught in the act and there was no denying it.

"I've been searching this camp for weeks looking for you and then I find you kissing some foreigner," motioning his hand toward the spot that Chaz vacated only moments ago. "How could you do such a thing?"

"You don't understand, it just happened," I tried to explain wanting to avoid the hurt in his eyes.

"Understand?" He pulled in close to me, blocking my path. "No, Matika, I don't understand how you can be ashamed of me wanting to do the honorable thing by you. I poured my heart out to you and you've crushed it like a worthless grape."

Reaching to touch his face, he backed away from me like I had a deadly disease.

"I'm so sorry, I didn't mean for it to be like this."

"What did you mean for it to be like? Would you have loved me more if I had taken you like a whore?" He was so angry. I had never imagined seeing him like this.

"Lutalo, just listen to me," I pleaded.

"You want me to listen to you?"

"I'm much better than this," his eyes swept briefly over me before he stalked off without so much as a glance back.

I was upset and relieved at the same time. I was angry at myself for breaking Lutalo's heart and relieved for not having to tell Baba about him. He'd placed so much pressure on me that I just couldn't live up to. I wasn't ready to be married to him. Lutalo needed someone else more accommodating, not me. At that point, I never wanted to get married, at least not yet. I felt like I wanted to live a little, like Suda had. Every day was always an exotic adventure for her.

There was a change in me that was both liberating and frightening. It was like passing a threshold not knowing what lay on the other side, but something exciting awaited me just ahead and I wanted to experience it all. I was finally in control of my life. Yes, Baba was there and so was Mama, but I still felt like I had some freedom to make choices that were best for me.

When I reached the wash area, Suda was already there waiting for me. "Where were you? What took you so long?" Taking the basket from me, she didn't wait for an answer as she began the laundry. "Hurry, Matika, or Mama will come looking for us."

Suda was more worried than I, which said a lot and made me very nervous. Although she was preoccupied with her own thoughts, I wondered if anyone would see the change in me. I felt like a woman now after having my first womanly experience. I felt alive.

We finished the wash in record time and ran back to the tent. Straightening my wrinkled dress, I entered after Suda. Mama was upset.

"It doesn't take two hours to wash clothes," her voice was shrill. Fear emanated from her eyes. "If Baba had come back and found you two gone…I wouldn't be the only one to get beaten."

"I'm sorry, Mama," I said because she was right. I could have gotten us all beaten. Mama was Baba's good and obedient wife. "It was all my fault."

"No, Mama, it was crowded. The women pushed us out," Suda lied. The only pushing that was done was by Suda. It's a wonder those women, whose eyes shot daggers at us, didn't do anything. She delivered the lie with such ease it scared me. "We wanted to make you happy so we took our time and did a good job."

I nearly laughed at that last statement. I imagined the stains on the clothes were laughing, too.

"Thank you, Suda, but don't do that again." She was only mildly placated with Suda's excuse. Mama then took the basket outside to hang the clothes to dry.

I felt guilty. In the future, I had to watch my time with Chaz or risk losing everything. It was hard because I lost myself completely around him. I couldn't let this happen again and I was thankful that Suda didn't bring it up.

Baba hadn't returned to the hut by the time we went to sleep that night. Suda was tossing and turning, which kept me awake as well. Every now and then she would get up and peek outside. I knew she was worried that Baba would run into Walyam, or worse, Walyam coming in first and Baba catching him in our tent.

Finally, Baba came into the hut and Suda settled down, allowing us both to get some sleep. That night, after I drifted off while reminiscing of the events from the day, I had a horrible nightmare.

I was shunned by my family because Baba found out about Chaz. I was all alone. Chaz kept calling out to me but I couldn't find him, unable to discern the direction of his voice. I was alienated. Then I heard sneering laughter that grew louder and louder, drowning out Chaz's voice, until I could hear him no more as it faded away in the distance. Walyam came out of nowhere and began beating me like he did that poor boy. No matter how hard I tried, I could not fight him.

I awoke that morning feeling tired and sad. I tried to think pleasant thoughts but I just couldn't shake the nightmare. Suda and I headed to school as usual, but the air around us was different. Something was amiss.

"Does anything seem strange to you?" I asked her as we neared the school.

"Yes, I hear something," she whispered, urging me to be silent. "Do you hear them?"

There, in the direction of schoolhouse, we heard people shouting. "Wait here while I check it out," she said bolting in the direction of the noise.

"Wait for me!" I yelled, running after her. I hustled to catch her but she was too fast.

When I neared, I saw masses of people running and protesting at the medical building. Some were throwing rocks at it, while others were looting supplies, furniture and file cabinets. They were shouting so loudly I couldn't make out anything they said.

I was afraid when I couldn't see Suda in the sea of protestors because the school was also being destroyed. Some of the foreigners being escorted away by American soldiers were fighting them off. Others were yelling out the window and frantically waving their hands for help.

"What are you doing here?" he demanded appearing from nowhere. He had a concerned look that spoke volumes of the severity of the situation.

"What's happening, Chaz?"

"They've run out of medical supplies and the people are angry that no one can be treated. We knew this was coming and tried to get the medical staff out last night, but they refused. They insisted on treating patients until the last of the supplies were gone. Look where that got them."

"Private Landry, move out!" a soldier shouted at Chaz as he headed toward the Humvee.

"Matika, we're leaving soon but I will meet you at our spot as soon as I can. I want to give you my address before I go so you can write me."

"Please don't go. I need you," I pleaded. He was the only thing that got me through this and oh, how I enjoyed every minute we'd spent together.

He looked over his shoulders before pulling me into his arms, holding me so tightly I could barely breathe. I didn't care. His touch was life to me and I needed every bit I could get from him. Pulling my chin up to his handsome face, he paused shortly before he kissed me with such a hungry passion that I knew he needed me as much as I needed him.

"This is way hard for me. I love you, Matika, with all my heart. Don't ever forget it." His declaration of love was like heavenly manna to my starving soul. He took the chain around his neck and put it in my hands.

"I love you too, Chaz. I'll write you every chance I get," I promised.

"We'll see each other again, I promise. I just know you are the one for me." He held me once again, but all too soon pulled away, leaving a void in my chest as he stole my heart.

"Please don't forget me," I mouthed after him.

CHAPTER TWENTY-SIX

An all-out brawl broke out between the looters. It was extremely dangerous as the crowd fought over the scarce supplies. My heart was torn between looking for Suda and fleeing back to the tent. In the end, after watching a man get trampled by the masses, I gave up my search, choosing to trust that she would make her way back as I ran to safety. Shots rang out behind me but I didn't stop or look back as I weaved my way through the multitude that headed toward the riot site.

"Matika!" he shouted, grabbing my arm forcefully, pulling me to a sudden stop. "Everyone is looking for you." Walyam eyes flared with accusation. "Where have you been?"

"I was looking for Suda at school."

"You were probably with the white man again."

I didn't deny it but I pulled away from him. Chaz's chain burned in my hand as I held it tightly.

"Come on," he said angrily, taking my free hand and pulling me toward the tent that was a few yards away. I didn't fight him because it would only add fuel to his fire; instead, I hurried to keep up with his long legs. Before entering our dwelling he firmly pinched my bottom, causing me to yelp in protest.

"I found her," he announced like a hero saving the world. "She could have been killed out there."

I wanted to slap him for his lies. I was nearly to the tent when he came upon me.

"Thank you, Walyam," Baba said with relief as he patted him on the shoulder. Walyam beamed, his eyes gloating. "I'm thankful to you once again." Then Baba came to me and struck me across the face, sending my head sharply to the side. My face stung, my pride wounded, I kept my head down to avoid seeing the satisfaction on Walyam's face.

"You are never to leave the hut without permission or an escort."

I struggled to hold back my tears and anger. "Yes, Baba." It was all I could say. Baba was angry at me because of Walyam's lies. I couldn't dispute anything he said for fear of him telling Baba that I was with Chaz, and then I would be in real trouble. Baba was worried about me, but not nearly as angry as he would have been if he'd found out about Chaz. My newfound freedom was gone in just a few words. That hurt more than anything.

"Walyam, I have business to see to. Can you watch over the women in my absence?"

"Of course, you don't ever need to ask, Baba."

How dare he call him that! He was *my* Baba, not his.

That pleased Baba and officially put Walyam in charge of us whenever Baba was gone. Suda could barely contain her excitement. Baba switched to Swahili and told Mama that Walyam would help protect us whenever he was not present, and that Mama would have to tell him her whereabouts whenever she left the hut. We were only allowed to leave with him to do chores and nothing more.

Baba then took Walyam outside. Mama kept us busy for a while straightening up the front area. It was midafternoon and I knew Chaz was waiting for me. I was dying inside to see him and was completely unfocused. I was useless and Mama chastised me more than once for making mistakes such as letting the fire go out while making soup.

Wanting to run out of the hut, I finally told Mama I needed to relieve myself and stole out only to run right into Walyam's thick chest.

"Where do you think you're going?"

"Walyam, please," I pleaded with him. "Just let me leave for only ten minutes." I had to resort to begging, which was a small price to pay to see Chaz. I had to have his address to write him when he left. I would never see him again if I didn't.

"No, it's too dangerous," he said smiling down at me. He held a strong leverage over me and he knew it.

This was not going to work so I had to try another method. I needed to get to the point. "Please do me this favor or I may never see him again. I need his address so I may write him."

"Why should I let you?"

"I have helped Suda many times to see you. I've said nothing to Baba about you coming into our hut when he is asleep. Walyam, you know I would do it for you."

He looked at me with such intensity that I thought he would say no.

"Fine, I will meet him and get his address. Tell me where he is now."

Although I was skeptical of his intentions, I had no choice but to tell him. "He's at the water pump."

"Okay, go inside."

I watched as he headed in the direction of the water pump before I went back into the hut.

This was the longest wait of my life and I didn't know what to expect. I hoped that Walyam would get Chaz's address for me, but I couldn't trust him. Frustrated and feeling helpless, there was nothing else to do but pretend to read.

"I think Baba is starting to get around," Suda said quietly in her broken English so Mama wouldn't understand.

"Come around, you mean."

"Yes, and I owe it to you. Sorry that happened. I think Baba is heating up to Walyam."

"Suda..." I couldn't even bring myself to correct her. I was irritated and didn't want to talk at all and her happiness at my expense did nothing to aid the situation. "I'm reading."

"Sure you are. You have not turned a single page the whole time," she said in Swahili as she got up.

By the time Walyam sauntered into the tent hours later, I was at my wit's end. Wanting to pounce on him with questions, I was forced to wait until the right moment. He saw it in my eyes but he chose to completely ignore me, sitting on Suda's mat stretching his impossibly long legs, staring at the ceiling like it was a divine piece of art.

My opportunity to speak to him alone arose when Mama went to help her friend and Suda excused herself to use the latrine.

"Did you get it?" I asked after Suda left the hut.

"What are you talking about?" he asked sarcastically, turning away from me.

"Walyam, you know what I'm talking about," I touched his arm to get his attention.

He looked down at my hand before I pulled it away. "He wasn't there, Matika."

"No!" He was lying to me. I couldn't believe him. Chaz wouldn't do that. My heart was torn asunder. My life would never be the same again. Sinking down on the mat I lay there, weeping with my back to him.

"I waited for two hours and he didn't show."

"Why?" I cried harder. Why was he tormenting me?

"I went to their camp. The foreigners are all gone, Matika," he said, having the decency to sound like he was almost regretful. Almost.

He put a comforting hand on the small of my back. I was so upset that I barely noticed as his hand traveled down my hips to rest on my bottom. Although it wasn't Chaz's fault, I felt abandoned and this was a sample of what was in store for me. From now on, I would have to make sure I was never alone with Walyam.

I was glad when Suda came in. I felt Walyam's hand snatch away, his demeanor changed.

"What happened?" Suda asked Walyam.

"I don't know," he responded, discreetly moving away from me.

"Matika, are you all right?" she asked hovering over me. I couldn't answer her past the lump in my throat or through the hole in my heavy heart.

"Just give her some time. She's upset."

For once, I was thankful to Walyam. I had to be alone in the worst way and under our current living conditions this was the closest I was going to get. They left me alone for the rest of the evening. I didn't eat the soup Mama made for the evening meal, and everyone assumed I was upset about getting in trouble with Baba.

"Everything is shut down. No school, no clinic. We are on complete lockdown," Baba said when he returned that evening.

"What about the food supplies?" Suda asked. Food was already low and without the school…

"There is nothing as of yet and there won't be any more rations until they get some supplies in. There is a curfew in place and no one is allowed to walk around after dark. They keep us here like animals. Several people were killed today and many more injured. With no doctors or supplies we can't even attend the wounded."

"All the foreigners are gone," Walyam added.

"We need to get out of here soon. I fear conditions are only going to get worse. Walyam, you are welcome to stay here as long as you like."

"Thank you, Baba," Walyam responded.

"I managed to get some books for you and Matika. I'll take charge of your studies."

I didn't acknowledge anything Baba said but lay with my back to them as they discussed the changes that would affect our daily lives. I didn't care about anything anymore. The moon could have fallen and I wouldn't have moved from my mat.

For days I lay there, only getting up out of necessity. We had run completely out of food and hadn't eaten for days. I ignored the churning in my stomach. I was tired of life. Wanting to die, I contemplated the best way to kill myself. Only Walyam knew the truth.

"Get up, Matika," Baba said entering the hut. Everyone was gone and frankly, I didn't even know when or where they went, nor did I care. "I'm not going to let you kill yourself over this. I could have lost you that day."

Baba clearly thought I was angry with him, but I loved him and didn't want him to feel that way. I realized then that I was being selfish, basking in my own depression when I needed to live for my family, not die for my own selfish reasons.

"I know Baba, and I'm very sorry for it," I turned over to see the relief and love in his eyes.

"Indeed you are," he pressed his palm lightly against my forehead before he headed out.

I held the chain that Chaz gave me. It was like holding a part of him. Looking at it for the first time I saw that his full name, William Charles Landry III, along with a series of numbers were engraved on the little plate that was lined with black rubber.

Feeling a little better, I washed up and prepared to be an active member in the family again. I was starting to get really hungry but realized there wasn't a single crumb to eat, with no rations for two days now. It was time to start a new chapter in my life. I needed to remove Chaz from my mind and do what I could to help my family. This was my family that was starving. I needed to move on and be a good daughter and sister, so when Walyam entered the hut alone I got my chance.

"Walyam, I have some things that maybe you can get food with."

"If I cannot bribe the guards with my supplies for food, what makes you think you have anything that they would want? Unless you wish them to use your body."

"Please look at what I have and see if you can use it." I chose to ignore his last statement and pulled out all the supplies Chaz had given me that were hidden in my basket. Walyam's eyes widened in surprise and I, too, hadn't realized how much I'd accumulated.

"What is this?" he asked holding up an MRE.

"It is the food the American soldiers eat."

"Interesting. They're going to like this." Putting it down, he sifted through the other items before he gathered half and put them in a cloth bag. "Put these away in case they steal what I have." Then as he was leaving, he said, "I guess something good came out of you giving yourself to that white man."

He was right. What was I thinking? I had acted shamelessly. Even Chaz didn't think me good enough to even say goodbye or give his address to me. If I hadn't seen him by the school I would have never even seen him again. I cursed myself for being so foolish.

Mama and Suda returned an hour later but looked very sad. Mama's eyes were swollen, like she'd been crying. She went straight to where she and Baba slept and closed the curtain for privacy.

"What happened?" I mouthed to Suda.

"Her best friend, Mayahna, just miscarried," she said quietly as she sat beside me. "It's because she has not been eating in order to give more to her children. Now her milk is dried out and there is nothing to feed her baby. With no milk, her baby will die too."

"I am so sorry." This was Mama's friend whose children I'd recently bathed. I felt guilty that I couldn't help her. Here I was mourning over Chaz when there were many others who were grieving the death of loved ones.

"Matika, it has gotten bad. Mama and I helped her with chores and the wash. The kids were filthy and soiled. They were crying from hunger but we had nothing to give them."

Baba didn't look much better than Mama when he returned empty-handed. With his shoulders slumped he looked worried. It must have hurt his pride that he couldn't feed his family. I wanted to tell him that it was going to be all right, but knew enough not to bring it up.

CHAPTER TWENTY-SEVEN

Within the hour, Walyam returned to the tent as if he had just saved the world, carrying a large bag of rice, grains and beans.

"Where did you get that?" Baba asked wondrously delighted.

"I had a few things for bribes," Walyam boasted.

Walyam took credit for everything, allowing Baba to pat his shoulder with approval while he beamed with smugness. I wanted to shout that it was what I'd gotten for a broken heart. This was all that I was worth to Chaz, but I wouldn't disgrace my family no matter how much it ate at my soul.

"Walyam, you'll always be welcome in my home."

"Thank you, Baba,"

Suda beamed proudly as she prepared the evening meal. Baba told Mama to help and she was more than content to do so. Mama made enough food for her best friend and her children, with Baba's permission. Although staples were scarce and giving to others would take away from us, it was in his nature to take care and command others. We pounded the oats and made flat bread for the next couple of days.

Before we ate, Baba gave thanks to Walyam and everyone expressed gratitude toward him. The food was bland because of the lack of spices but it was filling, putting Mayahna's children to sleep right after eating. Hunger kept them up many nights and they were exhausted. Walyam and Suda each carried a child while escorting Mayahna back to her tent before darkness fell.

For entertainment, Baba recited folklore of great battles and chivalry, but those old stories no longer interested me. There had been a time when I would have kneeled at his feet as he sat in his chair back in our hut in Uganda and hung on his every word. That time was over because I had seen the horrors of war and no amount of folklore could glorify it. Perhaps it wasn't considered masculine if Baba told stories other than of war, but still I considered it out of place. Even Walyam appeared uncomfortable, especially considering his background as a child soldier forced into violence, not to mention the loss of his family.

Several months crept by at a snail's pace. Walyam continued to barter for much-needed staples. Food and rations started to flow again and we were fortunate. I never strayed from the hut because that would mean I would have to be escorted by Walyam. It was bad enough that he looked at me hungrily and found enough opportunities to boldly touch my bottom or breast whenever the chance presented itself. He was so clever that no one ever suspected a thing.

True to his word, Baba took over our studies and was relentless. He had a college education from Kampala University that paved his way to a quick ascent up the military ranks. We were given so much math work and reading that when we had finished the books, he made up lessons of his own. Using pencils so dull that no amount of pulling back the wood could sharpen them, Suda and I used every blank page and free space between the margins of the books to do Baba's assignments.

Finally, the day arrived.

"Suda, Matika and I will leave in four days' time," he announced after the evening meal, during the time we normally spoke of things happening throughout the camp. He must have known we were leaving for quite some time, but chose to guard his secret until the last moment. Baba had always done that, much to everyone's annoyance. He was never forthcoming on any information, as if no one needed to know anything but him.

"I have arranged for safe transport to the airport."

Suda looked visibly ill and Walyam covered her hand with his. His expression was stoic as he listened to what Baba had to say.

"Not to worry," he said to Mama, who was now weeping, "In six months' time, you and Walyam will both join us. It is all done. Namazzi and some of your bothers will be coming, too."

That statement made everyone feel a little better but I wanted to weep for other reasons. I was so happy that I couldn't hold back my tears of joy. Leaving this wretched place filled with fond memories of Chaz and nightmares of Walyam's continuous harassment, I longed to forget far more than I could've asked for.

"Not to worry, little one. I shall see you soon," Mama hugged me close.

I almost laughed in her face, but immediately bit the inside of my cheek. It was so selfish of me not to think of her. I was so happy about leaving Walyam behind that I had forgotten that it was Mama who had to stay here with him.

We were never close and I knew I was to blame for putting up the barrier between us. After my own mother left us in Uganda to fend for ourselves, I couldn't trust anyone in that role again. If my birth mama couldn't love me, why would another who was not related by blood be able to love me?

The next day, while Walyam was distracted with Suda and Mama was with her friend Mayahna next door, I was given permission to go to the latrine. I was in no hurry to return to the tent and watch Walyam groping Suda as if I wasn't there. Suda felt comfortable around me but for this very reason, I wish she didn't. Walyam was…well…just being Walyam and found every opportunity to get under my skin.

Deciding to pass some time but not venturing too far from the tent, I walked around to get some fresh air. Everything was calm and a few people were milling around as I was, bored with nothing to do.

"So this is the area you live in," a familiar voice said from behind.

I just hated when people snuck up behind me. Was it so hard to note your presence by giving a simple warning, such as "Hi, Matika"?

"Lutalo, what are you doing here?" I asked turning around, hiding my irritation.

"Once again, I have to say that I've been looking all over for you." The camp was very big, like a small city, so finding someone was like finding an ant in a grass field. Just about every tent looked identical with few variations.

"Why?"

"I wanted you to know that I accept your apology and I have forgiven you for your indiscretions."

"Maybe I don't want to be forgiven!" I snapped, glaring at him.

"Don't play games, I know you want to be forgiven. The foreigners have left camp. You have had plenty of time to be ready for me as I have for you. I've come to seek your hand," he said encircling his arms around me, drawing me in for a deep kiss.

His tongue plunged into my mouth and his hand grazed my breast. It wasn't like the undeniable stirring in my belly from Chaz, or the way he made my body melt from the inside out. This was not in Lutalo's character. I was shocked. I felt nothing for him, no stirring passion, nothing. The only feeling I had was that I was betraying Chaz's memory.

"No," I said pushing away from him.

"There is no need to be shy with me anymore. Soon I will be able to give you so much more."

"No, Lutalo. I don't feel that way about you anymore. I don't even know if I ever did."

"What do you mean? I know that you still love me as I love you," he tried to kiss me again, pulling me back to him.

"Let me go!" I cried pushing against him. "Please, just listen to me," I began much more gently. "So much has happened and this is all too much for me, Lutalo. I don't feel the same way. You are a friend to me, nothing more."

"A friend that you love to kiss and has you practically begging for more," he said getting closer to me. "What kind of benefits should I expect to receive as your lover, provided what you have given to me as a friend?"

"How dare you!" I didn't stop my hand fast enough from slapping him in the face. We were both shocked.

I turned and ran the short distance to the tent but realized my error. Lutalo now knew where I lived and there was a possibility he could go to Baba if he chose to press a marriage between us. All he had to do was say that we had done something intimate. Baba would be very angry, but given the fact that we were leaving in three days, it was less likely that he would make me stay behind with Lutalo. He had many plans for us and I was more than excited for our new adventure.

That night we had the best evening meal ever in that horrid camp. Baba surprised us with a small portion of dried beef in the stew. The aroma wafted through the air far beyond our hut, inviting unwanted guests. Mama's friend came over with her children to share our stew because her husband had been unable to provide anything that week.

We stayed up late telling stories about our new life. Baba was very happy, which put us all in a good mood. I fell asleep with a full stomach, content that Walyam had finally left for the evening and happy about the future. I knew everything was going to work out.

A hand covering my mouth woke me from a peaceful sleep. I was pulled off the mat. I'd had enough. I must tell Baba about Walyam. He had gone too far this time, I thought to myself. Twisting my body away from him, I bit his hand.

"You bitch," he snarled, snatching his hand away.

It wasn't Walyam's voice. A hand slapped my face, sending me to the floor. I was swiftly gagged and tied like a stuffed pig. It was so dark in the tent, but I could make out two men carrying the fighting Suda out of the hut. When they dropped her she tore the gag from her mouth.

"Babaaaa!" she screamed, piercing the night's silence just before they pounced on her.

What was happening?

Baba rushed from the back of the hut, caught the man who had me tied, and drove his fist into his windpipe three times in fast succession. Choking and grabbing his windpipe, the man dropped to the ground. Baba went for the next man but was instantly halted by a rifle aimed at his head.

"Don't move or I'll shoot," said the gunman with an unsteady voice. His vibrating firearm betrayed his brave words.

Baba stood defiantly looking at him as if he were ready to strike. His fighting skills were impressive and had me in awe, but I prayed that he didn't go up against an armed man. Just then Mama peeped through the curtain in the tent.

"Get back," Baba ordered in a low voice. She withdrew.

"We have your daughter, General Naminiha. Come with us peacefully and she will not be harmed."

Baba's eyes narrowed. His gaze was steady. His hands flexed and his jaws tightened with tension. But behind that bravado, I saw that same look of concern in his eyes that was present when we reunited many months ago. There really was no option, but he stood there for what seemed like hours yet it was no more than a minute.

Slowly, he raised his hands and placed then behind his head. I watched him move like the world had stopped, except for his retreat. Not once did Baba take his eyes off the man holding the rifle. He didn't look at me as he stepped over my bound body, but acknowledged my presence with one graceful step. With his shoulders back, his head held high, he stepped out of the hut.

Baba was gang tackled to the ground as he breached the door. There was no need for that when he clearly didn't put up a fight, but even surrendered willingly. Three men quickly bound his hands and dragged him out of sight.

Again, my family was torn. I couldn't handle it. Not knowing what to do, the tears came streaming down my checks. This was unbearable. We were so close to freedom, so close to happiness, I could smell it. Something much bigger than our lives here was within our reach but now…

Two men entered the hut. They didn't forget me. Why should they? It was only fair when they had my sister and Baba. One threw me roughly over his shoulders like a sack of rice while the other dragged the now-unconscious, or dead, thug out of the hut.

CHAPTER TWENTY-EIGHT

They dumped me in the back of a truck about five tents away. Not a single person stepped outside to question the armed men. People stayed hidden in the shadows, unwilling to get involved.

This wasn't the first time a person was taken from their tent in camp. It was a nocturnal occurrence that was only whispered about. We weren't citizens of Kenya and were treated no better than the hyenas, especially after the foreigners had fled. The guards viewed us as leeches that only took away from their precious country. They used us many ways to their benefit, such as free labor from the men in the day and taking advantage of women and young girls in the night.

"Are you all right?" Baba asked looking concerned, scanning my body for injuries when the truck pulled away. He was tied but had managed to sit with his back against the truck's side. Suda, bound, a thick cloth around her mouth, was at his feet. Her tear-filled eyes were wild and full of anger.

"Yes, Baba," I replied, nodding my head. Biting my lip, I refrained from asking him what was going to happen to us.

Two men were sitting in the front of the truck while the others were trailing closely behind in an old jeep.

"You must be strong. Don't tell anyone who I am no matter what. If you do, as I have said many times, it will be the end of us. They may threaten to kill you or hurt you to get you to talk but as long as you don't, you will not die. Pain is only temporary but death is forever."

"Baba, I'm afraid," I said breathlessly, my heart racing. I tried to inch my way closer to him but the truck veered sharply, throwing me against the sideboards, farther away.

"You're strong, Matika. You've been through much and will survive this," he said glancing down at Suda.

She stopped her struggles and swept her lashes up to look at Baba.

"Listen well," he finished.

The truck screeched to a halt, its wheels barely stopping before a metal barrier where three sentries were on post. Two men manually lifted a red-and-white metal bar that served as a gate while the other stood inside the adjacent guard shack, lifting a hand to his mouth to cover a yawn.

We had been taken to the east side of the refugee camp to a collection of flat-topped buildings with white plastered walls. I had never ventured here. On the guard shack two spotlights beamed down on us, a cloak of mosquitoes as thick as the morning mist bathed in the glow.

"Asleep on the job again?" the driver asked rudely to the overweight guard in the shack who'd waddled to the truck.

"What's your business this time of night?" the portly guard asked, clearly vexed at being awakened or addressed so rudely.

"My business is none that you need be concerned with. Go back to sleep," the driver mocked as he drove though the barrier.

The truck skidded to a halt at a second building, a plume of dust filling the air around us. The jeep pulled up next, the engine killed. All the men got out of the vehicles but one stayed behind with slumped shoulders, not moving. He was quickly forgotten as the others approached. Baba's back went ramrod straight as the men swarmed the truck.

"We will kill them if you put up a fight," the leader of the group said to Baba as he pointed a rifle at me. His stoic expression left no uncertainty about his seriousness. Men gathered around the truck and waited for the leader's subsequent nod.

It took four men to drag Baba out of the truck. They were taking no chances with him as they carried him to the building. The one behind in the jeep was a hard reminder of the danger Baba posed. Three men were clad in a Kenyan uniform while the others were dressed in civilian clothes. Two men lifted Suda, who went out kicking, landing a swift blow to the poor man holding her feet.

I was plucked from the truck bed by my hair and pulled close to a man who wore a Kenyan uniform that was completely soaked with fetor sweat. His body odor was so potent that a blind man could track his scent from kilometers away.

My balance failed me when I briefly stood as my capturer tried to adjust my body, sending me roughly to my knees, the sharp rocks biting into them with a vengeance.

"Pick her up, you weak fool!" the leader growled through clenched teeth, barely keeping his patience. He had the rifle still pointed at my head.

"Yes, sir," my captor responded. He lifted me in his arms, grunting as he made his way up the wooden steps of the building, holding me too tightly to his round belly as he panted louder than a woman giving birth to twins. He was short and it was a wonder he could lift his tree-trunk limbs, let alone carry me to the threshold.

With each of the five steps he took I was prepared to fall with him on top of me. When he finally made it over the last one he was wheezing loudly. We were the last to enter the building.

Inside was a nicely decorated hall with polished, dark wooden floors that reeked of a very strong disinfectant on top of lacquer. Pictures of different planes and artillery lined the plastered walls. Two tables held model figurines of soldiers carved out of aromatic sandalwood. A lone electric light bulb hung on a thin wire from the ceiling; it gently swayed from the disturbance caused by opening the door. Boots clicking loudly on the wood created an echo that disrupted the quaint surroundings.

"Hurry up," the leader said holding open a door as the soldier huffed and puffed along his way.

The door opened up to a dimly lit dirt courtyard surrounded by single-story buildings that were all connected. A wooden walkway wrapped around the inside with short intervals that dropped off into nothing.

Still tied up, we were taken inside a room at the far end that had a series of double desks in neat little rows. It was a classroom, but one that was meant for adults, not children. Although it was still dark, light streamed in from the courtyard and through the open door and glassless window that stretched over half the wall.

The leader walked over to the movable blackboard, which he pushed aside. Nearby, a cabinet protruded from the wall, no more than fifteen centimeters, which perhaps housed school supplies, ammunition or guns. It was narrow, no taller than the top of the shortest man's head.

Unlocking the padlock with one hand, the leader stepped aside as he nudged the door open with a booted foot, pointing his rifle at

Suda. It was a secret door, in the least expected place. The training room provided the perfect cover, unlike a small kitchen or latrine that would have attracted human traffic. With a slight nod, the others began to climb down a staircase. Going down without turning around and facing the steps first would have been an impressive skill.

Suda didn't put up a fight as the men lowered her down, but stayed as still as a doll disappearing into the dark cave. Baba, much larger than Suda, was led down next without much aid. There simply wasn't any room to carry his large frame down the small passageway since he was taller than all the men, with broad shoulders and a muscular build that was attributed to years of physical training and genetics. Even with our minimal food supply he had managed to maintain most of his weight.

When it was time for the solider to go down with me, I was shaking like a leaf. I just knew I would fall to my death in the abyss. He cradled his sausage hands tightly around my legs as he lumbered his way to the opening. He was too wide to go down with me. There was no way he could safely get us down, and my thoughts were confirmed when he mistakenly cracked the side of my head against the door frame.

"You fool! Wait here," the leader said in an irritated voice. He looked over his shoulder before turning back to the opening. "Take her down," he ordered when one of the men came back up.

"Yeah, yeah," the man who was not wearing a uniform replied with a sarcastic lilt. He wore a hat that he tipped with his first finger as he approached me. "What are you going to do with this one?" he asked, lifting me over his shoulders. His hand was centered too high up my thigh, his thumb barely a scant few centimeters away from my most intimate part, my thin night shirt hardly a barrier.

"That's none of your concern. You just do the job I pay you for, nothing more, nothing less," the leader growled, slowly raising his gun to the civilian's head.

There was a silence that followed, lasting far too long as they stared each other down. I couldn't see either of their faces but there were only two outcomes to this scenario and I hoped for the one that didn't leave me falling on my face. The civilian took a steadying breath before turning with me on his high shoulders, and then ducked down the dark passageway without another word.

At the bottom, my nose was assaulted by the foul odor of rot, decay, filth, and urine. The ground was greatly disturbed, causing the air to be thick with dust that made my eyes water and tickled my nose and throat, which begged for a sneeze that refused to burst forth.

A soft glow came from a single flashlight that was strapped to the beam above. Baba was tied with his arms behind a beam, the veil of light shining down on his head that hung chin to chest. Blood trickled from his nose and down his lips in a thin stream. Suda lay not far from him with her legs and hands still tied, her mouth gagged.

Without windows or openings, no fresh air or sunlight could seep through the darkness. It was cool now in the wee hours of the morning, but by midmorning it would get extremely hot and stuffy in this life-size oven. The space was very small, slightly bigger than our tent, with an array of strange tools mounted on the walls and an empty bucket for a toilet that looked as though it had never been clean in its long life.

With no water to speak of, my throat was parched. It was difficult to swallow the lump that had formed from the dust that collected in my mouth. With nothing else in the room besides the two wooden beams, one of which was occupied by Baba, it completed the hopelessness of our situation.

I was unceremoniously dropped and barely kept my head from hitting the ground. The men quickly left us alone. When the door shut the men's footsteps were muffled, at best letting us all know that this room was made to keep sound from entering…or escaping.

Baba was unconscious. For a moment it was so quiet, the only sound was Baba's ragged breathing. I hoped he was okay. The flashlight above him created dark shadows in all corners of the room. I felt so alone, even with the two of them present.

"Ahem," mumbled Suda sternly, clearly giving me an order.

Although my hands were secured behind my back and my feet were bound, I wasn't as restricted as Suda. Her hands and feet were tied together, preventing much of any movement, and she looked uncomfortable.

"Ahem," she insisted.

I began to inch my way to her. The ground was dusty and looked as if the loose dirt hadn't been swept in years, creating soft layers that were crawling with insects. When I made it to Suda, I used my teeth to try to remove her gag but it was too tight. Instead I worked at the knot at the back of her head. It took a good fifteen minutes to finally get it free.

"Oh, finally," she cried letting out a sigh of relief. "Are you all right, Matika? Your head is bleeding."

"Yes, my head was hit on the way down. Is Baba all right?"

"They beat him," she seethed between clenched teeth. "I think we can untie each other and when they come down, we can give those bastards a nasty surprise. We'll pay them double for what they did!"

"How do you expect us to fight? We have nothing and they have guns."

"We have the element of surprise. Come now and I'll untie you."

"Why do you think they've taken us?" I asked as I made my way closer to Suda's hands.

"Why do you think?" she replied irritably. "We are here because they must have found out about Baba. To think that we were so close to leaving this place drives me insane. Walyam doesn't even know what happened. My soul would never rest if I died without seeing him again."

"He will know because Mama is still there and she saw everything. They didn't take her."

"They wouldn't be interested in Mama. They know she has only been with Baba since he arrived at camp. It's us they can use to manipulate him. Matika, you must not give in to them no matter what. Baba needs us to be brave. Yah! What kind of knots are these? How dare they do this to us!" Giving my hand a forceful pull in frustration, she bent lower to get a better look. This process was taking a lot longer than it should with her hands tied.

"Still, Baba has not been in Uganda in over a year. What good would he be to them?" I asked leaning forward, trying not to block the dim light that swung idly over Baba.

"He knows enough. He leaves every day for a reason, so I'm sure he has kept up with what's going on in Uganda. It could be some top secret information about key figures or even the president. That would be something that the enemy would want."

I sat there in stunned silence for several minutes as Suda worked diligently on her task. I had never even considered such a thing nor realized how important my father was or the information he possessed. It was a scary thought. What was worse still was my imagination about how they had planned on getting the information out of him – or us. I glanced up at the tools on the wall, instantly wishing I hadn't.

"Come now, Matika. Untie me."

With my hands now free, the blood rushed to them. I twisted them, attempting to get the blood circulating faster and was rewarded with sharp stab of pain in my right hand.

"Move away from me now. Someone is coming," Suda's hurried voice sent a chill down my spine.

CHAPTER TWENTY-NINE

I crawled away from her just as the door was thrust open. A rush of fresh air poured into the abyss, giving temporary relief to the stuffiness. The silence was deafening as no one so much as breathed; our captor stood at the threshold and waited on us as much as we waited in agonized silence for his decent into our prison.

When he finally took a step I put my hands behind my back as if they were still tied. When he came down Baba began to stir slightly, sensing his presence, but then succumbed once again to the heavy fog. It was the leader of the group, with a shiny pistol in his right hand pointed at Baba. He didn't look at Suda or me but focused his attention on Baba.

Two other men came as well; one wore a uniform like the leader, the other was in civilian clothes that consisted of dark pants and a short-sleeve T-shirt. The uniformed man was clean-shaven like his leader but his uniform was in a sordid state. He must have had a job that required physical exertion. His hair was neatly trimmed as befitting a soldier, and he appeared to be in his late twenties. The small room seemed to be swallowed up by the three of them.

The other looked like a laborer hired to harvest your crops, but would run off with your chickens if left alone. He appeared to be in his early thirties, unshaven, plain of face, with a short, thin frame. His features were mouse-like with beady eyes no bigger than a fingertip. Like a dishonored man, he never made eye contact with anyone but steadily shifted his gaze around the room like one who had lost it all yet did more than what was needed to survive at any cost.

"You must remember to keep him conscious," the leader instructed the men without taking his eyes off Baba, lecturing his men like students being prepared for a test. "He must stay conscious to feel...to hear... to see everything."

"Yes, sir," the beady-eyed man replied. The other man had his eyes trained on me.

"Get him up!" the leader barked to them.

The men jump forward and lifted Baba higher on the beam to a standing position, one on each side of him, securing his limp body so he wouldn't fall back down. Baba awakened and struggled against them but there was nothing he could do.

"Where should we start?" the leader asked, pointing his gun at Baba's head, then slowly lowering it to his chest, and finally pausing on his *makende*. The question was not directed at anyone in particular but meant for his pleasure.

Lowering his pistol, he looked straight at Baba. "What is your name?"

"Piss off!" Baba spat, blood and spit running down his month.

With a scowl, the leader lunged forward and struck him with his pistol across the face, sending sweat and blood across the room.

"What's your name?"

Stoically, Baba remained silent.

Two more blows flashed across his face and to his abdomen. Baba doubled over and was pulled upright by one of the men. Blood oozed from his nose and his left eye was swollen shut. It was hard to watch.

The interrogation wouldn't end. On and on they beat him like there was no tomorrow. They asked questions about locations of individuals, diamonds, money and weapons. The leader was frustrated and worn out from his heavy-handed blows, but Baba held fast, giving no information, grunting in pain when he was struck, particularly in the gut.

The two men holding Baba seem to take no pleasure in their task, keeping their eyes trained straight ahead.

I couldn't stand to watch it any longer and turned my head away. The constant thud of fist on flesh filled the room like a drum as Baba was pounded like a dusty rug. It sickened me. When I looked again I couldn't believe it. His face was a bloody pulp, barely recognizable. This couldn't continue. He was going to die if they didn't stop. I needed to be strong but I couldn't any longer.

"You're going to kill him!" I cried out, my voice high-pitched in terror.

"You filthy pig!" Suda's voice followed mine.

The leader turned and considered her words for a moment, briefly looking down at his once immaculate boots now covered with blood and dirt. His sweating chest heaved up and down, perspiration pouring down his face as he lowered his hands and looked at Suda.

"You won't talk," the leader said looking back at Baba, who didn't seem focused at all, "but I can get your daughter to talk for you."

He grabbed Suda and dragged her by the arm right in front of Baba. He kicked her hard in her stomach and she yelled in pain.

"You hit like a woman!" she screamed.

He lifted Suda by the collar of her dress and sent a swift blow across her face. He asked the same questions he had asked Baba but she didn't say anything. Then he got close to her face and yelled, "Where are the weapons?"

Suda head-butted him in the face, making his nose bleed. Dropping her to the floor, he cradled his face, the rage in his eyes gutting her on the spot. She began to scoot away, afraid of his next move. Even the men holding Baba were shocked and seemed to be contemplating whether they should go after Suda.

The leader grabbed a strange tool mounted on the wall. The instrument, as long as a forearm, had a pointed tip and a device near the handle that rotated it.

"What pleasure do you gain from hitting defenseless women? A child, no less," Baba said with disdain through swollen lips. These were the first words that he had uttered. It was as if he had awakened from the dead.

The leader turned, surprised by Baba's remark, his nostrils flaring with fury. For a long moment he stood ready to pounce, his hands shaking. The muscles in his face were twitching but gradually he gained his composure.

"I will be back. If you don't talk then, I will rip her insides out..." he said pointing the strange tool only centimeters away from Suda's abdomen, rotating the pointed tip, "very, very slowly."

"Let's go," he said turning to the men.

The men promptly let Baba go. He bravely stood there even though he looked ready to collapse. The men ran up the stairs after their leader as if being summoned by Satan himself. As soon as the door shut, Baba collapsed, sliding painfully down the wooden beam before hitting the ground.

"Oh, Baba!" I cried crawling over, not bothering to free my legs. Tears stung my eyes as I wept for him. I was afraid to touch him; his body looked so broken, filled with pain. His eyes rolled in the back of his head, his mouth opened, struggling to breath.

"Untie me," Suda commanded, now sitting up.

Coming over to her I did as she said. I freed my legs as she attended to Baba with confident hands, freeing him, as well. She laid him down gently, placing his head in her lap. There was no water to wash his wounds so she did the best she could, tearing a large piece of her dress to cleanse him.

"You mustn't cry," she whispered, focused on Baba.

That was like asking a river not to flow. She was right, I had to be strong from for him because the last thing Baba needed was to worry about me. Grounding out the tears with the backs of my dirty hands, I tried to hold them back.

"What can I do to help?" I sobbed, failing at sounding normal.

"Get some rest. I will watch him." Her voice was steady but she didn't look up at me.

I turned away as I saw a tear drop onto Baba's face. She needed her time. I crawled over to the far wall, lying down on the hard ground, trying to fall asleep. It was difficult to pretend to sleep as fear and anguish coursed through my mind. Sometime later, Baba's breathing became even and Suda let out a sigh of relief. She sniffed a few times, crying in silence, confirming the severity of his injuries.

I found myself dozing and though I tried to stay awake, the mental exhaustion overwhelmed me like a thick fog settling in a valley.

The pounding of boots on the wooden floor above awakened me. I sat up quickly and crawled over to Suda, who had fallen asleep slumped against the beam. Baba still rested on her lap, his face much more red and swollen. Even in sleep his expression was pained.

"Suda, wake up."

The door opened once again. My heart pounded strongly against my chest cavity and I was afraid it would crack. It was happening all over again and much too soon. Baba would die and then what would happen to us? I felt Suda's body tense as her eyes shot open, her expression anxious.

The same two men came down cautiously; the soldier carried a gun that he trained in Baba's direction. The civilian carried a bright flashlight, the beam pointed at Suda. She shielded her eyes with her hands after awakening only moments before. "Haven't you done enough to him?"

He ignored her, then shined the flashlight at me, which caused me to do the same.

"Take her."

CHAPTER THIRTY

The civilian promptly came forward and pointed his gun at me.

"You make one move and I will shoot her dead."

A rush of ice water flowed through my veins, chilling my blood as an overwhelming numbness enveloped me. What could they possibly want with me? I looked over at Suda, whose face was ashen. She swallowed, closing her large eyes briefly before looking up at me.

"I don't know anything," I pleaded, facing the men. "Please don't take me away."

The civilian pulled me away from Suda, whom I found myself clinging to for dear life. It was no use. Before I knew it I was being led upstairs.

"You'd better not touch-!"

The door silenced her voice.

It was early morning in the world and the sun was close to breaching the sky. The birds chirped as they frolicked in the dew-filled trees that gave off a refreshing scent. I wondered briefly if it had only been hours or perhaps an entire day that we missed being trapped below. Time was meaningless in eternity.

The men took me through the classroom onto the wraparound platform that proved to be older and more dilapidated than I'd previously thought. Like ancient voices the boards popped and cracked, and in some places were missing, as if they had swallowed the people who dared to travel over them. One particularly heavy soldier came to my mind.

There were few men around but perhaps it was too early. Something smelled delicious so they must have been waiting for their morning meal. My stomach ached for food but more than anything I was so thirsty. I couldn't figure out why such thoughts roamed through my head as I was being led to the unknown.

Walking to the adjacent building in the opposite direction of the entrance, one man flanked each side of me. I couldn't help but glance back several times. It was like being pulled farther and farther down a lake, knowing that even if you were ever freed you'd be too far down to swim to the top that was cruelly out of reach.

"Please tell me what's happening," I began, "because I have done nothing wrong. We have done nothing wrong."

"Shut up," the soldier ordered. He had put his gun away but squeezed the back of my neck, letting me know that his orders must be followed.

Both men looked uneasy and fatigued. It was evident that they had had little sleep and by the looks of it, perhaps none at all.

I was taken through a series of very small corridors with whitewashed walls. Then the soldier pushed me into a room, shutting the door behind me. This room had four work desks, two by two, each holding a dusty old typewriter.

There he stood in the corner, looking out the window. I immediately recognized him, even with his back to me. His stance was more sure than normal, but a welcome sight in my hour of need.

"Lutalo!" The word rushed out as I ran over to him. "I'm so happy to see you."

He didn't move until I was within arm's length. Turning around swiftly, he had a stoic look on his face, stopping me dead in my tracks.

"Strange, the last time we spoke you didn't want to see me again," he said with a smile that never touched his cold eyes.

"You have to help us. I don't know what's going on, but my family and I are locked up like prisoners. We are being treated worse than animals."

"Calm down, Matika," he soothed. "Everything will be fine in the end. You'll see. Justice will be finally served."

With that he reached up and touched my cheek gently. It was strange how he could be so calm. He knew something. I could feel it.

"Please, please help us. They're going to kill Baba-" I started, and then promptly shut my mouth. In my frantic state of mind it took me a moment to realize his last comment. "What do you mean 'justice will be served'?"

Pushing his hand away from my face I searched his eyes.

"Matika, I want to thank you."

"Thank me for what? Lutalo, what are you talking about?" I asked completely puzzled. His tone told me that I would be devastated by what was coming.

"You have finally given me the revenge that I've been searching for my whole life. My life's labor has finally bore fruit. Baba will finally receive the justice that has been long overdue."

"What are you saying?" My heart was pounding sharply.

"Baba is a thief, a tyrant and a killer!"

I was slowly backing away from him. This wasn't happening. He didn't seem to notice me as he raged on.

"That's why he fled Uganda. He deserves nothing less. Death will be dealt slowly. He will remember the pain in the afterlife."

"It was you who told them," my voice shaky, barely above a whisper.

"Yes," he confirmed with a prideful smile. "You must not mourn the devil, Matika. Our Baba will never breathe again. He took my mama away from me so it is only fair that I make sure he meets his maker. Not to worry. I still love you, even knowing that you are the daughter of the devil."

"My Baba is your Baba?"

I couldn't have heard correctly. Feeling my face lose its color I squeezed my eyes shut, willing his words to go away.

"I have known since the moment you told me who he was. At first I thought you were mistaken but soon found your story to be true. I spent months looking for you. You and I will be married and I'll take from Baba what he took from me."

"But you're my brother!" My eyes flashed with rage at his sick implications.

"No one will ever know. I'll never acknowledge who you are. I will take it to my grave and so will you."

Nooo! A voice screamed in my head. It hurt to respond. If my chest was pierced a dozen times the pain wouldn't have been as great as the betrayal he had launched that burned through me like hot oil. With a numb face and watering eyes, I just stared at him, unable to look away.

We stood there, eye to eye, as a sea of emotions stormed through me. What had I done? Each time I had trusted the stronger sex I was led down a path of betrayal and pain. Pain so great that I wanted to die from it. I knew something was seriously wrong with me that I gravitated toward these men who would only seek to harm me in the end.

Men who appeared kind, said nice words to me to bolster my confidence and spent countless hours building me up to the highest peak, molding me like the finest clay, taking away my pain and uncertainty. Yet these same men ripped my heart out with their bare hands. With a single shove, they pushed me over the highest cliff to the lowest valley, my body bashed by rocks the whole way down the cliff.

What had I done to deserve such a plight? I was so stupid, vulnerable, and worst of all…an easy prey, like a wounded animal leaving a trail of blood in its wake. I felt more exposed than if I were naked before a crowd of men. I had been brutally twisted like a wet garment through every emotion. What made a bad situation simply unbearable was the fact that it was all my doing. I could blame them all night long, but it wouldn't change the decisions I'd made. I offered my thoughts to the wolves, had lain down and invited them to devour me whole.

I couldn't take it for another moment. I felt my chest muscles constricting tightly under my skin, cutting off my oxygen. Failing to draw in a deep breath because air wouldn't go past my constricted throat, I continued to meet his eyes that now grew round with concern, but I no longer cared what happened next.

It was over. All over. There was nothing left but my will to live that could be taken from me and this game of life would soon come to an end. Slowly my vision clouded, as if looking though water, my wheezing lungs thirsty for a breath that was not forthcoming.

I felt my body give way faster than my mind that welcomed the eternal darkness only moments after I fell into Lutalo's strong grasp. The last thing I heard was his deep voice calling my name from far, far away.

CHAPTER THIRTY-ONE

In this dimension of nothingness there was peace. There was no sound, thought or feeling. Nothing. I wanted to stay and embrace the comfort it offered. Like a warm blanket on a chilly winter's night, it wrapped me in a cocoon and protected me from the elements, leaving no part of me exposed.

"Matika," a voice from afar called to me. It came from all around me and threatened to breach my swathe of unconsciousness. I begged to stay, not remembering how I got here or where I came from but I knew I didn't want to go back, not now, not ever. My life was a violent struggle for existence that I no longer wanted.

"Matika!"

My world shook violently. The blankets surrounding me were torn apart. I was fully exposed. My head ached severely.

"What did you do to her!" Suda's voice broke through the fog, lifting me from unconsciousness.

Reality slammed me awake. All the memories of what had transpired unlocked with dreadful vengeance. I didn't want to come back and face my family. No!

"It's okay. I'm here," she coddled.

I hadn't realized that I'd spoken out loud.

Opening my eyes, I found myself back with Suda. Baba was a mess, close to death, laboring for every breath he took. Lutalo was there with a raised pistol. On the outside he looked relaxed, but his tight grip on the gun noted otherwise. His eyes revealed emotions that horrified me, the emotions of a person intent on a kill.

"Please don't do this," I begged weakly positioning myself in front of Baba. I looked at Lutalo but tried to avoid his bloodshot eyes.

"Don't try to protect him, Matika," he spat, clicking the hammer back. "He deserves nothing less than swift justice."

"How does he know your name?" Suda asked shrewdly. Nothing slipped past her.

"You never even told your sister about us!"

He was raging. I didn't know what to say to him. I was stuck because if I answered him, everyone would know what I'd done. I was helpless.

"If you didn't bother to tell your sister, you weren't going to tell him."

With all the strength he could muster, Baba raised up. I didn't need to look at him. I felt the nerves in his body coming alive, like an old lion crouched in a thicket of tall elephant grass. He was waiting, ready to pounce.

"What's going on, Matika?" Suda asked.

She was so close to me now. Everyone waited for my response. I could say "Yes, I was going to tell him," and anger my family but appease Lutalo. I could say "No, I was not" and anger Lutalo but maybe save face with my family. What did it matter? He was going to kill Baba and probably me, but Baba was all I cared about.

"Yes, I was going to tell him," I blurted out.

"You lie!" he fumed coming face to face with me. He pulled back the trigger and raised the barrel of the pistol, shaking it in front of my face.

"I'm not lying," I said as evenly as I could.

"Tell him what, Matika?" Suda's voice was as unstable as I felt.

"Yes, tell him what?" Lutalo repeated, jamming the gun against my forehead.

"I…I…" I couldn't do this. I felt Baba's hand weakly grasp my arm. I looked down at him. My heart wept at the pain I'd caused him. I had betrayed him. I was his daughter, his own flesh and blood. The truth would be his death.

"Tell him now! I want him to know everything before he dies!" Lutalo shouted.

"Baba, I'm so sorry…," I said sobbing uncontrollably. I couldn't finish. I realized that he was going to kill Baba no matter what I said.

"What did you do, Matika?!" Suda's voice pierced my ears.

"Tell him how much you love me and that we are going to get married."

"We can't get married. It's wrong, Lutalo!" I countered, but that caused the blood vessels on his head to pulse angrily.

"It's right that I get something from that murderer. He took everything from me! I will have a mother for my children since he took away mine." He moved the gun from my face and pointed it at Baba.

"How could you kill her?!"

"Lutalo?" Baba's asked, his voice barely a whisper. In that moment everything stopped. It was so quiet that one could hear the breath of a beetle.

Baba dispelled any doubts I had about Lutalo's story. There was a small part of me that wanted to believe Baba had known him from another place, another time, and that Lutalo had lost his mind.

Lutalo lowered the handgun slowly, as if an invisible force tugged his arm down. A gamut of emotions played across his face, each warring with the others for dominance.

"You remember me," he responded in a tone as low as a base drum, his countenance unreadable.

"Umph," Baba grunted. He attempted to sit up further but fell back in agony.

"I was nothing but a bug under your shoe," Lutalo said kneeling only centimeters from Baba. "I only lived because you permitted it."

Suda was ready to attack; I could see the flame in her eyes. Silently she communicated, swiftly focusing on Lutalo's gun and then back at me. It was like she wanted me to get ready to seize the weapon. I looked back at her with wide eyes, terrified. It was a crazy move. She returned a frustrated stare as she directed her attention back to Lutalo.

"I bet that after you killed my mother, the only family I knew, you never gave me a second thought. All these years I lived for this day. To see you crawl on your face like a dog and beg for forgiveness. What do you have to say now, mighty Baba?"

Baba didn't speak but looked him in the eyes. There was a long silence as Lutalo waited.

"Beg for forgiveness and I will let you die quickly."

"Lutalo, please don't do this," I begged, pulling at his arm.

Before I could move, he backhanded me swiftly, driving me to the ground in a heap.

Suda jumped to her feet, ready to strike. I had to do something before I got her killed too.

"Do you think you're better than me? I'm your son! Your blood runs through me the same as your other children."

"You're not my brother," Suda said, shocked despite the conviction that filled her voice. Her eyes bulged, threatening to pop out of their sockets.

"Oh, I am. That is nothing to be proud of. Our Baba is a thief and murderer, among other things."

"Your mother was a whore," Baba said.

Lutalo struck Baba across his swollen face.

"Beg for forgiveness!"

"No!" I was on my knees instantly, wrapping my arms around Lutalo's ankles. "I will do anything you want, Lutalo. Please, just don't kill Baba."

Resting my forehead against his muddy shoes, I submitted to him, putting my life, my body, my soul in his hands. I knelt in defeat.

"I will be your wife, your servant, your willing slave if you let him live. I will be anything you desire me to be. There is nothing I wouldn't do for you. Have mercy us."

"At least Matika will speak for you. After all, she led me to your home. It was destiny. She wanted me to find you. For that I will keep her forever."

"You are sick!" Suda spat on the floor, disgusted at the revelations.

"I hear that you are a wild one. You need to be tamed. I'll make sure that the others tame you soon enough."

"Get up, Matika," Baba said forcefully. "Do not kneel to him."

I pulled away at Baba's command. His tone evoked obedience that few disputed.

"I've won this game; it's over," Lutalo said to Baba.

"Get ready," he said looking at me with a contorted hard face. "I'll be back to take you to our home within the hour. I can't have you embarrass me looking like a filthy rat."

Lifting my hands, I subconsciously touched my hair, letting out angry clouds of dust. Dirt was in my nails and covered every inch of my exposed flesh. I would wager that it continued under my night dress, as well.

He left us, ascending the steps quickly. For a while, neither of us spoke as Suda quietly attended to Baba. Moments later, a small-framed old man lumbered down the stairs carrying two buckets of water and some linen cloths tucked under his spiny arms. He looked to be a kitchen hand with the amount of soot on his clothes and skin. Smelling like smoke from hours of tending to a charcoal fire, his curly hair was as white as the cloths he carried peeking out of the soot that covered it. His mouth hung with a sunken jaw showing missing teeth.

The man stayed silent. After he put the buckets down he pointed to one of them, motioning with his hands to his mouth, letting us know that one bucket was for drinking. Then pointing to the other bucket, he used cloths that he freed from his underarm, rubbing it against his dirty skin for washing.

Such a small detail was so important because drinking bad water would make you very ill, even kill you. There were several instances at the refugee camp where people got very sick and died from drinking contaminated water. Children who got diarrhea from bad water had little chance of survival. It was far worse than the worms that infected every bowel movement.

"I have a plan," Suda announced after we'd all drank greedily from the water and cleansed Baba's wounds.

"You need to wash up right now," she said handing me one of the cloths. "You need to look your best."

"What plan do you have?" I asked as I worked on ridding the dirt from my face. I was almost afraid to ask, knowing it would mostly involve me.

"We need to get a message to Walyam before it's too late. You have to tell him where we are and what happened."

"How will I do that? I don't even know where Lutalo is taking me. I'm sure it won't be near Walyam's tent."

"When he comes back for you, you'll need to convince him to take you back to the tent. If he's not at our home, you need to have Mama, or her friend, pass the message to Walyam."

My hands shook as I washed the dirt from the rest of my body, saving my hair for last. I needed to look presentable. When I was done the water was as black as the night sky, but I felt lighter, cleaner after washing; the dirt had weighed me down like a second layer of skin.

"What if he doesn't take me?" I asked, my mind racing with doubt.

"You must make him listen to you. If you don't, there's no chance for us." Suda looked down at Baba, who began to stir.

"I really don't know if Walyam can even help us." I wanted to say "will" instead but held my tongue. I'd done enough to put my family here; there was no need for further insult. Deep down inside, I felt he couldn't be counted on.

"He can and he will," she said.

"In a hole, under the sleeping mat…" Baba's voice trailed off below a whisper. His chest was rattled by a cough that produced a spittle of blood that ran down the corner of his month.

"Rock…take it."

"Baba, take what?" I asked when he didn't continue, but his eyes closed and he slipped into unconsciousness. I hoped I'd heard him right.

"Take what Baba?" I asked trying to shake him awake but getting no response.

"Let's go!" Lutalo called from the top of the stairs.

Before I stood, Suda squeezed my arm, digging her nails into it as she looked up at me. She looked as desperate as I felt. She had hope that Walyam could save us but doubted that I would succeed in getting the message to him.

"You're a woman. Make him take you," she said in a quiet but no less forceful tone.

I nodded at her briefly before heading to the floor above where Lutalo waited impatiently to take me to my new home.

CHAPTER THIRTY-TWO

Pride is a powerful emotion that can be both good and bad. Being proud is represented by the self-esteem or conceit that arises from an act, possession or relationship. Pride can be ugly, sad, strong, happy and beautiful depending upon the person and its use. Best of all, pride can be manipulated and twisted into an emotional prison where only it can close and open the mental locks.

Lutalo's source of pride was evident as he victoriously guided me out of the building with his head held high and shoulders thrust back. Men watched with envy as he glided past them, his hand resting snugly on the small of my back, signaling ownership that was freely given instead of taken. I fueled his fire by covertly making eye contact with a few of them, causing them to look at me more intently, their lascivious gazes were not missed by Lutalo. He puffed his chest out even further, as if campaign ribbons of gold sat upon it.

"The two of us together are perfect," he said as he opened the jeep door for me to slide in. What looked like a polite gesture was merely a disguise for ensuring that I wouldn't run away and embarrass him. He shouldn't have worried. There was too much at stake to run. He had me by the throat with nowhere to go.

"Yes," I acquiesced politely, feeding his ego even more, setting him up for the question I was about to ask.

Once he closed the door, he strolled around the front of the car, slowly swiveling his head, never taking his eyes off me. He climbed into the car, his eyes searching my face before he put the key in the ignition. It took him three tries for the engine to fire-up before we finally backed away from the building.

As we pulled away, I felt a deep dread knowing what I had to do and guilty relief of being out of that underground room where I was helpless to save Baba. Down there, I was watching him die as the breath of life was draining out of him. It was unbearable. At least I had a chance to be of some help and maybe even save them. I had gotten out of tough spots before, I could do it again.

"How far are we going?" I asked after we exited the gate.

"Not far. About fifteen minutes away. Tonight we are going to stay here but tomorrow we leave for Uganda," he announced after turning a corner too quickly, sending me against him.

"Uganda! Why would we go back there?" Panic seized my voice.

"Do you honestly think that I would stay here? I have so much to offer my people and the Liberation. I've done great service and finally have the opportunity to redeem myself. The colonel will be most pleased with me. I'll be promoted for sure. He's meeting us at the border."

Lutalo's mention of the colonel instantly made me sick. Returning there was not an option. The colonel would kill me and there would be nothing Lutalo could do to stop him, assuming that he would even try. I had to rein in my fearful thoughts and calm down or I would pass out again.

"Lutalo, I need to get my things from my tent. Could we stop there first?"

"No. It's in the opposite direction. There are a few things that I need to take care of before leaving in the morning."

"Please, I don't have anything to wear," I begged like a child asking for Mama's sweet bread. "My night dress is not suitable for travel."

"I like you just the way you are," he said glancing down at my ill-fitting, short night dress. His eyes smiled even though it didn't reach his lips.

"Don't worry, I'll buy you new clothes in Uganda. Besides, it's bad luck for a new bride to wear her old clothes."

"Yes, but I have personal items that cannot be replaced. It would please me greatly to have my things." I reached for his arm to get his attention back on me instead of the road.

"Fine, I'll have someone get them for you later."

Panic filled my heart. He had an answer for everything. I had to think of something fast or I was going to fail my family again. I loathed thinking what he had to take care of before we left tomorrow.

"They won't know what's mine," I snapped in a salty voice that was unknown to me. "Besides, you wouldn't want any men touching your bride's personal things. That would be disrespectful."

His brows furrowed as he thought it over. It was clear that he didn't want to return to Baba's tent, but he also didn't want another man's hands on my belongings. Just when I thought I'd lost the battle, Lutalo made a hard left.

"Fine. Consider it a wedding gift."

"Thank you," I said calmly, barely hearing my voice over the drum beat of my heart that was now housed in my ears. My hands were shaking uncontrollably so I hugged my arms across my breasts.

"Are you cold?" he asked taking a hand off the wheel, spreading his arm wide for me to come closer to him.

I wasn't cold. It was quite hot outside, but this was a moment of truth. If I hesitated even slightly he would see through me and know that I despised him.

"Yes," I said sliding into his embrace, snuggling closely to him.

I tried to relax my rigid body that was stiffer than a board while looking at the path ahead. There was no way I could remember the route back to that building, especially after starting out in one direction and changing course several times. It all looked the same, from the trees to the dilapidated buildings to the tin-roofed shanties. Even the people looked the same as they milled about.

Soon we pulled up a few yards from the tent and Lutalo killed the engine. I saw Walyam from a distance and made brief eye contact with him before moving away from Lutalo. Of all the times for Walyam to leave me alone when I needed him. I had to talk to him, but first needed to figure out how to make Lutalo wait in the car so I could be free to search under the sleeping mat for whatever Baba wanted me to find.

"Make it quick," he snapped making no move to exit the vehicle.

"You're not coming in?" I asked biting my tongue, wanting him to think I didn't mind but stopping short of offering an invitation.

"I would never willingly enter his slum domain!" He looked uncomfortable as he shifted in his seat. Then, crossing his arms over his chest, "Hurry, and don't make me come in and get you."

I quickly got out of the jeep and stumbled over my feet as I burst through the tent flap. Inside, the tent was destroyed. The floor was littered with our clothes, personal items and toiletries. Every jar, basket and box was thoroughly ransacked. Even the sack of grain was torn and its contents spewed all over the floor as if someone had kicked it across the room in frustration.

I went to Baba's section and slowly pulled back the curtain, afraid of what I might find. Mama was not there. Thank goodness. The condition was much of the same as the rest of the tent. Baba said "it" was under the sleeping mat. Quickly, I got on my hands and knees to search the area where the sleeping mat would have been had the room not been destroyed.

The dirt floor was hard and solid, just like the main room. Taking a stick the width of a thumb I began digging in random spots. Everything looked the same. Nothing yielded results. I had to hurry; it was only a matter of time before Lutalo came in. Where was Walyam when I needed him? The stick broke and I tossed it to the ground in frustration. There was no use. Baba must have been out of his mind; after all, he had suffered several traumatic blows to the head.

Taking a closer look, I saw a slight elevation in the dirt about the size of a palm. Immediately, I grabbed the closest thing I could get my hands on, which happened to be a wooden comb, and began to dig. It wasn't long before I reached a small plastic bag. Pulling firmly on the bag from its confines, I tore it open. There was a slip of paper folded into eights and a handgun. Unfolding the paper revealed that it was really a map that held glittering rocks that fell to the floor, the colors fanning out across the hut. Diamonds! At least twenty lay on the ground, begging me to pick them up.

They were right about Baba, he did have diamonds. Was this the only gun or were there other weapons Baba had that the interrogators spoke about? Who was he? I wasn't sure if this was just a coincidence, but I grew very fearful because now I knew about something that could endanger us all. I was not strong enough to keep silent facing death and torture. How I wished I could go back in time…

A thump sounded on the wall of the tent.

"Matika," Walyam whispered.

"Walyam?" I asked to confirm it was him.

"Yes, it is me. I'm coming in."

I scooped up the diamonds before Walyam removed a loose wall board aside and entered Baba's room. He looked anxious.

"Where have you been? What's happened?" He came up and gave me a hug.

I embraced him as well, holding on to him tightly. I was never so happy to see him in my life. Finally, I pulled away.

"You have to help us. They're going to kill Baba. They beat him so badly and I fear that we won't last much longer. They have threatened Suda as well with unspeakable things."

Walyam's body tensed at the mention of Suda. His jaws clenched and his eyes narrowed. His love, protection, or ownership of her was apparent.

"Where have they taken her?" he asked through tight lips.

"A small military outpost, but I don't know where it's located."

"Tell me what you know about it. I may be able to find out where it is."

"There was a red and white gate with a guard that manually lifted it up to let us through. A group of buildings arranged in a square. There is one opening though a long hall that I could see. That's the building where they're holding Suda and Baba. Go to the right once you get past the hall."

I told Walyam about the classroom, our underground room and everything I remembered about our location. He took it all in, asking questions every now and then.

"Baba wanted me to give you this in exchange for helping us," I reached down and picked up the gun that was on the floor, offering it to him.

"Is that all?" he looked at me before reaching down and taking the gun, inspecting it with a critical eye.

"And these," I offered, opening up the hand that clutched the diamonds, flashing them briefly before his eyes.

"What!" he said, clearly interested as he reached for the jewels.

"Not until you agree to help us," I said putting both my hands behind my back, my eyes narrowing. I had to have his word that he would help us before I could part with them.

"Even if I agreed, you really don't know for sure. You just have to trust me."

"So you're not agreeing?"

"Of course I'll help you. Don't be silly, Matika. What kind of man do you think I am?"

"Please save them."

"And what of you?"

"I'll have to find my own way. Lutalo's forcing me back to Uganda with him. We leave tomorrow but I can't go with him. I'll be killed for sure. All I want is for my family to be safe, and if you can do that I will repay you with anything I have."

"Anything?" he asked, his eyes burning into mine before making its way down my body, leaving no doubt of his intentions.

"That is what I said. My word means everything to me as it should to you," I replied handing over half the diamonds. I couldn't part with all of them. "Take these and make haste."

"Matika!" Lutalo shouted impatiently not far from me, as if he'd gotten out of the vehicle.

"Hurry, you must go!"

"I will meet you at the east gate at midnight if all goes well. If you're late…," he paused, not finishing the obvious before turning on this heel. He swiftly exited the same way he had entered.

"Matika!"

"I'm coming," I huffed before picking up a handful of Mama's clothes and a few odd items hurriedly.

Running out of our home, I slammed into Lutalo as I stepped over the threshold, the impact caused my load to fall to the floor.

"Let me help you –"

"I got it –"

Our heads collided as we reached to retrieve the fallen clothes. Thankfully, the diamonds stayed in my hand, but I needed my arms full for further distraction.

"Ugh," he groaned pushing me away. "Let me get this."

Ever so slowly he reached down and one by one picked up each garment, caressing its fabric. I really wasn't sure what all I'd taken considering the limited time I had, but I should have taken just a little more time to be a bit more selective.

"This is rather large for you, wouldn't you say?" he held one of Mama's overgrown working dresses. Not only was it very large indeed, it was practically threadbare.

"What is this?" he said holding Baba's shirt out to me.

I was at a loss for words. I had taken a very old dress that was way too big, Baba's shirt, a collection of scarves and a cup.

"That's my brother's, who I may never see again."

"You took all that time to come out of here with these tattered rags and junk," he seethed through clinched teeth, suspicion spilling out.

"I'm sorry, Lutalo, but I don't have much. I really couldn't find anything because our home was destroyed and looted." It was not a complete lie, and was far from unbelievable. Our home was ransacked by our capture and looting was common practice in the camp.

"Let's go, my bride," he said handing the clothes to me.

CHAPTER THIRTY-THREE

During the ride I worked diligently, using a piece of cloth as a wrap for the diamonds and fastening them snuggly to the inside of my dress. Only when they were completely secure did I look around. Within fifteen minutes we reached Lutalo's dwelling. I tried hard to determine our location but it was difficult. At least when I escaped tonight, I'd travel east. If Walyam could free my family it would be my greatest joy.

Lutalo lived in a large, single-story compound with many windows. There were three exits that men entered and departed like bees in a hive, a double-door center and exits to the left and right. Rows of doors were on each side of a long, dimly lit hall with every other bare bulb blown. The hall was completely void of color other than dingy, piss-yellow walls and a concrete floor littered with peeling paint and trash. Every so often, the walls opened up to a soiled latrine, emitting the most vile odor imaginable that offered no privacy whatsoever, with stained toilets lined against the wall in plain sight.

It was an unusual place where many soldiers lived and shared quarters. Lutalo's room was not far from the center, near the main entrance, which would make it difficult for a covert escape. His barren room was small, with a few beds and wooden boxes that were even smaller. The whitewashed walls, now stained brown, were bare save for a solitary poster with torn edges. It was a picture of a man smoking and a beautiful woman with curves that resembled a snake. The words beneath the poster were too faded to read. There was little distinction from the plumes of dust and the cigarette smoke that filled the space.

A young man with a thin layer of boyish facial stubble, smoking a cigarette, sat on one of the three bunks.

"Leave us. Pass the word that we don't want to be disturbed," Lutalo ordered. The young man chuckled and clipped his shoulders before heading to the door, pausing to make a backward glance at me.

"You sure you don't want to share when you're done? You're out of practice and won't be able to satisfy that one," he teased, his eyes never leaving my body.

"Get out!" Lutalo pushed him through the door forcefully, slamming it shut.

"Let me know if you tire of him," he called through the door.

We were alone, encapsulated in a silent shroud. He stood there staring at me, intensifying my discomfort. He reached to touch my cheek but stopped when he was inches away, a puzzled look coming over on his face. Maybe he had changed his mind and reconsidered his action. I could only hope.

"Has anyone touched you yet? I need to know if you carry a bastard within you."

I thought about lying, because maybe he wouldn't want me anymore. But he'd get angry and might hurt me or, even worse, derail the plans for tonight in his rage, killing Baba. In the end, keeping him pleased and distracted was the prudent choice.

"I've not been with a man, Lutalo," I sighed lowering my head, resigned to go forward as planned. I slowly lifted my face to him.

Lutalo smiled, pleased with my response, and his face lit up like I'd never seen before. His shoulders squared even further, he raised his head higher, filling the room with his masculine presence.

"I haven't been with a woman and I'm not ashamed of it," Lutalo repeated as he reached out and awkwardly stroked my cheek with the back of his palm. "We are both pure. Perfect for one another. Lay with me," he finished as he turned and pulled the coverlet back on his bed.

It couldn't be like this. I wanted the first time to be with someone I loved, someone I chose, like Suda was able to. I wanted it to be with Chaz, even though he left me without a trace, as if his mere existence was a figment of my imagination. But now I had no choice. I had to do this for Baba. It disgusted me that I had to lie with my own brother, flesh of my flesh, blood of my blood. He would labor over me until he spilled his putrid seed, corrupting my virgin womb.

There was no way I would spend a lifetime playing wife to him. I knew that the whole situation was my fault, but still, if Walyam didn't succeed in getting my family freed, there was no guarantee that Lutalo would let them live. He had planned for us to return to Uganda, where I'd meet my Maker.

I chewed nervously at my fingernails as he used the coverlet from another bed to make a pillow. My fingernails were filled with dirt from digging but I didn't care as I tasted the salted earth.

"Come," he cooed reaching his hand out to me, his eyes at half-mast.

I shook in uncontrollable fear. My chest was beginning to seize again as it strained to draw a solid breath.

"Get over here!" he demanded.

Worse things could have happened to me while I traveled alone in war-torn Uganda. In fact, horrific things could have happened if Lutalo had not intervened. I should be counted among the lucky. Forever trying to see the good side of things was my only means of survival.

Shouldn't I be thankful and give him what he wants, I thought as I took his cool hand and allowed him to lead me to the bunk. Rigidly I lay on my back as he stretched out beside me.

"There, that's not so bad now," he offered, coming up on an elbow.

My eyes were trained on the stained ceiling. It was surprisingly more stained than the walls. I watched him through the corner of my eye staring at me. Ever so slowly he raised his hand and placed it on my flat stomach, and rubbed as he grinned slightly. I could sense his manhood growing.

When he eased on top of me, I was surprised at his weight. He felt a lot heavier than he looked. Reaching his hand to the back of my neck, he pulled me into a long kiss. My mouth was so dry. I dared not open my lips as his tongue roughly tried to gain entrance.

I yelped when he cruelly pulled at my breast, hurting me, causing my mouth to open just enough for his invasion. I felt like I was drowning, on the verge suffocation. Plunging his tongue back and forth made me want to gag. It was like being devoured from the inside out. I tried to pull away from him but found my hands were pinned under his wide chest, his full weight crushing me into the mattress. His body seemed endless and I tried to wiggle my way out from under him. It was hopeless; there was no stopping him short of a solid knee to the *makende*. That would only infuriate him and could be deadly.

Suddenly he broke his kiss and pulled up my dress, allowing my first breath in minutes.

"Wait," I croaked breathlessly, pulling my hands up to my throat.

"I've waited long enough, Matika," he said hoarsely as he fumbled with his trousers.

"But we are not married!"

I was panicked. He yanked down his pants to his knees, exposing his aroused manhood. I lifted my head to concentrate on his face. I didn't want to see him intimately; it was all wrong.

"We will be tomorrow," he said but without much bravado.

"But we are not today," I protested.

He lay back down on me, letting out a small sigh. I felt him, all of him, hard and warm with a velvety surface and cushioning springs of curls nestled at the base, pressed against my belly. It was odd to feel him like that. It was beyond my imagination to see Lutalo in such a heated state. He began to grind in an awkward rhythm that sent chills through my body, crushing me further into the bed.

He reached down between us and pressed his hardness against my intimate core.

"Please," I cried.

"Stop talking!" he hollered in frustration.

He fumbled around seeking entrance, but to my astonishment, he wasn't able to penetrate. Again he pressed and pressed, but his manhood lost its luster and was flaccid no matter how hard he tried.

"This is your fault!" he struck me across the face before pulling up on his knees. "Don't get up. I'm not done yet."

My face stung from his blow. I couldn't possibly understand how it was my fault that he couldn't make his manhood harden at will. Perhaps it was something I said or did. Suda often said that she could make any man hard. Not that I wanted Lutalo to be inside of me, but I had to wonder whether something was wrong with me.

He worked and worked at stroking himself and tried several more times to push his way into me, each time growing more and more agitated, but to no avail. He couldn't maintain his hardness. He covered my face with a dirty shirt but that, too, didn't work for him.

"We'll wait until we are wed tomorrow," he said in frustration, pulling up his pants.

With that statement I pulled down my dress and sat up. Lutalo looked perplexed and upset at the same time. I felt sorry for him. It was a weakness of mine when I saw someone distressed and Lutalo looked like a child after getting scolded. Lutalo wasn't more than a few years older than me. In his late teens, he had lived beyond his years. He had survived much, the loss of his mother, the rejection from family and being a child soldier forced to commit many atrocities that no one should endure.

"I'm sorry," I said softly reaching to touch his arm.

"What are you sorry for?" he asked without looking at me.

"For everything," I responded gently looking down at my hand on his arm. I really meant it. I was sorry for everything that had happened to him, to us.

Before I knew it he pulled me into his arms and held me tight. His body shook but I didn't hear him cry. His breathing was controlled at best, but I felt his tears falling on my head. That was my undoing. I cried with him. My grief spiraled out of control from a sense of utter despair to self-loathing. There was no end. Our lives could have been so much different together as brother and sister instead of this twisted existence.

He pulled me down so that I was lying on top of him as we wept together. We cried for very different reasons, but in this we were united. As seasons of tears overflowed from unbound hearts, as time ceased until our souls emptied themselves, we held on tightly for fear of drowning in our sorrow. I'm not sure how much time passed before our tears were spent and we were wet from their bitterness.

"You see, I need you and you need me. We are meant to be together. Don't you feel it?" he rumbled, his chest to my ear.

"Yes," I agreed.

"Matika, do you love me?"

"Yes, I do."

"Good. I need you by my side always. No one will ever understand me like you do. You have her eyes."

"Whose eyes?"

"Mama's eyes," he said putting his hand under my chin so that so he could look in my face. "She was so beautiful, just like you."

Lutalo was wrong. I had Baba's eyes, as he did, almond shaped, large, the color of coffee beans. Our eye lashes swept our cheeks with every blink and flowed like fans, curling ever so slightly at the end like a worn broom. It was one of the features that set our brothers apart from the rest of the village boys. Lutalo was deceiving himself to think that my eyes were like his mother's. Still, I didn't want to force him to see what he clearly tried to ignore.

"Thank you," was all I'd managed to say as I looked at him.

He kissed me on the cheek and held me in his arms until we were both asleep. Oddly enough, I felt comfortable and secure in his embrace. Mentally, I was drained and needed a reprieve, if even for a few hours.

"Lutalo! Lutalo!" someone shouted, awakening me with a start.

CHAPTER THIRTY-FOUR

I slid off Lutalo's chest, where I'd slept peacefully. It was pitch black in the room; only a faint sliver of light from the hall outlined the door at the bottom, where there was a seven-centimeter gap. I wondered how long we'd slept. It felt like early nightfall. I should have left earlier when he had fallen asleep, but now missed my opportunity.

Lutalo got up and silently padded to the door. His walk was always graceful and catlike, even after being rudely awakened and possibly startled. That was another feature that could be attributed to Baba. It's funny that now that I knew he was Baba's son, my brother, I could plainly see the similarities between them.

The bright beam streamed in as the door was opened, where two men stood waiting. The illumination behind them didn't allow me to distinguish them, but I suspected that one was his roommate who was here earlier; the other had a similar height and build.

"You're needed at headquarters," his roommate's voice boomed.

"Can't it wait until tomorrow?" Lutalo asked, letting out a yawn as he rubbed the sleep out of his eyes.

"It's urgent…he's here," the other said a bit too loudly as the cement floor in the hall echoed with activity.

My heart was pounding. Who was he referring to? Whomever he was, it sent Lutalo in a rush of activity. Leaving the door wide open, not bothering to pull the overhead string for the solitary bulb, he donned his shirt while I stayed on the bed unmoving, hoping to be forgotten. Fidgeting with the small buttons, he looked around for his boots that were strangely at opposite ends of the room.

There was an awkward moment when he couldn't loosen his laces enough to slide his bare foot into the stiff leather after multiple attempts.

"Here, take care of this," he ordered, tossing it to me in frustration. I rolled and without thinking caught it effortlessly before it touched the ground, to his surprise and mine.

The laces of the boots were as tight as newly braided hair. It took some effort to work my narrow fingertip through them in the dimly lit room. It would have been easier if I hadn't bitten my already short nails shorter.

"Thanks," he said when I returned the shoe to him. After putting it on, he stood up and headed for the door. Then he stopped and strolled back to me.

"I'll only be a moment. Stay here. I can't guarantee your safety if you don't."

"I'm very hungry, Lutalo," I added quickly, trying to buy more precious time. "Could you bring me something back to eat?"

"Of course," he replied before he pressed his lips against mine for a quick kiss, before closing me in the room he called, "Lock the door."

I got up and did just that. Hearing the many excited voices in the hallway and getting a whiff of sweet tobacco, I wasn't taking any chances. In the room alone, leaving the lights off, I looked out the small window that was covered with a linen drape. Unfortunately, the window faced another building that was an arm's span away. A soldier could easily see me if he looked out his window or happened to be passing by.

Turning away, I checked around the room, biting my non-existent nails. Dressed as I was, I was an easy target; going unnoticed would be impossible. I had to do something quickly or I would lose the only opportunity to get away. Then it hit me as I stared at a dirty pile of fatigues. I wrinkled up my nose at the pungent body odor that would be my best advantage. I also spotted a small tin case used to hold playing cards. It was perfect for the diamonds that needed a safer place and the small cloth that was wrapped around the stones prevented any noise from movement of the tin.

Running over to the clothes, I put on a green shirt and slipped the pants over my night dress, rolling them a few times at the waist so they wouldn't fall down. The uniform was so dirty it could stand up on its own. The shirt was much too large and hung low at the collar, exposing my clothes underneath, but it would have to do. I placed the tin in the breast pocket that hung much lower than it should have. Finding a hat, I hid my hair, carefully tucking each thick braid. Finally, I pulled on a pair of muddy boots that flopped with every step I took. Cautiously approaching the window, I peered out. A group of men passed by; one was clearly drunk, singing merrily as he was carried by another man laughing loudly.

Once they passed I slowly pushed up the window. To my horror, the window only opened halfway and wouldn't budge further. Despite several desperate attempts, it was stuck. I had no choice. Peering out once again, I began to slip out.

I panicked. My butt wouldn't allow me to pass through. The top half of my body hung toward the ground as I tried to grab a hold of something. I kicked with my legs, trying to gain momentum. Compressing my lungs, I tried to squeeze through, elongating my body. It was no use. I was as tight as a cork in a bottle of wine. I was stuck and couldn't retreat.

"Open the door!" someone yelled, banging on it with heavy fists. The voice was harsh and it was not Lutalo's.

"I know you're in there, I can smell you from here," he called out louder. "I'm coming back with the key if you don't open it."

Like a thirteen-pound baby coming out of the womb, I struggled even harder to push my way through the impossibly small opening. I dangled like a cloth out the window, unable to go backward or forward. I wasn't overweight, as a matter of fact I was on the thin side, like Suda. At that moment however, I felt like my bottom was as plump as a rhino's rump.

Footsteps echoed in the hall, a door creaked opened, then closed. More footsteps, followed by muffled speech and soft moans.

I reached and reached for the small bush that was at my fingertips but I couldn't get any closer. I rolled right and then left, trying to ease out but to no avail. Finally resigned to being punished, I let my body go slack and suddenly felt the tip of the bush. I reached again and grabbed one of the scattered bushes. I worked at pulling myself through, letting out a soft grunt as the sharp branches pierced my hands. Several heart-pounding minutes passed as I struggled to get out the window. Finally I fell to the ground in a heap, legs overhead, the pants ripped in the back of my thigh, making me wish I'd put on the uniform after I went through the window.

It was cool outside but I was sweating like an African Bush Hog roasting over a spit. Taking a moment to still my heartbeat, I lay there trembling.

"Where is she?" someone yelled.

I sprang into motion in the opposite direction than the group had gone earlier, leaving the dark and dusty building behind. There wasn't much time. Whoever entered the room knew I had escaped. Not only that, they'd tell Lutalo that I was gone. Panicked, I lost what little sense of direction I had. I couldn't remember which way we'd come from. The only thing I remembered was that there was one main road that was paved surrounded by other dirt roads that connected sections of the buildings.

One thing about this base, it was a lot farther from the refugee camp. It was also bigger and more spread out over a larger piece of land. There were many trees, and bushes. The tall grass wasn't maintained compared to the manicured lawns of the other base. Well-worn walking paths meandered between the buildings surrounded by tall elephant grass that made it difficult to take another route. Tall light poles near each building shone their brilliance like beacons inviting everyone's eyes to see me. I was trapped with nowhere to run.

A white bus, similar to the one I had traveled on to the horrid refugee camp, pulled up to a jerky halt, its brakes screeching in complaint. A mixture of men in uniforms and civilian clothes exited slowly. They looked tired, as if returning after working a long shift. With my head down, I headed toward the bus in a nearby parking lot a few buildings over from Lutalo's, hoping no one would notice me.

A boldness arose in me. I was scared but had nothing to lose. I wanted to try following the bus out to the main road. Lutalo had access to a vehicle so being on foot wasn't a good idea, but I had to get out of the area. With my luck he could be alerted at any moment. Immediately, he'd search for me and have someone dispatched to kill our father.

Briskly walking to the bus I brushed past the departing men without notice. They seemed too concerned about finding their beds than taking an interest in me. I probably looked like a short young man to them, frail and as thin as a stick with my ill-fitting fatigues. Walking with my head down and shoulders slouched did well to hide my breasts, which seemed to protrude like the mountains over Lake Victoria. I felt a stiff breeze flow through the backside of the torn pants.

The bus was pulled off to side of the road, idling, with the headlights shooting a thick beam down the dark road. There weren't many other vehicles around, and those that were present consisted of passenger vans, jeeps and a few trucks. Small groups of men and a few women were scattered about not far from the bus, next to the nearby flat-topped building.

The driver was writing on a clipboard, straining his tired, bulging eyes in the pale overhead light. I approached the open door. The grossly overweight man was wearing a khaki-green uniform. His belly was so big it rested on the steering wheel and provided the perfect desktop for his clipboard. His lack of facial hair added to the high gloss on his face.

"Out of service," the portly man called out in English before reaching for the lever and pulling the door shut in my face. He hadn't taken his eyes off his paperwork to spare me a glance.

"Please, I only have a question," I said respectfully in the deepest voice I could muster. When he didn't look up I pounded my hand on the glass door, desperate. Any moment now, Lutalo would be looking for me with a vengeance.

"I don't get paid enough to answer your questions," he called to me in a heavy accent, again not sparing a mere glimpse. Setting his clipboard aside, he put the bus in gear.

"I will pay you well if you help me," I called a little louder in English, banging on the glass door again.

"You don't have enough money," he looked down at me from his throne, his attention clearly engaged.

"I have more than enough, the likes of you've never seen."

"This better be worth it. Now let me see," he called pulling the door open.

I scampered up the four steps into the bus, nearly falling in the driver's lap. My chest was burning with anticipation and fear that was both overwhelming and determined.

"Leave this place first and I will show you a treasure."

"Where're we going?"

"Anywhere out of here."

"It better be worth it or I will throw you in the street while the bus is still moving," he threatened.

With that he closed the door and pulled out onto the road before I'd taken a seat. I chose one in the first row opposite the driver, trying to duck as low as I could but found the windows were even lower. I kept my eyes forward as we pulled away, but I saw people staring. There was no hiding aside from lying on the floor.

"Are you a deserter? You must be in some kind of trouble then. That's going to cost you much more."

I didn't respond to him, letting him think what he wanted. It took forever to get out of the area. Rows and rows of tin roofed buildings were followed by dirt and even more buildings. Walking would have been quicker than his slow-motion driving. Suddenly he stopped the bus in the middle of the road, killing the lights but not the engine. I shot up in the seat. It was time to negotiate and I had a diamond out and ready.

"Why the stick?" I asked spotting a sturdy dark piece of wood beside him.

"To keep order on my bus," he responded. "Don't try to change the subject."

"What time do you have?"

"What do you need the time for? It's late."

"Much depends on the time," I remarked smoothly putting on a mask of false confidence.

"Let me see," he said taking a supreme effort to squeeze his thick hand into the pocket of an extremely tight pair of pants to take out his timepiece.

As he grunted and squirmed, I briefly closed my eyes to keep from rolling them in the back of my head. He was as slow as mud running uphill.

"It's ten till midnight," he said putting his watch on the dashboard, not attempting the heroic return to his pocket.

I'm late!

"I need you to take me near the east entrance of Dadaab," I said squeezing the precious diamond like I was making a wish on a shooting star. Everything rested on this very moment. I held my breath and waited for his response.

"I can't do that. It's too far."

I held out the stone that sparkled in the moonlit night like the evening star.

"What is this?" he asked as his eyes shone in the face of the stone.

"A diamond."

"We'll see," he said. Lifting his hand up to the rear view mirror, he scratched the precious rock on its surface.

"It's real," he said in wonder. "Where did you get it?" His brow lifted to his hairline with curiosity.

"That's not your concern, but it's yours if you drive quickly."

"For this, I'll take you to the ends of the earth." Half his face was covered in a wide grin, his teeth making a mockery of oral hygiene.

"That won't be necessary. I'll settle for the east entrance of Dadaab. That's all you have to do and the diamond is yours."

"As you say," he remarked putting the bus in gear after stealing another look at the diamond before placing it in his breast pocket.

Once we were on the road again I could finally breathe. I was going to be late but maybe they would wait for me. I held tightly to that small ray of hope because there would be nothing left for me if I missed them, assuming they had escaped.

For what seemed like hours the bus weaved through the dark roads, passing tin-roof after tin-roof shanties toward the refugee camp. The air was stuffy, fueled with exhaust that was coming inside the bus instead of out the tailpipe. I held my forearm to my nose, using my stinky sleeve to filter the diesel fumes. I couldn't imagine how he drove this bus, day in and day out, without killing all his brain cells. I already had a headache after the first few minutes.

Seeing the lighted guard tower of the camp ahead about two kilometers away, I told the driver to pull over off the road. It was time. Trying to convince myself that it was the uncertainty of not knowing that made me feel so anxious. I wasn't sure what I was looking for. Would they be waiting in a car for me? If so, how would I know whom to approach? It was just too quiet, too peaceful. Something wasn't right.

CHAPTER THIRTY-FIVE

"You must wait here," I said standing on shaky legs.

"I'm not staying here! You paid me to take you to the gate so…here you are," he said extending his flabby arms to the darkness beyond, creating rippling waves of sagging flesh.

"Listen, I'll give you another diamond if you wait for me."

"These roads are dangerous. Many have been attacked here by those savage refugees from the camp."

I was insulted. If anyone was a savage it was the men who guarded the camp posing as peacekeepers, yet stealing the precious aid destined for us, watching and at times participating in brutal rapes and beatings. Truly he must know these things.

"For two diamonds…Will you wait if I give you two more? I won't be long. No more than a half-hour."

"Three," he said holding up his fat fingers. "I feel a desperate need to find my bed and my evening meal grows cold."

It was funny to imagine what kind of woman waited for him at home with his meal ready at this hour. Would she be upset at this delay or asleep in bed? She must be an excellent cook in order for him to maintain his hefty weight. I found myself smiling at the picture I'd just painted.

"Make it quick. What will it be?" he asked pulling me from the image of his wife.

"I only have two left," I lied protecting the stones that were my family's passport to freedom. "They're worth more money than you'd see in a year, maybe two. Wealthy Americans pay thousands of U.S. dollars for only one of these." Another lie slid from my lips. I had no idea how much the diamonds were worth. In truth I'd never seen one before.

"Girl, I know you're up to something bad. Something very bad," he mused.

"*Wangie!*" I was shocked he'd known I was a girl.

"I don't want to hear about it and don't care, so spare me. I haven't got all night. If my wife wasn't pregnant again with number eight and complaining about our home, I wouldn't be here risking my life for the likes of you. I have it in mind to take your diamonds and throw you out…but that would be too much effort on my part. Besides, I'm not sure what you have concealed under that oversized uniform."

There was no way I'd let this man take the precious stones away from me. He would have to catch me first and by the looks of it he didn't stand a chance. Holding my eyes firmly on him, my shoulders squared, I felt empowered with a newfound confidence. I'd walked too many kilometers through jungles, been chased across savannahs, and crossed precarious rivers to back down now. I'd come too far and was at the apex of my journey. With my chin pointed skyward and my fists ready, I waited for him to strike.

He sensed my desperate resolve.

"All right, all right, but I'll wait for twenty minutes. If you're not back by then, I'm leaving without you," he said outstretching his hand in typical beggar fashion.

"When I return I will pay you," I said starting for the door, my heartbeat playing a fast tune in my ears.

"You will pay me now!" he demanded, lever in hand, refusing to open the door.

I'd be a fool to pay him now with no incentive for him to wait. He would drive away as soon as he got his greedy hands on the diamonds and there would be nothing I could do about it. Although he had me over a barrel, he didn't need to know that.

"All right, one now and one when I get back," I said handing him another precious stone, the smaller of the two, before he opened the door. Before I moved any farther, I secured the tin with the stones around my belly for safekeeping. I needed to run and couldn't risk losing the diamonds in the process.

The cool night air poured in as I stepped out of the bus; a refreshing sweet aroma of wildflowers and damp earth greeted me. I wanted to run to the camp as fast as I could, but I couldn't be reckless, so I jogged at a modest pace. I chose to stay near the road, at least until I got closer. The grass was too high; no telling what wildlife awaited there, especially the deadly snakes that loved the tall grass. I hated snakes. One day in our village a cousin was bitten by a deadly mamba and died that night. Why they were on this earth was a wonder to me. I didn't know anyone who liked them, except for the *sangoma* and my older brother Obiajula, who caught field snakes to scare us. He could be so cruel.

When I was more than halfway to the camp, I could hear the rumbling of the bus engine. I turned around to find it making a three-point turn in the middle of the road. My heart shuddered and skipped a beat. Even though it would take a while to maneuver such a large vehicle, it was just too far away to catch. He was leaving me and there was nothing I could do about it.

Turning around, I ran forward at a much faster pace. I couldn't look back. I convinced myself that my family was out by the gate, waiting patiently for me, but with a sinking heart I knew that was not the case. I could neither return to the camp nor the bus. I was on my own.

Tonight was cooler than usual, cold in fact. With a temperature that felt about eleven degrees Celsius it was more like an August night instead of April. The days had been hot, the nights clear and cold. A gentle breeze swept through the grass with a low hiss, sounding like a thousand snakes.

Drawing closer to the entrance with three guards in sight, I was stunned when a truck shot through the gate at a breakneck speed. The headlights glared, leaving me no choice but to dive into the grass to hide. It was itchy and moved underneath me like an undercurrent of rats and vermin. I quickly flipped from belly to back, cursing myself for not paying attention. I was so worried about snakes that I'd jeopardized everything.

The truck stopped centimeters from crushing my legs, its lights blinding as I stared at the grill. For some reason that I didn't understand, I couldn't run away. Tearing my eyes from its sunbeam lights was also impossible. Rooted in place, I put up a hand to shield my eyes from the laser assault while leaning on my elbow in an elevated position.

The truck door open and someone rushed out. I was caught even before I made it to the gate. Everything was off from the time I stepped off the bus. No, it was off from the time I allowed myself to fall asleep knowing I needed to run. This night was destined for a bad ending and no amount of diamonds could get me out of this mess.

Booted soles greeted the dusty ground with a soft thump. A tall silhouette with long legs in an upside down "v" meeting a narrow waist stood over me. Not bothering to protest or offer any resistance, I was pulled up on my feet. I accepted defeat. I was too tired of running, too tired to hide, and it was much too late.

"Are you all right?"

I didn't think I'd ever welcome the sound of his voice. It was Walyam! On impulse I jumped into his arms and hugged him tightly, burying my face in the crook of his arm. Letting his warmth sink into my bones never felt so good. He was so tall. I was overjoyed to see him.

"Is my family safe? How did you free them?"

"They're safe for now. There are many who were willing to do anything for diamonds. You gave me enough to also pay off the guards, which will buy us some time before they are forced to come after us. Come, get in the truck," his chest rumbled as he pulled away from me. He turned and headed toward the open driver's door bidding me inside. I slid in next to a weeping Suda, who embraced me tightly as Walyam climbed in behind me, shutting the truck door.

"Oh, Matika," she cried as she pulled away from me and did a visual assessment.

Suda was in shambles, her face bloodied, and her dress in shreds hanging loosely off her shoulders. Her red eyes provided a glimpse of the tears she'd shed. Aside from all that, her spirit was not broken. She and Baba had been through so much.

"Where's Baba?" I asked in a panic-filled voice. I turned to Walyam. "Did you save him?"

"We have to get rid of this truck as soon as possible. This is the general's personal truck and we'll be a target in it."

"Where is he?!"

Walyam ignored my question, which made me even more panicked.

"He's covered in the back," Suda said in a small voice, but what she didn't say was even more disheartening.

"Is he alive?"

"He is for now, but he's not doing well. We gave him the milk of the poppy so he would sleep without pain. I fear any moment could be his last, but we have to be strong for him. What they did to us was cruel and unthinkable, yet we are together now."

"Stop the truck!"

Walyam slammed on the breaks at my command. The truck skidded to a halt, disrupting a plume of dust that danced in the glow of the headlights.

"Are you crazy?" he yelled, glaring at me.

To my astonishment, the bus was still here. The driver had only turned around and parked on the other side of the road. The engine roared to life at our approach, emitting the most beautiful sound.

"Do you see that bus parked ahead? Come on, follow me," I said opening the door on Suda's side and pushing her out. Exiting the truck I didn't bother to close the door behind me.

"This bus will take us wherever we need to go."

"Are you sure? Is it safe?" Suda's eyes were large with worried disbelief.

"Yes, he gave me a ride here and I paid him to wait. You said that they will be looking for this truck so we better make it quick."

"Hurry. Help me with Baba," Walyam called as he jumped and landed on the truck's bed with a thud.

He didn't pull the coverlet off Baba but pushed him to the end of the truck for easier access. Suda and I helped Walyam carry Baba to the awaiting bus. It felt like carrying a lifeless body and I wondered if it was already too late. We lumbered over to the bus at a brisk but steady pace.

"Wait! Wait! What's going on?" the portly driver asked as we hoisted Baba onto the bus, laying him carefully in the aisle, not daring to sit him in a seat.

"Drive to this address," Walyam said showing him a small slip of paper. "Now!"

"That's an hour's drive and much too far. Why have you brought a dead body on my bus!" His voice was five tones higher. "I am not transporting that body anywhere and I don't care how much you pay me. That's not worth my life."

"I will pay you double!" I called to out to him.

"Absolutely, not!"

"I said drive!" Walyam demanded, shoving the pistol against the back of the man's skull. The driver winced in pain.

"Okay, okay, just calm down. I'm driving."

With slow movements and shaky hands, he put the bus in gear and pulled onto the narrow road. Walyam sat down behind the driver but kept the gun trained near the man's head, allowing him the needed space to drive safely. Suda and I sat opposite him. She looked out the window.

"I knew you were trouble," the driver muttered under his breath after some time. "I don't know why I waited for you. I was this close to leaving," he emphasized, putting forefinger to thumb. "Should have just gone straight home and let my wife complain about our little house all night, every night, year after year. At least I'd be alive to drive this bus for a meager earning tomorrow."

"Shut up!" Walyam bellowed in a low malicious tone. He was at the edge of his seat moving his head from left to right, vigilant as always.

"I was merely stating a fact," the man began again, "but I should have asked myself, 'What kind of a girl walks around carrying ice?'"

Walyam looked over at me and rolled his eyes heavenward. The big man was a parrot but there wasn't much he could do about it. Killing him or even hurting him benefited no one and left us without a driver and guide we desperately needed. Walyam lowered his pistol, expelling a deep breath instead.

"But nooo, I was too greedy," the driver grumbled to himself. The man continued on and on but neither of us commented on his rant.

A procession of military vehicles was headed straight for us, sirens flashing and horns blaring loudly. The vehicles were diving toward the camp.

"Can't you drive any faster?" Walyam asked.

"And get a ticket by the military police? I would lose my license. Then I'd lose my job."

"What good is having a job if you're dead?" The threat hung in the air.

The driver sped up a bit, and as he passed, the other vehicles slowed down to observe. We hadn't aroused their suspicion or else they would have turned around.

"It will only be a matter of time before they're onto us. They'll find the truck on the side of the road and know we're on this bus."

"How much time do we have?" Suda asked getting on her knees facing the rear of the bus as the lights faded out of view.

"Fifteen minutes at most…if we're lucky."

"Let's hope so," Suda replied.

"That was really smart of you to have this bus waiting," Walyam said as he looked over at me, his face genuine. "They would have caught us already. You're resourceful when you want to be…for a girl that is."

I felt the fire rush to my face at his compliment. Although unwanted from him, it was flattering, nonetheless.

"I didn't think I would make it back here in time. Thank you for getting my family out. I don't know how you did it, but you did."

"I had to call in some favors, but we're in no way out of danger. You're father's an important man and they're not willing to let him go so easily. His potential is much greater than what I could offer in exchange to keep them away."

"Look," the driver called out pointing at a spot in the road ahead. "A checkpoint. I've never seen one here before. This is the only way out of the area and I can't cut through the field in this bus. Look at the automatic rifles. We have to stop."

CHAPTER THIRTY-SIX

"Slow down," Walyam commanded.

The makeshift checkpoint shown like a beacon in the night. I could hear the diesel generator providing power to their lights.

"Slow down, speed up, he says. You know, you really need to make up your mind. This is all too confusing and I'm under a lot of stress."

"Shut up and let me think. You talk like a cackling old hen."

The diver let out a "hmph" but said no more as he slowed the bus to a crawl. We didn't have much time to do anything.

"Hide Baba under the seat. Walyam, you and Suda need to take cover, " I ordered taking control of the situation.

Suda didn't hesitate. She jumped over me and began pulling Baba toward the back of the bus and worked at hiding his large body. I was glad he'd slept because she was not gentle, banging his head on the metal seat brackets as she pulled him to the rear of the bus.

"I'm not hiding like a scared woman. I'll kill them if I have to," Walyam boasted.

"I'm off my schedule and it's suspicious for me to come from the camp without passengers," the driver added.

"You're a dead man if you give us away," Walyam interjected.

"I'm your passenger; I'm staying right here. Just leave it to me. I'm the only one with a uniform. Walyam, get in back. We don't have much time," I added.

We were almost upon the blockade, but Walyam refused to move from his seat. I had a plan that simply wouldn't work with him sitting in front.

"Walyam, please," Suda's desperate voice cried out from the rear.

"I will not," he said obstinately through clenched jaws that clicked in fury.

"You have blood all over you, Walyam. They will see it and know right away that something is wrong. Just hide and trust me as I have trusted you. If something goes wrong, you come out shooting. Besides, you would have the element of surprise."

I could tell he was weighing my words but we had run out of time and approached the checkpoint at that moment. I looked over as two armed and uniformed men came up to the door. Three others stood in front of a crudely made barrier constructed from flimsy red and white painted wooden poles. Each carried a flashlight strapped to their belts and assault rifles poised at us. As the doors were thrown open, I looked over at Walyam. He was gone.

"You were driving so slow. We thought you'd never get here," the first guard said as he came up the steps rifle in hand. The other soldiers waited below.

"This old bus has very bad brakes," the driver began, "I have to slow down early or else I won't be able to stop. I've been asking the company for new brakes for so long and they just look –"

"Let me see your log," the guard demanded, cutting him off.

The soldier, who was in his late twenties with neatly cropped hair that faded into a box at the crown, grabbed the sweat-stained logbook. His hands were long, his body filled with muscles showing through a well-fitted uniform. Perfect bone structure was covered with flawless, smooth skin. No facial hair obstructed his face. To top it off, he had the most precise eyebrows I'd ever seen, like he'd spent hours pulling out one hair at a time to make the optimal half-moon.

I imagined any woman would call him handsome, including me, which would make my job even more difficult. It seemed like he was used to women doing anything to please him. With flawless features and a seamless hairline, he wanted for nothing from the opposite sex.

The driver managed to look calmer now than on the ride here, except for the heavy sweat that poured from his head and down his neck, leaving a damp pool around his white-collared shirt. Despite his rudeness at the beginning, the driver wasn't a bad man. Like anyone else he wanted to get ahead in life, better his living situation and provide for his family. There was a lot to be said about a man who pleased his wife, let alone listened to her complaints. Most men would never consider the wishes of their spouses. I truly felt bad for judging him so harshly and exploiting his vulnerability.

I was learning so much about men and what I wanted in one. If I could piece together the perfect husband he'd contain an assortment of traits that I admired. He'd be as strong as Baba, as kind and gentle as my oldest brother, as caring as the bus driver and as resourceful as Walyam. I was astonished that I'd want anyone remotely resembling Walyam, but I couldn't ignore what he had done for me and my family throughout the year.

Most importantly, my husband would be as passionate and loving as my Chaz. Just the very thought of him melted my inner core. His gentle touched burned my skin and evoked feelings of passion in me that I never knew existed. When he looked at me, it was like I was the only woman in the world.

"Your entry reads here that you made your final stop at the base at 23:30. Why are back here with a passenger?" he asked returning the log. Then he looked over at me.

There was a lot to be said about being a woman. Granted, we were not equal to African men in many respects, actually none at all, but we had something that all men wanted. Sure, men could take it just as easily, but what was better than having a woman desire you. Suda uttered the words to me before I left with Lutalo, "You are a woman." She had spoken it with authority. I didn't have faith in her words at first, until I got Lutalo to take me back to get Baba's diamonds. Only then did I start to understand that I could use my womanly assets to my advantage.

"He came back for me," I said in a sultry voice that wasn't my own. It was lusty and full of the promise of ultimate pleasure. I didn't even bother to hide the fact that I was female and promptly took off my hat and gave him what I thought was my best smile.

"That's not your uniform? You're not in the service," he said eying me with suspicion.

My heart was racking my ribcage. I couldn't breathe. Also, at any moment, Walyam could pop out, guns blazing, and not give me a chance to work my plan.

"You are right, I shouldn't be impersonating a soldier," I replied breathlessly, which sounded more like a moan than the fact that I couldn't get the air out of my lungs. Reaching to stroke my breast I stood and moved closer, only a few centimeters from him. His eyes blazed with hunger.

"I must be going. I have somewhere I need to be," I said smoothly.

"Where do you think you're going at this hour?"

"I have an appointment with someone on the base and I can't keep him waiting."

"I can give you more pleasure than any other soldier. Come here, babe, and I'll show you what I can do."

He reached out and caressed by my toned bottom, pulling me to him. With his other hand he grappled at my breasts firmly. "Very nice," he said smoothly before bending down to nip at my lips.

"I would love to see what you can do for me. You are so handsome," I said using the most seductive voice I could muster. Standing on my toes I reached up and licked him from his throat to his ear. "Unfortunately, I fear that the appointment tonight is far too important to be ignored."

"Who are you seeing tonight?" He asked pulling back with a suspicions eye.

"He is so important that disclosing his name would cause a scandal."

"You lie! No one cares about a scandal from a camp whore," he replied with furrowed brows and narrowed eyes, pulling back from me.

His words had stung more than they should considering I was no whore. I wanted to slap the sneer off his smooth face. My plan wasn't working. He was right. No one cared about who slept with whom. This was especially true for senior officials. As a matter of fact, it was expected. Having a mistress was as normal as having multiple wives. Women were like cattle to be used and traded at will.

"I'm not some uneducated country wretch. You don't know who my father is," I said haughtily with chin in the air, eyeing him with disdain.

"So...what do I care?" He started pulling at my uniform, the bus driver completely forgotten. He was going to take me right here and now with an audience.

"Nor do you know who I'm betrothed to, Sergeant *Stinnas*," I said emphasizing his name printed on his uniform, for which I prayed I'd pronounced correctly.

That got his attention. His eyes snapped open wide. An angry father could be appeased but defiling a bride-to-be to an important man would be dangerous and could cost his life. A man's pride for something that was his alone was a force to be reckoned with. I could be engaged to his superior for all he knew.

"Stinnas, make it quick. We have company."

I followed his stare to the back of the bus where several headlights were visible through rear window. They were coming for us!

CHAPTER THIRTY-SEVEN

"Look, I really have to go. Now!"

"Fine!" He fumed even though the tent in his pants cried out in complaint. "Go and tell no one." With that he headed to the exit.

Heavy breaks screeched to a halt. "Stop that bus!" a soldier yelled jumping out of a truck.

"Drive now, before it's too late!" I cried to the driver before Stinnas' foot hit the ground. We simply couldn't wait a moment longer.

The driver had the bus in gear, gunning the accelerator, not bothering to close the door. Just as we were about to make it through the checkpoint another vehicle screeched to a halt in front of us. Men snaked out of the trucks surrounding the bus.

"Get your hands up!"

"Oh, no!" the driver cried completely forlorn. "This just keeps getting better."

"I've checked the bus. It's just a girl," Stinnas remarked in a bored tone, lazily waving the men back with his hand. "There is no need to be alarmed. We didn't see any of the suspects from the description that came through tonight."

"Stand down, Sergeant," an officer ordered as he pushed Stinnas aside.

"Yes sir."

"Up with your hands," he ordered the driver as he boarded the bus.

The driver's hands shot up to the sky, creating a wave that traveled through the flab of his arms. Mine reluctantly followed. We were caught. Perhaps I should have let Walyam take care of this. What was I thinking? I had become too full of myself, too confidant.

An officer with a red stripe on his shoulders appeared on the bus, pistol in hand. He peered down the aisle but didn't advance. Using his flashlight he quickly scanned the rows. Then, he blinded me with his light as I remained standing. There was nothing I could do at this point.

"It's just a girl and she's alone!" he called eying me with intense professionalism. He pointed his pistol at my head.

More footsteps. The driver cursed softly under his breath.

"Leave us!" The order was sharp and clear.

That voice. I couldn't quite place it but I'd heard it before. Was it one of the captors that had stormed our hut? Whoever it was had frightened the soldier, and without a hint of hesitation he disappeared as if he never was.

"So…we meet again," his tone was as harsh as gravel.

It was unfathomable. The colonel had found me.

With many ribbons on his chest he stood in front of me. He was as I remembered him, save for a deep scar that ran across his face that puckered at the edges of his sadistic smile. A scar that had I put there no less.

His nails ran lightly over my skin, creating a toxic current coursing through my veins. Although I wanted to pull away, I couldn't move. Afraid, I struggled to keep my eyes on him, consumed with the nightmare of my escape from this man. Terror tried to gain traction and rip me from the edge of consciousness. I had to fight my emotions but it was a losing battle to stay calm.

"First, I will cut you open from navel to nose," his acrid voice singed my ears. He lifted a nasty knife and turned it back and forth, the moonlight on its shiny blade a beautiful thing, as shiny as one of my perfect diamonds. The colonel had used this knife to cut, maul, and kill his victims, whoever they might be. He was a merciless killer without a shred of humanity in those vacant, soulless eyes.

The skin on the back of my neck crawled, feeling every single leg of a phantom spider prancing across my nape. Then a subtle rustle stirred from the rear of the bus, bringing me back from the grips of paralysis. He brought the knife swiftly to my belly. I was in shock. I couldn't believe it pierced through the layers of clothing, reaching into my tender flesh like soft butter and doubling me over. Terror ruled me like a master puppeteer. Tears flowed freely from my eyes. I hissed as the pain raced through me, making my head buzz and heartbeat flicker. The metallic smell of fresh blood filled the air around me as my clothes were instantly soaked.

Alerted, the colonel turned his head quickly to the rear of the bus at the sound of metal hitting metal. I would not stand there and be gutted alive without a fight. Knowing I was no match standing face to face with him and his formidable weapon, I still had to find a way. Using the small window of opportunity, I fell to the floor, found a piece of metal and landed a solid blow to the colonel's shin. He grunted sharply but didn't drop the dagger.

"You bitch!" he cursed but recovered quickly and assumed a fighting stance, ready to pounce.

I quickly crawled under the seats toward the rear to get away but made it only two rows. He was too quick. Facing him was my only choice or I'd risk getting stabbed in the back. I rolled over. Where was Walyam when I needed him?

The colonel came down on me wielding his weapon, slicing through the air. I kicked wildly with booted heels, sending the knife and shoe flying in the driver's direction. In an instant his body pinned me to the floor, his bony hands around my neck. I fought with everything I had, with a will to live that surpassed my fear of dying. My hands, like claws, dug at his eyes with a renewed furry.

The colonel released my throat and started to reach for his pistol in his holster. He provided just enough space for me to knee him in the *makende*. The force wasn't as hard as I'd wanted, but he howled in pain. His frame, though skinny, was tough as steel. I moved from under him to escape but he recovered too quickly. I put up my hands in defense, but it did little to prevent the closed-fist blows that struck across my face in quick succession. My brain was rattled from the skull pounding and fought a losing battle against my heavy eyelids.

What happened next was chaos. Shots ranged out from the back of the bus. The colonel shuddered. Windows exploded. The bus shook and men yelled orders. Dragged by my shoeless foot, the colonel pulled me toward him slowly. His other arm hung limply at his side, bleeding profusely. Despite his wound, he refused to escape the bus without me. His men needed to be careful and not hit him as they riddled the bus with rounds of bullets. There was only one way onto the bus and it was a deadly risk, as Walyam's aim was true and a great advantage.

"Drive now!" Walyam bellowed.

Once more the bus was thrown in gear, but not before a soldier bravely jumped though the open door. *Snap!* Only one bullet. The look of shock and wide-eyed terror was on the man's face as a red plume appeared in the center of his forehead. Walyam's aim was deadly, dropping him to the ground like a bag of sand.

As the bus was being fired upon, the driver screamed in protest but continued to operate as he managed to sink below the windshield, escaping the spray of death. Bullets ricocheted from the floor to the ceiling. The sounds were deafening and threatened to rupture my eardrums. We ran over something. A pothole? A soldier? It was hard to tell and I imagined that the driver didn't even know for that matter. His visibility was grossly compromised with his body submerged under the steering wheel.

"Follow us and the colonel's dead!" Walyam called out to the soldiers.

With that, the bus barreled down the road and the shooting stopped.

The colonel was very dangerous and was still intent on killing me, but Walyam was in the rear of the bus with his back to me, watching for soldiers with his gun perched on the backseat, like a sniper ready to fire.

"Kill him now!" I wanted to scream but my throat closed and wouldn't cooperate.

The colonel was steadily pulling me closer to him as he sat on the aisle floor, holding me like a rag doll, a human shield. With my back flush against his chest, I slumped in his arms, fighting the heavy fog in my head that wouldn't lift. I screamed for help, but only managed a weak moan.

It was like a nightmare I'd often had as a small child, one in which I couldn't move or cry out for help as horned demons with sharpened claws as long as their arms would enter our hut and attack me. I'd wake up kicking and screaming, covered in a cold sweat in the middle of the night. My eldest brother comforted me, because Mama would be angry at me for waking her.

The silver gleam of the knife near my ankle beckoned me and I tried weakly to reach for it with my foot as I struggled in the colonel's tight grip. The heavy fog was lifting slowly, my body's strength gaining some momentum. Focusing my energy, I threw back my head and nailed him in the face with my skull, exploding his nose like a melon. Blood splattered everywhere, yet he still wouldn't loosen his grip. His purpose was clear, my energy was now spent, but I had to keep fighting.

The bus swerved suddenly and the weapon slid closer to me. I inched it with my foot, bending my knee to get the precious metal closer to me. Eons passed but I was too dazed, too off balance to work more swiftly. I had to reach it before it was too late.

"I may die but I will kill you first," he growled, pointing his pistol at my head with a shaky hand, cocking the hammer.

Finally, I grabbed the hilt of the knife. Without hesitation, I pulled forward, whirled around and stabbed him in the side of his throat. He let go of me then and I scampered away, never taking my eyes off of him or the gun. A deep red stream poured out of him in rivers that quickly pooled on the floor. His life essence was flowing from his body and he hovered on the brink of death. The colonel didn't even seem rattled as he lifted his pistol again and aimed his gun to complete his mission before dying. I tried to take cover, but it was too late. With an unsteady aim he pulled the trigger.

CHAPTER THIRTY-EIGHT

Two shots fired. A window shattered behind me. Smoke poured from the colonel's gun as we looked in each other's eyes. Blood flowed from his head moments before he fell over dead. Walyam had shot him. I felt my body for the fatal wound.

"Are you okay, Matika?" Suda's worried voiced was welcome music to my ears. "Oh my gosh, you're bleeding!"

"I'm fine," I said with more authority than I felt. With the adrenaline flowing through my veins, I felt no physical pain. I took my first long solid breath but was unable to tear my gaze away from the colonel. I was afraid that at any moment he would awaken and kill me, yet deep down inside I knew that he was never coming back.

My feelings were mixed about his death. It sickened me that I had seen him die before my eyes, an image I would never forget. Although Walyam had ultimately ended his life, he would never have recovered from his severed neck. I killed him. I was ashamed of the power I felt within me. It was so intense. It was the ultimate feeling of control, a control that was intoxicating.

I wrestled with the moral struggle of ending a man's life, which was devastating no matter the reason. I felt terrible on so many levels and no amount of reasoning could take away that feeling.

Finally, my fear of him was put to rest. He would no longer be able to terrorize, hurt and kill others. A known tyrant was dead and the world would be a safer place. More importantly, my family was free from him and in the grand scheme of things, it was all that mattered. I did what I had to do to survive.

Suda helped me out of the uniform that was sticky with blood. Looking through the tear in my dress we both saw that my abdomen now sported a slice as long as a pinky just below the navel. Only then did I feel the pain and my brain registered the injury. My head throbbed, and my face stung and felt too large for my body. I was sore all over and my wound burned like it was being pierced by a hot poker, with an endless flow of alcohol being poured onto the exposed flesh.

"There's a first aid kit back here," Walyam said to Suda as he was moving the colonel's body to the back of the bus next to Baba. Two enemies side by side – one dead and the other near death.

"Why can't you throw him off the bus? I don't want to have to ride with a dead body," Suda complained, wrinkling her noise in disgust as she retrieved the kit.

"What's one more dead body to you anyway? You might as well collect another. I've seen more dead bodies tonight than at a funeral," the driver trumpeted over his shoulder.

"That's the only reason they're not following us now. As long as they think he's alive, we're safe."

"Take us to this address," Walyam said to the driver, showing him the paper again. "It's a safe place and we need to get there as soon as possible."

"That address is on the other side of town and I highly doubt that it's a safe house. No place in this town is safe for you."

"What do you care? Just do as you're told. We don't need trouble from you," Suda said eying him suspiciously as she returned with the kit in hand.

"You seem to be forgetting that I was shot at and I'm still offering to help you. If I didn't care in the least, I wouldn't have driven you out of that mess. I could have gotten off the bus instead if I wanted to. Come on, I was almost killed because of you," he said turning his head, briefly making eye contact with her. "You can call me Kubwa by the way. At this point we should be on a first-name basis. Remember, we've been shot at together and that should count for something."

Kubwa meant "big" and it was a fitting name for him. I wondered if he acquired that name later in life because I couldn't imagine a mother naming her newborn child *Kubwa*.

"I do have a cousin in Nairobi. That would be safer for all of us."

"How do I know if I can trust you, Kubwa?" Walyam asked, plopping down in the seat behind the driver.

"Now that I'm involved in helping you, I can never work for the company again. They will know it's me because I'll be the only driver who hasn't returned to base. In fact, I'm done in this town. Besides, I don't know your whole story, but from what I've seen, those soldiers are up to no good. Honestly, this wouldn't be the first time. You were lucky to get away. I know that area of town and it's full of officers from the base."

Walyam let out a curse as he ran his fingers over his neatly cropped hair. There wasn't much to be said. It could possibly be a trap that awaited us either way. Still it was better to take a chance in Nairobi than near the refugee camp. "Ok, let's go to your cousin. If you try anything, I'll kill you."

"There you go with those threatening words again. I throw myself out there and look what I get in return. Some people are so ungrateful."

"Thank you, Kubwa," I said to him and I really meant it. "My name is Matika."

"You're welcome, Matika. I couldn't let a girl like you get taken by them. I'm also thinking of myself and my family, too, so don't thank me too much," he regarded me briefly, cracking a crooked smile for the first time. "Besides, with what you gave me I will have plenty of time and money to look for another job. You owe me another so don't forget it."

"I won't. What about your family?" I asked in concern.

"I'll call my wife right away and let her know where we're heading. I have to get my family out of here. It won't be safe for any of us now. She will be pleased so long as I don't die tonight, in which case she would kill me again. My wife can get pretty angry."

All talking stopped when Suda pulled down my dress to my waist with no regard for privacy. She seemed to forget that I was no longer some shirtless little girl, but what could I say to her as my face flushed two shades darker. In light of everything, I felt very uncomfortable being exposed in front of Walyam, who used this moment to gaze over at me, his eyes unreadable as he watched Suda work. The driver, on the other hand, kept his eyes on the road.

What luck! The little tin box of diamonds had kept the knife from going all the way through me. I untied the tin from around my waist and held on to it.

"You are very lucky, Matika," Suda remarked.

My body was covered in bruises and cut badly, yet I still wanted to hide from Walyam's watchful eyes. Suda surveyed my injury and then cleansed my wound. Once all the blood was cleared away it didn't look so bad. Still, I wanted to cry as she used the needle to put in a few well-placed stitches, but I wouldn't in front of Walyam. When she was done I pulled my dress up quickly, thankful for more than one reason.

"It will leave a scar but you will heal nicely," she said patting my leg with confidence.

"Thank you," I said and sat in a seat a few rows back. I was so tired and needed some alone time. When Suda went back to tend to Baba I was relieved because I wanted so badly to see if he was still breathing, but the fear of seeing the colonel's body prevented me.

We headed out of town and only stopped once about an hour into our journey to refuel. It took a lot of effort for Kubwa to get off the bus. He was crippled and used a stick to help him walk. I wondered what had happened to him or if he was born that way. I looked at him stunned. He never complained or showed any sign of his disability. It must have been very difficult for him to find a job and for him to find one as a driver was nothing short of a miracle. I suddenly felt really bad that I had jeopardized his future.

We watched in shocked silence as Kubwa slowly made his way with a pronounced limp to the station attendant. He paid for the gas because none of us had any money and using diamonds would arouse suspicion. He didn't have much and could only fill half the tank, but again, he didn't complain. Kubwa also called a neighbor to get ahold of his wife and spoke rapidly in a tribal language that I couldn't understand. Walyam followed and stood guard over him to make sure he didn't run.

We drank water from the outside hose and filled a few containers for Suda to cleanse Baba's wounds while she made use of the first aid kit. I did what I could to clean the blood from the bus. Walyam worked at wrapping the colonel's body and then broke out the cracked windows to make the appearance of them being open. I tidied up the glass debris when he was finished, throwing the trash out the windows.

Exhausted, my body could fight it no longer. Curling up on the seat I fell into a deep sleep plagued by nightmares of the colonel's dead body coming alive and attacking me with the butcher knife. The gash flowed with blood so vividly, and the edges of severed flesh that met with the bloodied meat were too real to be a dream.

I snapped awake, clawing at the air. I looked around to be sure the colonel was not standing over me. Feeling nauseous, I began to gag and dry heave. Although eating was the least of my desires, my body demanded compensation from the stress and exertion of the last forty-eight hours. The hunger pangs were crippling.

When my stomach finally decided to subside from my throat, I sat up, not bothering an attempt to sleep again. The sun was rising, and a sweet melody in a deep baritone circulated throughout the bus. I peered over at Kubwa, who was singing gaily, tapping his finger against the steering wheel.

"He's been going at it for hours," Walyam complained, his voice groggy. He was across from me with his forehead resting on the seat in front of him, where Suda lay, his hands covering his ears.

"It doesn't sound so bad," I replied, giving Kubwa the credit he deserved.

"That's what I thought for the first half-hour, while you, on the other hand, slept. Then he just kept going on and on and on…" Walyam lifted up his head and shouted, "Oh, for mercy's sake, he's driving me crazy!"

"How do you expect me to stay awake?" Kubwa fired back. "The radio doesn't work. In fact, it has never worked for as long as I've had this bus. It is a long drive and I've been up all night with no one to talk to. And since we are on this discussion, I'm hungry!"

"Augh!" Walyam slammed his fist in back of the cushion, startling Suda, who shot up in her seat.

"How close are we to your cousin's?" I asked changing the subject. That seemed to get everyone's attention as they waited for Kubwa's response.

"About twenty minutes away. This traffic is madness," he said waving his fist in the morning air.

It was. We were in Nairobi and although it was early, the traffic and diesel fumes were horrendous. Cars and trucks were at a standstill. It was even more difficult to maneuver a bus through it when everyone kept cutting each other off. For a moment, I thought that maybe our bus would stand out with all the bullet holes, but some of the vehicles around us were in worse condition. Scooting closer to the window I pressed my forehead against it, viewing the streets that were lined with telephone poles, the wires dropping dangerously. It was so much more crowded than I remembered.

Then, as if on cue, we were in a very nice area that was full of buildings that seemed to reach the sky with rows of shiny glass. The cars were also lot nicer, and the men wore business suits, while the women wore colorful Western dresses and skirts.

I spotted a group of finely dressed young women sitting outside a café enjoying breakfast. With their manicured nails and straightened hair they looked so happy, without a care in the world. Yet, here I was, a filthy mess, covered in blood and grime, running for my life with a dead body in tow. I felt self-conscious and quickly turned away in case they'd make eye contact with their up-turned noses at me. I was too feeble to handle their condemnation. With a relieved breath, I was thankful when the traffic light changed and we were once again lumbering down the road.

CHAPTER THIRTY-NINE

Kubwa's driving skills were impressive, but it still took an hour to reach our destination on the other side of the city. His cousin was expecting us and was outside when we approached the house. After some creative parking, Kubwa got out and embraced his cousin, a man with a kind smile who was surprisingly shorter than Kubwa. We followed him off the bus as two young men carried Baba inside the house. Then one man drove the bus away while the other followed in a car. Suda and I were immediately ushered into the house by a young boy, as none of us were fit for viewing by nosy neighbors. Walyam hung back with the men.

The house was very nice, the nicest I'd ever seen. It was large and tan, filled to the brim with children of all ages wearing blue-and-white school uniforms. Every room had furniture, much of which I'd never seen and wondered about its use other than decoration. Many tables and square cases with little doors on them lined the walls. What stole my attention was the amount of lighting. It was midmorning, yielding plenty of natural light, yet at least two lit lamps with ornate shades were in every area of the home. Also, it was so clean I felt completely unworthy to be in it.

A short woman in her mid-forties greeted us in the "family room" after shooing away curious children. She, too, had a kind, knowing smile that crinkled the corners of her eyes. Dressed in a dark blue skirt and white coat she looked like one of the refugee doctors.

"Welcome to my home. I'm Laya, Kubwa's cousin. Don't mind the children. I will introduce you to everyone once you get settled. Come this way," she said kindly, her eyes twinkling with love as we followed.

"Are you a doctor?" Suda asked as we were led to a bathroom on the first floor with a standing shower, a white porcelain toilet and matching sink. Two thirsty towels that hung on the walls were simply too nice to be used on our filthy bodies. A wonderful fragrance came from a small bowl of richly colored purple woodchips and dried mulch on the sink.

"No, I'm a nurse but I will take good care of your father. You can use anything you see. I'll bring you a change of clothes and leave them outside the door for you. Don't take too long or the hungry men will eat the entire meal I've prepared. Kubwa will have no mercy," Laya warned before closing the door behind her.

I wanted to burn the shredded dress as I stepped out of it. Suda must have felt the same way as she ripped out of hers. We quickly got in the shower together, using an abundance of sweet-smelling soap and shampoo that worked nicely on our skin and hair. It felt so good to unbraid and wash all the grime that flowed from our hair and bodies, a muddy river of filth whirling around the drain.

Within ten minutes, Suda got out of the shower and wrapped herself in a soft, fluffy towel. I stayed in and let the water continue to run over me. I wanted to live in the shower forever and it would take more than food to entice me. The water suddenly turned hot when Suda flushed the toilet before opening the door to get the clothes left for us.

Grudgingly, I turned off the faucet and stepped out of the shower. The bathroom was steamy and oh, so comfortable. Laya had left each of us a dark blue knee-length skirt and white-collared shirt, the same uniform as the children. Although the shirt stretched around my bust, it fit nicely.

"Oh, much better," Laya beamed as we stepped out of the bathroom. "I hope you feel refreshed. Now let's get you two fed."

The large table was laden with food. The smell, strong and intoxicating, made me unsteady on my feet as my hunger bloomed with a ravenous strength in retribution for being denied.

"Poor thing! Here, let me help you," Laya said as she put her arm around my shoulders.

When we entered Walyam looked up from his meal, where he sat quietly eating. Wearing a clean shirt and pants, water dripped from his hair from a recent shower. Kubwa wore a large red robe that looked like a dress. No doubt they didn't have clothes that fit him. Talking loudly through a mouth full of food, ignoring our arrival, he was engaged in deep conversation with his cousin, who offered a brief nod.

Biting my lip, I avoided looking in Walyam's direction as I was seated at the table. I was still embarrassed that he'd seen me partially naked. Even though the situation was extreme it didn't take away the discomfort. Suda sat beside Walyam while Laya served our plates. She was very pleased to feed us.

"Eat up. You two are skin and bones. You fit my daughter's uniforms and she's younger than you both," Laya said.

With that I put my head down and quickly inhaled the food before me. Unfortunately, I ate too quickly and got a really bad stomach ache.

I longed for a second helping, even though the meal sat like a brick in my belly.

After the meal, Laya gave us a blanket to put on the floor in the family room. We were encouraged to sleep and not to worry because she would see to Baba's needs. I was so exhausted that I fell asleep before my head hit the floor.

The next few days flew by. Baba made a speedy recovery with the help of Laya, who turned out to be an excellent nurse. Although she made him stay in bed, he was eating and walking around on his own, with only two broken ribs, a broken nose and facial swelling that finally went down, revealing dark purple bruises and welts.

Kubwa's wife arrived with their brood of children on day two. The three bedroom house was busting at the seams with children bouncing off the walls. Between Laya's six, her older son's two, and Kubwa's seven, I didn't know who was whom. We ended up sleeping in shifts because there weren't enough blankets and linens to accommodate everyone.

Kubwa's wife was as I imagined her. She loved Kubwa and fussed over his every move, making sure he took care of himself. He did the same for her. She was only four months pregnant but her belly looked like a water buffalo ready for birth. Still, she moved around efficiently and managed to take care of her children with ease.

In turn, Kubwa doted on his wife, seeing to her every need. It was clear that they both loved each other above their own life. It was amazing to see that much affection between them. A loving couple, they looked longingly at each other as if they were alone instead of in the midst of a dozen children. They even moved with the synchronization of two people who know each other well, each very aware of the other's needs, while caring for their family. Even Laya looked at them with envy.

Kubwa and his cousin were instrumental to us. Baba was able to correspond with the embassy and get our papers in time to make our original flight.

On the night before we were to leave, Baba called me and Suda into his room. Until now, I had avoided Baba, feeling ashamed about everything that had happened. He was hurt because of me. I hoped he didn't remember everything Lutalo had said when we were in the basement.

"You are both very good daughters," Baba said as we entered the room, shutting the door behind us. "I couldn't be any more proud of you."

Baba sat in a small chair in the far corner of the room. His bed was neatly made with several oversize pillows on a floral print blanket. The feminine décor, a total contradiction to his nature, took nothing away from his masculinity. The room was dark, lit dimly with a small lamp on the pink dresser.

"Oh, Baba," Suda went to sit on the floor in front of him, sobbing. She had been very emotional lately, maybe because she was going to leave Walyam behind.

"No need for tears," he said sternly. "All is well. We leave first thing in the morning."

"Must we leave so soon? You are not doing well," Suda sputtered between tears.

"I'll be fine," Baba grunted.

I felt awkward standing by the door while Suda wept. Baba looked stoic, unyielding to her emotional display. When he looked over at me, I cast my eyes to the floor. I was so afraid to make eye contact with him. The shame I felt was so intense it nearly brought me to my knees.

"Suda, say your goodbyes to Walyam while I speak to Matika," Baba said as he gently pushed her away.

"Yes, Baba." Suda left the room rubbing her teary eyes with the back of her hand.

Once she left, it was so quiet. Baba was looking out the window lost in his own world, while I stood like a statue by the door. For a long moment he sat looking out the window. I thought that he may have forgotten about me and I couldn't stand the silence any longer. It was driving me crazy wondering what he was thinking. The anxiety was nerve-racking.

"Baba, I'm really sorry about everything. If you forgive me, I will never be disobedient to you. Please, listen to me," I cried kneeling before him. "I truly didn't know about Lutalo. I would never have done anything to harm you. You must believe me."

"I said it once and I'll say it again. Get off your knees. We do not beg to anyone."

Instantly, my back was ramrod straight as I got to my feet. He was looking up at me.

"Sit down," he ordered, motioning his hand to the neatly made bed.

"Yes, Baba," I acquiesced, sitting on the soft bed. I ran my hands nervously over the floral blanket, pulling at the loose thread, still afraid to look at him. I had only slept on a bed once with Lutalo briefly and for the life of me, I couldn't remember what it'd felt like. This bed was so high and narrow it made me wonder how someone sleeping wouldn't fall off.

"I met Lutalo's mother when I was in the capital," he began, not at me but through me, in some distant memory. "She was very beautiful, like your mother, like you. She got pregnant right away. I wanted to marry her and do the right thing. I offered to take her back to our village and build a hut for her and our child. She wouldn't hear of it. She said she didn't want to be tied down because she wanted a career in business. Though I was in the field more often than not, I provided for all her needs and Lutalo's, sending him to the best schools money could buy. I had a house for her worthy of a queen.

"In truth, she was seeing how far up the ranks she could go. As a colonel then, I was not enough for her so she began setting her sights on others. Soon she found herself in a web of deceit and her ambition led to her demise."

"Did you…" I couldn't finish. The thought of Baba killing a defenseless woman in cold blood was unthinkable.

"Matika…," he was shaking his head at me, like he was wiping away a bad memory. "She had gotten involved with a very powerful man. When he found out she was sleeping with others in the battalion, he had her killed. I was ordered to dispose of her body and kill Lutalo too, who had shrewdly hidden himself so they couldn't find him.

"No one knew he was my son. Lutalo found me as I was…getting rid of his mother's remains. I wasn't going to kill him. I had to hide him and get his mother's remains back to her family for a proper burial. They were coming back so I had to have him help me."

"Baba…" I was sobbing. I felt so bad for Lutalo and was relieved that Baba hadn't killed Lutalo's mother.

"Sending him away was the hardest thing I ever did. I gave his family money to bury her and take care of Lutalo but it wasn't right. Her blood was on my hands and I had abandoned my son."

"You did everything you could for him," I defended, wiping away my tears.

"No…I should have sent him to our village," his words were final and there was no changing them.

"You are the bravest and best daughter a man could ever hope for. Come here."

He reached for me and I slid into his outstretched arms, mindful not to hug him too tightly.

"I saved these, Baba," I said pulling away and handing him the tin of diamonds with the knife wound in the middle.

"What is this?" he asked opening the tin. His mouth dropped and his eyes lit up in surprise. "My diamonds! You are a very smart girl, Matika!"

He marveled at them for a few moments, turning one over in his hands. "Now get a good night's sleep because we leave first thing in the morning," he said in a pleasant tone, clearly pleased with the valuable stones.

Despite my best efforts, I didn't sleep that night. Early in the morning, before the sun broke, I went outside to sit in a plastic chair and waited for the house to awaken. I was ready to leave, but there was a least an hour before the sun would rise.

"You owe me and I always take what is owed," Walyam said in my ear. Repulsively, he trailed hot kisses down the side of my neck.

"I know," I acquiesced before he walked away.

Once again, hatred of him flared up. Old Walyam was back with a vengeance and I would have to deal with him, but not today. It could be months before he came to the U.S. Hopefully he would never make it, but that was highly unlikely if Baba was helping him.

"You must remember to keep in touch," Kubwa remarked.

I nearly jumped out of the chair, the seat sticking to my butt.

"I will," I smiled looking up at him, relieved. I hoped he didn't see Walyam kiss me. I felt so ashamed, helpless.

"I won't be staying here long but you may send a letter to me anytime at my cousin's home. He'll make sure I get it."

He gave me a card with the address that I clutched tightly, refusing to lose contact with this wonderful man like I did Chaz. I regretted so much that I didn't get to see him that fateful day.

"A word of advice, Matika. I wouldn't recommend you parade around dressed in male clothes in America because you never could look like a boy. They would think you are one of those 'funny girls' that like other girls. I don't believe they would think that very funny though," he said looking at me conspiratorially, desperately trying to contain his glee.

"I'll remember that," I promised him with a merry gleam of my own. "This is for you, Kubwa."

With joy, I handed him my last precious diamond that I'd kept from Baba. For Kubwa, I would give the clothes off my back. He was a noble man, a true friend. I was extremely lucky to have met him. Fate was clearly on my side that night when I came upon his bus.

"You have turned my life upside down, but for that I thank you," he said before pocketing the stone.

"Thank you for helping us. I guess this is goodbye."

"For now… I have a feeling I will see you again and my feelings are rarely wrong," he said as I hugged him. I disappeared in the folds of his flesh, but I didn't care. Pulling away, he patted me on the shoulder awkwardly before hobbling back in the house.

EPILOGUE

~~~~~~~~~~~~

It took everything we had to leave Kenya. With all our belongings gone, we had nothing but the clothes on our back. Baba managed to get cash for the stones that morning, although I wasn't sure how much. We finally boarded a nearly empty bus that had just unloaded a group of passengers and we headed toward the Nairobi airport.

Horrid memories of nights spent in the refugee camp seemed far away. It was strange that so many people were brought to that camp daily, yet we were among the few to leave. Singing quietly in the rear of the bus, I glanced out the window. The bus was set to go directly to the Nairobi airport but the driver made several stops, picking up more passengers, taking them to various locations, greedily keeping the money and other goods offered. The bus filled beyond capacity in no time.

From the bus stop we walked to the airport. Our flight was not scheduled to leave for several hours so we waited patiently in the airport with nothing to do. That night, as the throng of people had thinned, Suda and I went into the public toilet and washed in the row of sinks that provided clean running water. Little was said as we sat in the hard plastic seats the color of egg yolk, waiting to board our plan. Finally we boarded the plane bound for America.

It didn't matter where I would be a year or two from now. All that mattered was being closer to freedom with my family. Maybe, just maybe, I would find Chaz and we would be together, because he may have left me but he will forever be in my heart.

ABOUT THE AUTHOR

Latrice Simpkins has been passionately writing for over sixteen years. She holds a Bachelor's in Business from California State University, San Marcos, and a Master's degree in Management from Florida Institute of Technology. After serving in the U.S. Marine Corps for four years she began a career in civil service for the Department of the Navy as a Contracts and Grants Officer. Latrice is most notably known for providing grant assistance throughout Africa supporting the President's Emergency Plan for AIDS Relief (PEPFAR) program. She received a Letter of Commendation from the Commanding officer of Naval Health Research Center in 2012 for her outstanding work.

Latrice Simpkins currently lives in San Diego with her two beautiful young daughters. Her hobbies include working out, biking, collecting African art, and playing "zombie" Barbie with her girls.

www.ingramcontent.com/pod-product-compliance
Lightning Source LLC
Chambersburg PA
CBHW062018170626
46813CB00001B/214